A Cruise t

Lawyers on a cruise ship are being murdered and it's not a punchline. There's not just the killer to worry about, there's also an assassin, a code of silence, and several people who are not who or what they claim to be.

A story of betrayal, threats, double-crosses, and conspiracy.

And that's just how the lawyers interact with their colleagues.

It's also a story of murder, theft, terrible puns, and one rather conspicuous thermos.

By Mike Bowerbank

Thursday, September 4, 9:27pm: Vancouver, BC

Charles Lautzen was about to die.

He wasn't aware of this yet, though he probably should have been. There had been threats made and two of his fellow partners at the firm had already died this week.

But those were only accidents, weren't they?

A number of rather graphic threats had been received by the firm, some of which were directed at him but he dismissed them outright. Anything worth having required aggressive moves and being aggressive tended to upset small-minded people. Threats, however graphic and anatomically inaccurate they may be, were all just part of the game. If there was one thing Charles Lautzen didn't care about, it was people who issued threats. Or just people in general.

Money, on the other hand… now that was worth getting excited about. He was a deal-maker and he was anticipating a significant windfall from the most recent venture he'd put in motion. He figured it would be the easiest money he'd ever made. All he'd needed to do was apply the right amount pressure to the right people in the right places and then just sit back and let fear and greed do the rest.

In his mind, there was nothing like a large pile of money to silence the small, sadly neglected part of his brain which occasionally wondered about trivial things such as ethics. He was thus easily able to push aside any consideration of that group of small-thinking colleagues who opposed the deal.

'Think big, live bigger.'

'Bold actions yield the best dividends.'

Those were his mottos.

'Know when to quit' and *'don't overdo it'*, however, were not.

Charles, who would insist on being called 'Chuck' by his friends if he had any, believed the threats and warnings were ultimately the sort of silliness that wasn't worth his valuable time. When you bill your clients at more than five-hundred dollars per hour, you don't care about threats. Even his own clients threatened him from time to time, though this was most often when his billings arrived in their mail.

He couldn't wait to begin his late-evening routine of fast driving and hard partying. He got into his Porsche 911, started up the car, and revved the engine, hoping the distinct noise would both impress and annoy anyone within earshot.

He exited the parking garage of the office building and turned onto the street. Once he had gotten up some speed, he screeched over to the long, curving on-ramp which led to the bridge. As had become his nightly custom, he put the car into top gear and he accelerated rapidly along the on-ramp, always looking to beat his speed record across the bridge into the city. Charles loved the adrenaline rush of fast cars and to him there was no such thing as 'too fast'.

'Chuck' had developed a feel for his vehicle so he was aware of a correlation between his increasing speed and his having to fight the steering wheel for control. He came to the conclusion that something was not quite right with his car and it would likely need a wheel alignment done. That meant making an appointment with the over-priced mechanic at the dealership later this week. No matter.

They'd just better have my car fixed before the cruise this weekend, he thought. *I'm not about to miss a party like that.*

He was about to miss a party like that, of course, because he had less than a minute left to live.

Charles was now heading into the ramp's final curve before it merged onto the bridge and by then his car was shuddering. He couldn't maintain control so he stepped hard on the brake. As he did so, he heard a loud *thunk* noise and his brakes became unresponsive. His car went into an uncontrolled spin, crashed through the flimsy guard rail, and then soared out into the open air. The exhilaration of being airborne was to be short-lived.

And so, as it happens, was Charles.

As his car began the final few seconds of its nosedive towards the jagged rocks below, Charles was startled to discover his first thought was that this incident would likely have a negative impact on his vehicle's resale value. The thought he had immediately after that was: *I'm going to die*.

The car hit the rocks and both of Chuck's predictions came true simultaneously.

He was the third lawyer to have died that week.

He would not, however, be the last…

Friday, 8:22am: Seattle, WA

"Listen, I have a plane to catch so we really need to wrap up this meeting," Malcolm Mercer said, pinching the bridge of his nose, "and even after twenty minutes I still have absolutely no idea what it is you want us to do."

The client, Mrs. Belanger, was sitting across the desk from him in one of the small meeting rooms he and his wife Mary rented at the business centre on those occasions when they needed to meet prospective clients. Belanger was an older woman, though she would have bristled at being described as such. Because of carefully-applied layers of makeup, top-quality hair dye, and fashionable clothes, she was of the mistaken belief she could pass for a woman in her mid-thirties. She did have Malcolm fooled, though, as he believed she was at least eighty when she was, in fact, sixty-eight.

"It's perfectly simple," the woman huffed. "You people deal with the unusual, so find Walter, talk to him, and ask him who murdered him."

"He's dead, ma'am."

"I have it on good authority such things haven't stopped you people before."

"Okay, let's start by reviewing what you've told me so far, shall we?" Malcolm sat back in his chair and sighed. "Your husband was sick with cancer and two days before he died, a mysterious visitor came by his hospital bedside and was with him for over an hour. Your husband's doctors informed you two days later that he'd killed himself but you believe it was foul play."

"It's perfectly obvious to anyone with half a brain he was murdered," Belanger sniffed and looked down her nose at Malcolm. "All I'm asking you to do is talk to Walter directly so he can tell you that himself."

It was at this particular moment that Malcolm came to the conclusion that having an option on their website allowing members of the general public to book their own appointments was a well-intentioned yet ultimately terrible idea. It was much too early in the morning for this sort of nonsense.

"We're investigators, lady, not fortune tellers," Malcolm made sure she saw that he was looking at the clock on the wall. "When we take a case, we put together logical and methodical theories based on what evidence we're able to collect. We then systematically narrow it all down to the most likely options, test out the theories, and then come to a sensible conclusion. We don't just put on a silly hat and hold a séance."

"It's outrageous you're trying to make this so complicated," Belanger emitted a loud, exaggerated sighing noise. "Just ask him who forced those dreadful pills down his throat."

"We can't talk to the dead," Malcolm exhaled, trying hard to remain patient. He'd wished that he'd had more coffee as his headache was worsening. "Even if we could, I'm not sure a statement sworn postmortem would be admissible in court. Any witness statement we enter into evidence is subject to potential cross-examination by opposing counsel. The merits of your case may be negatively impacted if the person being cross-examined needs to be contained in an urn. So if you don't mind, Mrs. Belanger, we…"

"Don't."

"Don't what?"

"That dreadful accent of yours," she tut-tutted. "I simply loathe the appalling way you are pronouncing my name. It is pronounced 'bay-lon-jay', not 'bell-anger'."

"You're lucky I don't pronounce it 'pain in the ass' for the sake of accuracy," Malcolm no longer made the effort to hide his annoyance, as the pounding in his head continued unabated. "Did you review our fee schedule?"

"Yes, and it is as outrageous as it is unacceptable," Belanger snapped. "I'm requesting a simple task and I won't go above five hundred. I don't just hand out money willy-nilly, you know. Walter worked hard for everything he had."

"Yeah, even his ashes were urned."

"I'll pay you five hundred, as long as it includes all fees and taxes. Any simpleton could do it for that amount."

"Then get any simpleton to do it for five-hundred," Malcolm stood up and put on his jacket. "Our fees are not negotiable, which is lucky for you because I'd triple the price just to get rid of you."

"I expected better service than this."

"And I expected that you'd have left before now, but alas, it seems we're both leaving here disappointed."

"This is completely outrageous."

"Yes, it certainly is," he walked to the door and held it open, making a sweeping gesture with his free hand to indicate she should be heading in that general direction. "Look, I have a flight to catch and I have to hurry, so either hire us or don't hire us. I don't care which one you choose but make the choice."

Friday, 11:13am: Vancouver, BC

Malcolm opened his suitcase and began piling his clothes on the bed while continuing to brief his wife, Mary Bristol, on his conversation with Mrs. Belanger. "So then, in the taxi on my way to the airport, I did some preliminary work on her case and put together a mission brief."

"Wait a minute, back up for a minute," Mary said. "I thought you said Mrs. Belanger stormed out of the room muttering we were outrageously expensive."

"Yeah, but I guarantee you she'll hire us anyway," Malcolm opened the bottom drawer of the dresser and tossed his clothes from the bed into it. "The stakes are too high for her and we're the only chance she has. I can't think of any other legitimate contractors who could take the case, bearing in mind she wants them to take a sworn statement from the cremated ashes of her dead spouse that can be entered as evidence."

"From what you've told me, it's in Mrs. Belanger's financial interest to prove murder," Mary glared at the haphazard way Malcolm had dumped his clothes into the drawer and decided not to say anything about it. "His insurance policy didn't cover self-administered suicide so she's at risk of missing out on a hefty insurance pay out."

"That's why she's going to hire us," Malcolm noticed the look on Mary's face so he tried to make the piles of clothes in the drawer a bit neater. "She wants us to try to find some solid evidence of foul play so she can send it in to the insurance company to support the appeal she launched. Her husband Walter had stage four cancer and there is no stage five. I can understand why he may have viewed suicide as being preferable to a slow and painful death."

"Doctor-assisted suicide is legal here in those types of terminal cases," she looked at the contents of the drawer and then flashed him a glance which indicated he'd only made the mess worse. "What's strange to me is that his contract would have covered a doctor-assisted ending due to a clause in his policy stating it covered death while undergoing any lawful medical procedure performed by a licensed practitioner. The insurance company was closing that loophole but Walter died before they could do so."

"Right, so then why would he commit suicide illegally and bequeath nothing to his estate when he could have done it legally through a doctor and gotten a sizable pay out?"

"Good question," Mary nodded. "So, are you sure we should take the case before hearing back from her?"

"I'm sure of it," Malcolm said as he pulled his clothes out of the drawer and refolded them and began to put them back into the drawer in a more organized fashion. "However, we had to drop everything and fly north so I've already contracted it out to Sammy Mendoza."

"He's one of the better detectives we've worked with," Mary admitted while giving an approving nod to his decision to fix his clothes. "How much will that set us back?"

"He said he can have the case wrapped up in a day or two," Malcolm closed the drawer quickly in case anything else got noticed. "It will be three hundred plus expenses, so add on another couple hundred. It turns out Mrs. Bell-Anger was right. Her job really could have been done by someone else for five-hundred and I'm really amused by that."

"Did it occur to you that you should have first discussed this with me before contracting it out?"

"The case is a big nothing and I didn't want to waste your time with such a pain-in-the-ass client," Malcolm said, hoping not to be stepping on any verbal land mines which might get The Look to make a dreaded return. "Besides, I didn't think you'd mind."

"I wouldn't have minded at all if you were in the habit of letting me know what you're wanting to do before going ahead and doing it."

"So," Malcolm clapped his hands together and rubbed them. "What do we know about this new client your parents want us to meet?"

"Don't think I didn't notice you changing the subject," Mary glared at him briefly but then paused and relented. "At the moment, though, I don't have anything else to add. I don't know anything at all about the new client, to be honest."

"Do you at least know if the client is your mom's friend, former colleague, or some other family member?"

"I have no idea whatsoever," Mary shook her head. "All Mom told me was she had a new client for us, that we had to drop everything and see her immediately, and that our job would be to protect someone named Mrs. Harrington. Aside from that, I know nothing and my normally-chatty mother is suddenly tight-lipped and saying she would only discuss it with us further in person. She said she'll tell us everything when we go downstairs."

"As long as it gives us a break from our usual cases which have all that supernatural crap and other inexplicable nonsense in them, I'll be thrilled."

"But that's what we do. It's our niche."

"Then I should have paid more attention on 'Career Day' at school," Malcolm muttered. He paused from tending to his suitcase and looked around Mary's childhood bedroom. "I never understood why you hated growing up in this room as a kid. It's a nice room."

"Yes I know, but I thought of it as a prison cell at the time," Mary admitted with a sheepish grin. "I was a troubled young woman. The years have sure added some perspective."

Malcolm pulled his well-worn brown leather jacket out of the suitcase and hung it up in the closet.

"Wait, you brought that old tattered thing?" Mary stared at the jacket. "You don't need it now since you have the new one I bought you."

"The new jacket's great and you know I've been wearing it. I brought the leather one along just in case."

"You brought two jackets 'just in case' yet you only packed three pairs of socks and underwear?"

"I knew we'd be with your mom," Malcolm said. "The first thing she asked me when we got here was if I had any laundry she could do. I'm forty-one but she always talks to me like I'm five."

"Trust me, she wasn't this willing to do laundry when I was five," a wave of memories involving heated arguments came rushing back into the forefront of Mary's mind. "She became a completely different person somewhere in the thirty-three years since then. Are you ready to head downstairs to find out about the job?"

"Sure, but where's Alyssa?"

"As soon as Mom and Dad saw her, I haven't been able to get her back from them," Mary chuckled. "Alyssa is certainly not complaining about all the extra attention she's getting."

"By the way, I only needed the bottom drawer of the dresser," Malcolm pointed. "You can have the other three."

"No, it's fine, I only needed two. I'm always happy to share with you."

"What we do isn't sharing," Malcolm looked up at her. "You know that, right?"

"Not true. We share almost everything."

"No, we only share things in theory," he said. "Three-quarters of the bed is yours, along with eighty percent of the space in the bathroom."

"I never said it was an *equal* share, but it still counts. It's based on need. You get a hundred percent of the space in the gun cabinet, for example."

"And when we eat out?" Malcolm continued. "You order so little and end up eating half of mine."

"You often order things that look so good and I want to try them. Besides," Mary winked, "calories don't count if you eat off of someone else's plate."

"I'm not sure it works that way."

"It does when you're a woman."

"Speaking of food, did you see the dining room table downstairs?" Malcolm said as he exited the bedroom with Mary behind him. "Your mom said she would put out a light lunch but there's enough food out there to feed the entire US Marine Corps."

"You do remember my mom's Latina and my dad's Italian, right? It shouldn't still be surprising to you that there's always a lot of food around. Let's go."

"You always look so gloomy when you come here, Malcolm," Irena Bellantoni – Mary's mother – said pinching the cheeks of his face. "Don't you like Vancouver?"

"Nah, the city's fine, Mrs. Bellantoni," Malcolm hugged her. "Aside from your husband, though, nobody in this town knows how to make a half-decent pastrami on rye."

"I see you have your priorities straight," Mary said.

"Before you go home, Malcolm dear, I'll take you to a deli that will change your mind," Mary's mom flashed a broad smile.

"Sounds good Mrs. B. I'll hold you to that."

"I'd like to hear about the new client you have for us, Mom," Mary said, sitting down in one of the wooden dining room chairs. "Especially the part about why it was so 'drop everything and get up here' urgent."

"Of course, Maria," her mother sat in the chair beside Mary. "But first, Malcolm, dear…"

"Yeah?"

"Can you go and find Leo? My husband is never here when I need him. I think he's with Alyssa in the greenhouse out back."

"Alright," Malcolm left the room and headed outside.

"Maria," Irena said in an urgent whisper. "I need you to speak to your sister."

"Amy hates me, Mom, and you know that," Mary's tone was blunt. "We haven't spoken a single word to one another in two decades. I sent a couple of cards and a few emails when I first left home, but after the first year of being ignored, I got smart and gave up."

"It's very important you try again."

"Mom, this morning you said you had a new client for me but instead I'm starting to suspect you just lured me here to try to get me to patch things up with Amy," Mary folded her arms. "I was supposed to go to Baneridge to help review patient files at Miralinda Hospital and instead I ended up hastily rearranging several weeks' worth of projects in order to come up here and meet with you. I don't appreciate the deception so I'm suitably annoyed right now."

"Maria, if I had asked you to come up to talk about your sister, would you have done so?"

"No, I would have flatly refused," Mary said, unfolding her arms and now drumming her fingers on the table. "Partly due to the sheer futility of such a request and partly because I'm busy with things that are actually possible for me to accomplish."

"So you understand I did what I had to do in order to get you here without telling any lies."

"Mom, *you did lie*. You said you had a new client for me."

"But I do have a new client for you and her name is Sarah," her mother patted Mary's hand. "Oh, and just so you know, your father and I will be the ones who will be taking care of your fees and expenses on Sarah's behalf."

"Who's Sarah?"

"I'll get to that, Maria," her mother soothed, "but first I need you to know there's a corporate law firm downtown where lawyers are dying off. Three have died in three days and they're worried more will follow."

"Is it the firm where you and dad used to work?"

"No, it's McKenzie Ferguson, not our old firm."

"Okay, so what does this have to do with Malcolm and me?"

"It's the firm where your sister works as a legal secretary."

"So far, we have a Sarah, a Mrs. Harrington, my sister Amy, and the law firm where Amy works which is losing lawyers, yet nothing which links those items together. You're speaking in riddles, Mom, so I'd appreciate it if you started giving me simple, straight-forward answers. Let's start with this Mrs. Harrington we're supposed to protect. Who is she? A friend of yours?"

"No, Maria," her mother took in a deep breath before she continued. "Mrs. Harrington is your sister."

"Unless you're keeping a big secret from me, Amy is the only sister I have and her last name is Colvin."

"Not since she remarried," her mother said.

"Remarried?" Mary's mouth was agape for a few seconds. "You mean she's not with Brett anymore?"

"No, their divorce was finalized nearly ten years ago."

"Ten…?" Mary's mouth opened and closed a few times before she was able to continue. "Why am I only finding out about this now?"

"I couldn't tell you because Amy doesn't want you knowing anything about her life," Mrs. Bellantoni began to fidget in the chair. "She hasn't come around to accepting you and Malcolm yet. She was furious when she found out you were alive. Oh, that came out wrong but you know what I mean."

"Not really, but it doesn't matter. She and I haven't been close for nearly thirty years so the silence of the past twenty has been for the best. I don't see any of that changing now. She's really got the hate on for me and she's too stubborn to change how she feels."

"She's your family Maria," her mother pleaded. "You should try harder to connect with more people."

"I'm an introvert, Mom," Mary gave her mother a look of disbelief. "Nothing makes me happier than canceled social plans so I can stay home and *not* connect with people. So who is Sarah?"

"Sarah is Amy's second child. She's our granddaughter and your niece."

"How many kids does Amy have?"

"Three," Irena said. "You saw Ryan when he was born, but she's since had Sarah and Crystal."

"What would one of her kids need my help with?"

"Sarah's eighteen, Maria, so she's a young woman now," her mother beamed. "She wants your help because she believes her mother is in danger. Your father and I believe the same."

"Then Sarah will have to hire someone else to help," Mary folded her arms again. "Amy hates me with a passion so she'll never accept my assistance. We've been estranged for so long now the chasm between us is probably too wide to be bridged."

"But once your father and I are gone, Amy will be the only family you have left."

Yes, once you're both gone, I'll have nobody left except Amy... and Malcolm, Amy's new husband, my daughter Alyssa, my nieces Sarah and Crystal, my nephew Ryan, and several dozen aunts, uncles, and cousins in both Argentina and Italy. How will I ever cope without any family?"

"Sarcasm causes wrinkles, dear," her mother frowned. "Don't use it."

Friday, 11:38am:

Mary was kneeling on the bedroom floor and sliding her emptied suitcase under the bed when she heard someone knocking on the doorframe. She looked up and saw a young woman standing in the open doorway. She was around Mary's height, five-feet four inches, and had an athletic build. The woman had sandy-blonde hair tied back in a ponytail and wore a burgundy-coloured blouse with blue jeans.

"Hey," the woman said. "So, you're my long-lost Aunt Mary."

"Oh, hi, you must be Sarah," Mary stood up and walked over to her. "It's nice to meet you."

"Same."

"So, um," Mary said, "how's high school?"

"I just started college this week."

"Then how's college?"

"I don't know yet because *I literally just started this week*," Sarah smirked. "You're really bad at making small talk, aren't you?"

"Yes, I really am," Mary wrung her hands as she shifted her weight from one foot to the other. "And this conversation somehow got even more awkward than it already was."

"Nah, forget it," Sarah said. "Small talk is just a superficial waste of time anyway, so I'll get right down to business. Mom is in danger and Grandma said you can help her. Is that true or not?"

"I'd love to help any way I can, but your mother won't approve of me being involved in anything you have in mind."

"Then it sucks to be her because she's going to have to deal with it," Sarah smirked. "Besides I'm eighteen, so let's face it: knowing she won't approve only makes this more appealing."

"How exactly do you think I can help her?" Mary asked. "What kind of danger is she in and what role would I play in preventing it?"

"People at the firm she works at are getting killed, right?"

"Yes, I've heard."

"Okay, and you know the cruise those lawyers and their biggest client are going on?"

"No, I wasn't told anything about that," Mary shook her head. "What cruise are you referring to?"

"Okay, so like the partners and administrators do a big, fancy retreat every four years and they take their biggest client, FIRST, with them."

"FIRST?"

"Yeah, it stands for Fully Integrated Robotics and Software Technology," Sarah leaned against the doorframe. "Anyway, four years ago, it was an extended weekend in Vegas and this time it's a cruise up north to Prince Rupert. They spend half the time plotting strategy and setting goals for the next few years and the other half partying their drunken asses off while schmoozing with the major players at FIRST."

"Ah, so it's a booze cruise?"

"Sort of, yeah," Sarah nodded. "Anyway, Mom's going to be on that ship so I want you on it too so you can keep her safe in case more bad stuff happens."

"I thought you said it was just for the firm's partners, clients, and administrators."

"It is, but during the sober moments, they need someone to take meeting minutes and help coordinate stuff," Sarah waved her hand in a dismissive fashion. "Besides, Mom assists that Stacy chick who was made, like, head of her practice group after the other guy decided to take his car for a short flying lesson off a bridge. Because Stacy's now the boss chick of the group, they chose Mom – her assistant – to be the one to help out. She tries to hide it, but I know Mom's completely freaking out about going on the cruise."

"Of all the people to pick to protect your mom, I'm the person she would be least likely to accept help from," Mary sighed. "I'm sure she'd rather be guarded by ravenous cannibals who were salivating and brandishing cutlery than by me. So… why?"

"Grandma told me you're this amazing kick-ass karate chick and that Uncle Malcolm is like some kind of badass gunslinger dude. That sounds like awesome protection to me."

"I somehow doubt your grandmother used the term 'kick-ass karate chick' to describe me."

"Look, Mom and I fight all the time and she is a constant pain in my ass, but at the same time I care a lot about her. Especially since dad left."

"Why did your father leave, if it's not too personal to ask?"

"He hooked up with some sleaze he met in an online hook-up room and then ran off to Halifax to be with her."

"I'm so sorry to hear that," Mary said. "Is he in touch with any of you?"

"Oh yeah, he's in touch with me, Ryan, and Crystal, but not Mom."

"Does he at least send money to help out?"

"Since Mom remarried, money's not an issue," Sarah said. "Even so, he's paying for my tuition and Ryan's too. When Crystal graduates, he's promised to fund her post-secondary as well."

"That's something, I suppose."

"Yes, it's *something* but even though we're old enough to mostly take care of ourselves now, raising the three of us on her own for those years was really stressful for Mom. She's having all kinds of problems keeping it together these days, even with my step-dad helping. My ex-dad shouldn't have left all the stress to her. I mean, go get marriage counselling or whatever, but don't leave us alone like that, right? Anyway, I want you to make sure nothing bad happens to Mom. We've already lost one parent, so we don't want to lose her as well."

"How does your step-dad treat you all?"

"He's pretty awesome but he's only been in the picture for like five years," Sarah said. "Because of him, things are way better financially. He makes an effort with us when he's not working on deals – and he works a lot – but he's still way out of his depth on a lot of things."

"At least he's trying."

"I know," Sarah nodded. "He's pretty cool. Mom once told him you and Uncle Malcolm were big-time criminal scumbags but he doesn't seem concerned about any of that. He said if anything, that was a plus. Besides, he's so worried about Mom he'll accept help from anyone in the family who is willing to offer it."

"I'm still worried about how your mom is going to react when she finds out I'm involved in this."

"Grandma, Grandpa, and I are going to put some serious pressure on her, and I know my step-dad will as well. Whether she wants you on board or not, you'll both be on that ship."

"Gee, what could possibly go wrong?"

"You roll your eyes just like Mom does," Sarah's wry grin broke into a full smile. "You're definitely her sister. Aunt Mary, we've only known each other for like, ten seconds, but I need you to do this. I grew up not having you in my life and I'm not afraid of using guilt if I have to."

"Wielding guilt as a weapon, just like your grandmother does," Mary chuckled. "I'm not the only one who is definitely related."

"So will you help me or do I have to talk about how my childhood left me permanently scarred and traumatized because my aunt wasn't there for me?"

"Of course I'll help you, Sarah. How could I say no to my scarred and traumatized niece?"

"Cool. I'll go tell Grandma."

Sarah turned on her heels and headed down the hall toward the stairs. She passed Malcolm on her way.

"Hey," Sarah nodded to him.

"Hey," Malcolm nodded back and then entered Mary's room.

"Who was that?" Malcolm said, gesturing with his thumb toward the hallway.

'Our client, Sarah."

"That's our client?" Malcolm's eyes bugged out. "She's just a kid."

"She's our client regardless."

"Whatever," He shook his head. "As long as somebody pays our bill, I'm not going to complain."

"Um, about that," Mary said. "This isn't an official mission from ARIES. If we take this job without approval then we're freelancing and we're not allowed to do that. Director Waterman will have a fit if she finds out, and she always finds out."

"Then let's get her approval."

"We can't do that either. We're not allowed to do jobs for family members because it's a clear conflict of interest."

"Then let's not call it a job," Malcolm shrugged. "Think of it as just doing a favour for your parents and your niece."

"It would be a *paid* favour, and that's what freelancing is by definition. It's strictly forbidden in our employment contract."

"Then we don't accept any payment from them at all," Malcolm leaned against the wall. "We just do a good deed by helping your niece and not charging your parents for it. Doing them this favour is no different than if we were helping out with chores around the house, as any good house guest would."

"And you'd be okay with that?"

"Your parents do a lot for us," Malcolm said. "Sure, I'm totally okay with it."

"Then that's sorted out. But working with my sister after twenty years... I don't know if I can handle that."

"What's the big deal?"

"When we were kids, my older sister could do no wrong. Everything came so easily for her and she didn't pursue any of her talents."

"This isn't about you and Amy."

"She could play instruments, she was a competitive swimmer..."

"Okay, apparently this *is* about you and Amy."

"Then, just as she got good at a lot of things, she just quit them all. I was interested in everything but had the talent for nothing."

"You have many talents," the volume of Malcolm's sigh was in direct proportion to the high level of exasperation he was feeling at that moment. "Should I list them or do you feel the need to delay us further with your self-pity?"

"I just want you to understand where my insecurities come from."

"I already know where they come from," Malcolm said. "They come from inside your head and nowhere else. Amy doesn't do this to you, you do it to yourself."

"By the time you and I started dating, she'd already been married and popped out my nephew Ryan."

"So what?" Malcolm cried out. "Don't measure your own worth based on what other people are doing. Besides, she's three years older than you are, so she had a head start. And based on what your parents told us, that first marriage of hers didn't work out so well. Also, you'd dated other guys before I came along."

"I'd dated *one* other person, but still..."

"But what?"

"But I never feel that I'm good enough. I always feel second-best."

"Not with me you don't," Malcolm massaged his temples as his headache began to flare up again.

"I know, and you're right," Mary realized she was being negative and perhaps even petulant. She was feeling wretched and was worrying she was making Malcolm feel unappreciated. "But I always used to feel as though I was living in her perfect shadow."

"Then you should have stepped out of it."

"It wasn't as easy as you make it sound."

"Yeah, I really think it was as easy as that."

"How would you know?" Mary challenged. "It's easy for you to say that because you had no rival siblings. You were an only child."

"Nothing about my life was ever easy," Malcolm snapped. "Even when my dad was alive, times were tough and we struggled. When he was killed in the line of duty and then mom had her breakdown, those miserable and screwed-up years of my childhood became my fond memories. Forgive me if I don't express any sympathy for someone who managed to reach adulthood with both of her parents alive." Malcolm then let loose a long, frustrated 'argh' sound. "I'm sorry I snapped at you, it's just..."

"It's okay," Mary hugged him. "I know we're both in our trigger zones."

"Come on," Malcolm kissed her forehead. "I'm going to take something for my headache and then we should head downstairs. Your mom has lunch waiting for us."

Friday, 12:53pm:

Lunch was probably delicious but Mary was too distracted to properly taste it and too nervous to enjoy it. After helping with the cleanup, she retreated to the solitude of the dining room and began pacing back and forth. She sat down for a moment and then stood up again to continue pacing. She wrung her hands and could feel a pulse drumming in her head. She realized she was biting her lower lip so she forced herself to stop doing that. She was then startled by a loud voice behind her.

"What is she doing here?"

Mary turned around and saw her sister Amy, hands on her hips and standing in the dining room doorway. Amy had straight, shoulder-length auburn hair with a few strands of grey in it. She looked as though she probably had a fair complexion, though it was difficult to know for certain as her face was currently red with fury.

Everything Mary had been rehearsing to say completely vanished from her mind and she could feel her ears turning red while her heart rate accelerated.

"Amy," her mother said, coming up behind her. "I need you to talk to your sister."

"Mom, you said you needed me to meet a Ms. Bristol."

"Yes, Amy," her mother said, patting Amy's shoulder. "Mary Bristol is your sister."

Amy turned from her mother back to Mary. "But the thug's last name isn't Bristol, it's Marksmann."

"No, his last name is Mercer now."

"Oh my God, I can't even..." Amy sputtered. "Then where did the surname of Bristol come from?"

"It's a long story," Mary said.

"I'm not a bit surprised," Amy all but spat the words. "Everything with you is a long story."

"I'm sorry to hear about you and Brett."

Amy rounded on her mother. "You told her about my divorce? Mom, I told you she is to know *nothing* about my life."

"Amy, I'm getting her to help you stay safe on that cruise," Irena soothed. "Too many bad things have been happening at your work and your father and I are worried about you."

"I don't need her help," Amy pointed at Mary. "As I told you on the phone two days ago, the firm is handling it."

"And since you told me that, how many more lawyers have been threatened or killed?"

"Too many, but..."

"Then it's settled," her mother said. "We're hiring them to help keep you safe."

"Them?" Amy's eyes bulged. "You mean the criminal is coming too?"

"Of course," her mother said. "Be nice, Amy, he's your brother-in-law."

"Don't remind me," Amy groaned. "More like a brother-*out*-law if you ask me. I don't want help from my sister and I certainly don't want the thug's help either."

"We ask so little and we have done so much to help you," her mother sidled up to her. "We were there for you when Brett left, and…"

"Stop right there, Mom," Amy raised both of her hands. "If this is going to be the start of a long list of things you can hold over my head, then don't bother. I'll just capitulate now and save us both several hours. But as soon as we get back, I want them both gone for good, capiche?"

Friday, 1:18pm:

Amy was in a tight embrace with her husband Christopher and he was gently rocking her back and forth.

"I thought you'd take my side in this, not my mother's," Amy pouted. "Everyone's against me on this, so I've been guilted into being stuck on a ship with Mary and the criminal. I hate my sister so much right now."

"I'm English, darling, so I know all about motivational guilt," Christopher said. "You know deep down they need to be with you on the ship."

"I know what you're trying to do, but why her? I mean, I understand why you say she needs to be on board, but I'd rather not have to deal with her at all."

"I must say that you're terribly harsh on your sister."

"She deserves it," Amy pulled just far enough away to look her husband in the eyes. "She's made so many lousy life choices."

"Amy, my dear, we promised to be honest with each other no matter what, right?"

"Yes. Why? What are you about to say?"

"Isn't it her life and therefore only her business what choices she makes?" he gently stroked her hair. "I mean, as long as she is willing to accept the inevitable consequences of her actions, isn't that all we can expect of anyone?"

"She ran away from home to be with a hitman when she was eighteen and until recently we thought she was dead."

"Yes, you told me all about the shadier side of your family, though I believe you said Mary's husband was more of a mercenary than a hitman."

"Okay, fine, he's not an actual hitman," Amy buried her head in his chest. "But he's this awful New York gangster type who is an honest-to-God vigilante and she ran off with him. With everything she's done, by all rights she shouldn't even be alive."

"That certainly is a drastic lifestyle choice, but once again I feel compelled to come back to the whole 'her-life, her-choices, her-consequences' theme," Christopher said. "Besides, I'm terribly worried about you. I'd feel much better knowing there were people on board who were committed to protecting you, no matter who they are or what their pasts may have been. Perhaps people who were able to run in the darkness and come out of it in one piece are just the sorts of people we need for this. Sarah and your parents brought them into this and I've come to see how this will be a net benefit for our situation. As such, I've already made the necessary arrangements so you'll have to accept it and get on with packing."

"You really think this is a positive development?"

"Absolutely," he patted her back and then let her go. "I'll be back shortly, my dear."

"Where are you going?"

"If you'll excuse me, my dear, I think it's prudent that I get the measure of the people I'm sending with you. I'm going to go and introduce myself."

There was a knock on the open door to her bedroom, so Mary looked up from her reading to see a man standing at the doorway. He was a well-dressed man in his mid-forties.

"Mary Bristol, I presume?"

"Oh, hi," Mary smiled, put the book down, then stood up. "You must be Amy's husband. I'm sorry, but I don't even know your name."

"It's Christopher," he smiled, extending his hand. "I'm delighted to finally meet you."

"I'm happy to meet you as well," Mary clasped his hand and shook it. "I like your English accent. Are you from the Sussex area?"

"Yes, from Brighton," he beamed. "Accents change every ten miles in England, so consider me suitably impressed by your knowledge of British linguistics. Amy has told me so much about you, though I question her assertion that you are a clear and present danger to western civilization."

"Yes, please do take everything she says about me with a grain – or perhaps *a brick* – of salt."

"Ms. Bristol, I wanted to meet you because I fear the worst for Amy."

"Please call me Mary," she smiled at him. "Have any threats been directed at her?"

"None that I have been made aware of but obviously she's going to be in close proximity to people who have been the recipients of such attention while she's on that bloody ship. If, heaven forbid, something terrible were to take place on the cruise, then I'd feel better having family there to help keep her safe."

"You know Amy hates me, right?"

"Yes, she has made me abundantly aware of that trifling little detail," Christopher understated. "Regardless, I have always preferred to make up my own mind about people. I work in the financial sector so I've learned to see through peoples' masks and detect any insincerity, yet so far with you, all I see is a kind, well-spoken person who seems genuinely interested in helping her sister."

"I certainly don't want anything bad to happen to Amy," Mary said. "Our relationship is somewhere between terrible and non-existent, but I still care about her. I will do whatever I can to help, of course."

"That's all I could possibly ask."

There was a gentle knock on the door frame and Malcolm stepped inside the room. "Hey, Mary. Your mother says Amy's ready to take us to the firm now."

"Okay, thanks."

"Ah, and you must be my brother-in-law, Malcolm. I'm Christopher."

"Hey," Malcolm nodded at him. "Nice to meet you."

"Delighted. I understand you're from New York, am I correct?"

"Yeah, Queens."

"I've heard so much about you," Christopher's eyes twinkled. "If you don't mind me saying, you're not at all how I imagined the Antichrist to look."

"Ah, yeah; Amy," Malcolm sighed and shook his head. "I can't control what people think of me. It's a happy coincidence that I also don't care."

"A wise philosophy indeed," Christopher beamed. "You're willing to help, so that makes you a decent chap in my eyes. Allow me to say how much I sincerely appreciate the two of you taking this on. I'd do anything to protect my family. Please make sure Amy comes back in one piece."

Friday, 2:09pm:

Malcolm, Mary, and Amy rode together in the elevator as it slowly made its way up to the third floor.

"So, what exactly is it you do here?" Malcolm asked.

"I work for Stacy Metzner," Amy's tone could have put a layer of frost on Hell's ceiling. "She's a senior partner and I assist her with her legal practise."

"So, you're a secretary," he summarized.

"No," Amy threw a glare at him. "I'm a legal administrative assistant."

"As opposed to an illegal one?"

"Look, just pay attention," Amy snapped. "McKenzie Ferguson is a top-tier corporate law firm with more than a hundred lawyers and it's divided into six practice groups."

"I'll just refer to your workplace as 'the firm' instead of always having to say 'McKenzie Ferguson' if it's all the same to you," Malcolm muttered.

"If it helps," Amy said, "the couriers refer to the firm as 'McFergie' for short."

"Not the most dignified of nicknames," Mary added.

"Hmph," Amy grunted. "It's a lot better than the nickname they gave to the firm Dummett Asselstine."

The elevator doors opened and they stepped out into the lobby. They walked along the smooth wood flooring toward the firm's lobby. The reception desk in front of them was an L-shaped design with a smooth black marble surface supported by elegant black interwoven wood planks. Behind the desk was a beige wall, perhaps ten feet across, and it was adorned with a canvas painted with pastel shapes in various hues and all sitting inside an orangey-gold ornate frame. A small jade-coloured vase sat atop the counter and the green plant hanging out of it looked as though it had been severely punished for trying to escape.

As Amy walked past the reception desk, the young woman behind it saw her and spoke up. "Oh Amy, the sandwich Ms. Metzner ordered has arrived."

"I'll take it in to her, thanks," Amy said, taking the paper bag. "You confirmed no gluten with the deli, right?"

"That's what the delivery guy said."

"Thank you," Amy said as she resumed walking toward the wing where her workstation was.

The three walked silently along the cherry-coloured hardwood floor, passing offices and secretarial stations along the way. The smell of coffee induced a craving in Malcolm and it reminded him he had a headache.

At the end of the hallway was a corner office, larger than most others. Amy knocked on the frosted-glass door and then opened it. She walked in, followed closely by Mary and then Malcolm. The woman sitting at the desk didn't look up. To Malcolm it appeared as though she were trying to bore a hole into her screen with her intense and steely eyes. She had straight brown hair, parted on one side with a stylish barrette. Her austere expression hadn't changed in the slightest since they entered.

"Your lunch arrived," Amy placed the bag on the corner of the desk.

Stacy Metzner didn't answer or respond in any way. She continued to stare at her computer screen while typing. The dull white walls of her office were adorned only with framed diplomas and certificates, with neither a single piece of art nor photograph to be seen. The only decoration on Stacy's rosewood desk was a bronze plaque which read 'When you've got them by the balls, their hearts and minds will follow'. She stopped typing, looked at her screen for a few moments and then looked up at the people in her office.

"If you're going to be looking after Amy, that's fine by me but don't be interfering with our workflow," Metzner said in an abrupt and curt voice.

"Don't worry, Ms. Metzner," Mary said. "We'll be discrete."

"And you," Stacy said with a nod toward Malcolm. "Try to stay out of sight and not be a distraction for everyone. You don't exactly look like you fit in, so next time you show up here it would behoove you to be dressed in office attire which acceptably aligns with our corporate dress code policy."

"Just so we're clear," Malcolm said, "you're judging me based on my appearance, correct?"

"Yes, I am," Stacy's response was testy and resonant. "People will always be judged on how they present themselves, so expect to be looked down upon by anyone who has the misfortune to see you."

"It's so sad," Malcolm said with mock wistfulness. "We have so far to go as a society. We abhor racism, yet we still allow people like you to be openly intolerant of gluten."

"If there's nothing further," Metzner said, "take your wry wit and stale humour out of my office and make sure you close the door behind you."

As Stacy was uttering the last syllable, a loud 'bong' sound rang out every few seconds over the public address system.

"Is that the fire alarm?" Mary pointed to a device on the ceiling where the noise was emanating from.

"It's the intermittent bell, meaning we have to be ready to evacuate while they investigate the source of the alarm," Amy said. "If it proceeds to rapid bells, then…"

The tone immediately changed to a continuous bonging sound.

"Okay, everyone," Stacy stood up. "Those bells mean we evacuate."

"No, it doesn't," Malcolm said while closing Stacy's door. "It means *everyone else* evacuates."

"It's probably just a drill," Amy made certain her frustration with Malcolm was made clearly evident in her voice.

"Three days, three dead lawyers," Malcolm replied. "This is day four and there's not a fourth body yet, so we don't have the luxury of assuming it's a drill."

"Do we stay here or evacuate?" Mary asked Malcolm. She had to raise her voice due to the noise. "I'm not sure which course of action is wiser."

"We stay here where we have control over who comes and goes," Malcolm said while pulling the venetian blinds down over the windows. The alarm was making his head pound again which only served to put him into a higher state of agitation. "With the blinds closed, the only way to establish a visual on Amy or Stacy is through this office door. There's too many people outside milling about and there will be some confusion. There will be too much going on for us to be able to keep our eyes looking in every direction and on every possible threat. So whether this is a drill or not, we stay right here."

"But what if the threat is inside the building right now?" Mary said. "If we stay here and they attack then there are no witnesses or bystanders to help us. Or what if there's a bomb or an actual fire? Or gas? We face potential perils either way."

"Yeah, we do," Malcolm said with a quick nod. "We'll make a plan to evacuate the building just in case, but until that is our only remaining option, we stay in this office where we can provide better protection."

Mary turned and was able to see movement through the translucent frosted glass in Stacy's door. She leaned close to Malcolm. "There's someone in the hallway and it looks as though they're heading toward us."

"Get down behind the desk with them and stay out of sight."

Mary and Amy went behind Stacy's deck and crouched down. Stacy looked in bewilderment as the two women took refuge beside her.

"That means you too," Malcolm said to Metzner. "I'm trying to save your life right now, if it's not too much trouble for you."

Stacy fired an angry look at him then slid out of her chair and huddled with Amy and Mary.

Malcolm retrieved his gun and switched off the safety. He pressed his back against the solid wall beside the door. He saw the door latch move down and the door began to open. Malcolm grabbed the person's wrist and yanked them inside the office, spun them around, and then pressed them up against the wall. The woman was wearing a yellow safety vest and an orange helmet strapped around her chin.

"What is your purpose here?"

"I'm... I'm supposed to make sure everyone has evacuated," the woman said, her voice in panicked gasps. "Don't hurt me, please."

"I'm sorry, I was just being cautious," Malcolm released his grip and patted the woman on the shoulder. "Great job. Keep it up."

"Is Stacy Metzner out of the building?"

"She knew what to do when the alarm sounded," Malcolm chose his words carefully.

"And, um, are you supposed to be here?"

"Yes, I'm part of the team holding this surprise drill to make sure everyone evacuates the building."

"You need a gun for that?"

"I take the fire code extremely seriously. Don't you?"

"Yes," the woman nodded with exaggerated enthusiasm. "Very much."

"You're doing a great job," Malcolm smiled. "Don't tell anyone what you saw here. Off you go."

The woman skittered down the hallway, no longer interested in checking offices.

Moments later, to the relief of the pulse in Malcolm's head, the alarm bells were silenced and there was a voice over the PA system.

"Attention, attention, this is the Security Desk," the male voice said. "We are investigating the cause of the alarm. At this time, we'd like everyone to continue the evacuation of the building as a precaution. Thank you."

That voice sounds familiar, Malcolm thought, though he couldn't place it.

Stacy Metzner stood up from behind her desk and advanced on Malcolm.

"What the hell do you think you're doing, you paranoid nut-job? You assaulted a member of the staff, you have my assistant in a panicked state, and you scared the bejeezus out of me as well.

And what kind of idiot brings a firearm inside an office building? I want you out of my office and off these premises or I'll call the police and tell them you're an armed lunatic. Just so you know, I'll also be asking our Fire Warden if she wants to press charges against you."

"You're all alive," Malcolm shrugged. "That's my job."

"We're all evacuating the building right this minute," Stacy glared at him. "When this is over, I don't want you coming back inside."

"Then at least let me lead the way," Malcolm opened the door.

"I certainly don't want you behind me, so go right ahead."

Malcolm led the way down the hallway, following the illuminated exit signs overhead. Mary was behind him while Stacy and Amy were side-by-side behind Mary.

"Your brother-in-law is a complete psychopath," Stacy said.

"I know," Amy said.

"Family dinners must be a real treat," Metzner grumbled. "I can't imagine what mayhem would ensue during dinner if someone dared to ask him to pass the potatoes. Does he throw the guests against the wall and frisk them as they arrive too?"

"We don't hang out socially," Amy said.

"I can understand why," Stacy scoffed. "It's a relief to know I can get a restraining order within twenty minutes if I want one. I wouldn't be surprised if he has a criminal past."

"He does," Amy said.

"Then why would we let him act as our protection?"

"Because," Malcolm said as he walked. "I'm much more likely than you to understand how an assassin thinks and operates. If you want to continue breathing, shut up and follow my lead."

As they drew near to the exit stairwell, Malcolm saw a sign which stated the north stairwell was out of order and to use the south stairs.

"To hell with that," Maloclm muttered as he reached for the handle of the door leading to the exit stairwell. He pushed down the latch and opened it and then immediately held up his hand. "Hold up, everyone."

"What now?" Amy snapped.

"There's somebody on the landing below," Malcolm said, and then added, "And it ain't pretty."

"Let me see," Stacy pushed past Malcolm and stood at the metal railing. She looked down to the landing below and saw the crumpled, motionless body of a woman. There was some blood on the floor of the landing beside the woman's head. The deceased was dressed in a light grey business suit with matching ankle-length skirt. Her long brown hair was covering her face.

"Everyone stay here," Malcolm said. "I'll check it out."

Malcolm walked down the concrete stairs, being careful not to step in any of the small droplets of blood on the way. As he arrived at the body he knelt down beside it. Stacy pulled out her phone and punched in a number.

"Yes, Stacy Metzner here. I need you to call for an ambulance right away. There's an injured woman on the north-side stairwell between the second and third floors." Metzner returned her gaze to the stricken woman on the landing. "I can't tell from here, but she's not moving, so at the very least she's unconscious." She paused. "Yes, and do it immediately."

Stacy put her phone away and then called down to Malcolm. "They're calling for an ambulance and sending a security guard with a first aid kit."

"A waste of time," Malcolm called up to her. "Dead people don't need First Aid, they need Last Rites. Everyone stay up there. The fewer people we have walking through a crime scene the better. By the way, do you still think I'm being paranoid? I'm asking for a friend."

Malcolm gently brushed the hair away from the deceased's face. "Anyone recognize her?"

"Oh my Lord in heaven," Amy gasped. "That's Janine."

"Does she work at the firm?" Mary inquired.

"Yes," Amy put her hands over her mouth and there was a horrified look in her eyes. "Janine Andrews is a lawyer in the Tech Group. Are you sure she's dead."

"Yeah," Malcolm said. "Looks like her neck's been broken."

"A broken neck?" Stacy's puzzled expression appeared to be identical to her annoyed one. "Then where's the blood from?"

"There was also an impact to the back of her head," Malcolm pointed to the victim's skull.

"There's a bit of water at the top of the stairs here," Stacy pointed. "It looks like she slipped on it. She must have fallen down the concrete stairs and hit her head on the way down."

"Right," Malcolm rolled his eyes. "Amazing how there's been one unfortunate fatal accident every day."

"She just fell and hit her head on the way down, that's all," Stacy's testy reply reflected her impatience with what she still viewed as Malcolm's over-zealousness.

"If she just slipped, then why is there blood spatter *at the top of the stairs?* See those small flecks of blood sprayed on the wall beside you? That means she sustained her injuries right where you're standing. She was already dead and bloodied before she 'fell' down to here."

The door at the foot of the stairs below burst open and a man in a white shirt and black pants burst through. He was carrying a large red bag with the words 'first aid' printed on the side of it in large, white letters. As the man took the stairs two at a time to get up to the landing, his black tie swaying back and forth.

"Everyone please stand back while I…" the raspy-voiced guard froze. "Oh my God. Malcolm?"

"Well, well, if it isn't Ad…"

"It's Whitlock," the out-of-breath guard looked carefully at Malcolm. "My name is Devon Whitlock, remember?"

"Oh, yes, of course," Malcolm said. "Good to see you again 'Devon'. We have one Janine Andrews with a broken neck. She allegedly slipped and had a bad fall."

"Allegedly?" Whitlock asked as he snapped on a pair of rubber gloves.

"With all the accidents happening lately," Malcolm said, "yeah, I'm going with 'allegedly' for now, wouldn't you?"

Whitlock did a brief check of Janine's neck pulse and inspected her head wound.

"She's definitely deceased," the guard sighed. "Did any of you see how this happened?"

"No, it was already done by the time we got here," Malcolm answered for everyone. "But it's clear someone struck her from behind as she came through the third floor fire exit door."

"How do you know?"

"The blood spatters on the wall at the upper landing," Malcolm pointed up the stairs. "They fit with the nature of the head injury. A right-handed swing with a thin but heavy blunt object, like a metal rod or a pipe."

"So what do we do now?" Stacy asked from the top of the stairs.

"Let me call this in," Whitlock said in his gravelly voice. "The rest of you, please go back through the doors you came in from and then exit the building via the south stairwell across the other side."

"Why?" Stacy demanded.

"Because," Malcolm replied, "I doubt you'll want to have to answer questions from investigators. As I said a moment ago, this stairwell is a crime scene."

"It may be argued that any place you went to could be considered a crime scene," Stacy said.

"Please say nothing to anyone about this incident for the time being," Whitlock said. "We'll need to conduct a full investigation."

"Just remember, Mr. Whitlock," Stacy pointed at him. "Don't call the police."

"I won't, ma'am."

While Devon Whitlock began barking instructions into his walkie-talkie, Malcolm went back to the top of the stairs and faced Mary.

"There's a killer on the loose," Malcolm said. "Stick with Amy and Metzner and get them out of the building. Do your best to keep everyone out of sight."

"Got it."

"One last thing," Malcolm whispered. "The body is still warm. This death just happened no more than two minutes before we found her. Whoever did it is still nearby, so be vigilant."

Mary shuddered and then cleared her throat.

"Alright, everyone, this way please," Mary gestured to the doorway leading out of the stairwell and back into the hallway. They went through and the door slowly closed and then clicked shut.

"I didn't think I'd ever see you again," Whitlock said as he snapped some photos of the scene with the camera on his phone.

"Yeah, well I guess this isn't your lucky day."

"I disagree," Whitlock grinned. "I'm alive and breathing because of you. What are you doing here?"

"Lawyers are getting killed and I'm protecting one of them."

"Hopefully it wasn't this one."

"No," Malcolm said. "And what are you doing here?"

"I've been working in security for the past seven months, and I was posted to this building about four weeks ago. I've got a new name, new job, and the works."

"You're still smoking, aren't you?"

"Guilty as charged. How did you know that?"

"You have a pack of smokes in your shirt pocket, your breath stinks of tobacco, you got winded running up a single flight of stairs, and your voice is even more raspy than it was before. Anyone with eyes, ears, and a functioning sense of smell would have been able to make that leap."

"Ah, yes," Whitlock chuckled. "I suppose it was obvious. Stupid question on my part."

"While we're waiting for the authorities to get here, tell me more about what you've been up to."

"We're almost there," Mary said as she pointed down the hall towards the south exit stairwell.

"This is absolutely preposterous," Stacy fumed, marching alongside Amy. "I suppose you are also carrying some sort of illegal weapon?"

"No," Mary said. "I don't like guns."

Mary's voice and expression remained calm, but her heart was racing.

"Then you're associating with the wrong type of person," Stacy said. "So then tell me something. If you have no weapons on your person at present, how exactly are you planning on protecting us if there's a killer somewhere in the building?"

Mary had been asking herself that same question since before they had left the north stairwell. If she met up with a weapon-wielding, homicidal killer, she'd need more than a lot of luck. Mary was trying to regulate her breathing to keep herself calm but her mind raced while her adrenaline spiked after every corner they went around. Mary opened the stairwell doors and looked around, up and then down. "You let me worry about that, okay?"

"No, I'd like to know," Stacy followed Mary through the door, Amy behind her. "Are you going to threaten them with an eyeliner pencil? Wag a scolding finger at them? Come on. What's your plan?"

"If something happens, I'll assess the threat and respond appropriately."

"I'm not reassured by your lack of an answer."

"That's a real shame," Mary's voice lacked anything resembling sincerity. "Just know you're in good hands, okay? Now let's get out of here."

Friday, 4:12pm:

"You did great back there," Malcolm took a sip of his take-out coffee and savoured it. "You got them out of the building and they're both alive."

"Don't change the subject," Mary grumped as she and Malcolm walked along West Georgia Street in front of the Cathedral. "Why would Melanie Waterman be coming with us on the cruise?"

"She's not," Malcolm said. "I said our *supervisor* would be on board, not our boss."

"What supervisor?" Mary managed to blend an equal amount of bewilderment and frustration into her voice. "We don't have a supervisor."

"We do now," he took another drink. "We've just acquired one on a trial basis."

"What supervisor have we acquired? I don't recall doing that, so what are you not telling me?"

"Look, the more cases we work on, the more attention we'll inevitably get. The more attention we get, the more likely it is that people from our pasts will recognize us and decide they need to stop us from breathing."

"Yes, absolutely," Mary exhaled sharply. Malcolm normally spoke in direct and to-the-point bursts, so when he dragged things out, Mary knew something was going to be stated that she would likely not enjoy hearing. The longer the build-up, the louder she anticipated sighing afterwards. "But where does the supervisor fit into all this?"

"Here's the brilliant part," Malcolm glanced over at her. "We hire somebody to pretend they're in charge while we do all the actual work in the background as his 'assistants'. He gets the spotlight and credit, and we stay anonymous."

"Because of the way you're building this up, I assume the person you've hired may cause me some alarm."

"Hopefully not," Malcolm paused before continuing. "Remember my first job at ARIES two years ago? We'd just had Alyssa and you were off work at the time, but do you remember when I was sent out on a job that involved the Da Nang Cartel?"

"Yes, of course," Mary said with a nod. "I helped you write your report when it was over."

"The guy I have in mind was the key witness who I was assigned to keep alive and out of harm's way until the trial."

"Oh Lord no," Mary slapped her palm onto her forehead and the ensuing sigh was indeed one for the record books. "You're not talking about Adam Spender, are you?"

"Technically no, because once he was done testifying and the Cartel was sent packing, he changed his name to Devon Whitlock."

"You mean the wheezing security guard from Amy's building?"

"Yeah, that guy," Malcolm had anticipated the sigh but not one that could have been measured on the Richter scale. He came to the realization he would have a harder time selling this idea than he'd hoped. "They're one and the same."

"Is there a closed-captioning version of this conversation I could activate?" Mary covered her face with her hands for a moment and then let her arms drop to her side. "I'm having a lot of trouble following along here. Isn't Spender worried about the Cartel finding him?"

"Once they were put on the plane and sent back to Vietnam to face charges, no. He may have been the star witness for the prosecution during the trial, but with a new name and career and with everyone he testified against being an ocean away, he felt pretty good about coming out of hiding and starting over. He's been working in the security industry for the past half year."

"There is so much wrong with all of this."

"Like what?"

"Are you kidding me?" Mary's eyes widened in disbelief. "I have so many questions, I wouldn't even know where to begin."

"Try anyway," he said. "I'll answer as many questions as you can ask."

"Okay then," Mary took a deep breath. "For starters, can you trust the judgment of a person who thought the name 'Devon Whitlock' was inconspicuous?"

"That's not really a fair…"

"Also, where did he go to get his name changed?" Mary began counting her questions on her fingers as they crossed Hornby Street and headed towards Granville. "Going through normal legal channels would involve publishing an official name change announcement in the media so unless he's an idiot, he didn't do that. What makes him so sure that not a single member, informer, or affiliate of the Da Nang Cartel was overlooked in the round-up? How does he know there aren't more of them around? And – perhaps most importantly – why didn't you come to me first before agreeing to work with him?"

"The answers are I don't know, I don't care, the cops told him the entire Cartel was extradited so he's no longer in danger here, and because it didn't come to my mind, in that order."

"I know I'll regret asking this, but… the people you recommend us working with tend to have lengthy rap sheets. What's on his?"

"Hardly anything," Malcolm waved his hand in a dismissive gesture.

"Tell me what 'hardly anything' means to you."

Malcolm had hoped she wouldn't think to ask that, but deep down he knew it was too much to hope for. "Assault, assault with a weapon, grand theft, manslaughter, possession of narcotics, and carjacking."

"Gee, is that all?" Mary's laugh was triggered by derision more than humour. "For the record, your definition of 'hardly anything' is completely different than mine. Are you sure that's everything?"

"No," he knew he was in deep but it was too late to turn back now. "I forgot to mention he was also charged with unlawful confinement."

"This just gets better and better," Mary began massaging her temples. "How can you possibly believe this guy can be trusted to be our pretend supervisor?"

"Because he's a solid, upstanding citizen."

"Are you serious?" Mary's jaw hung slack for a moment while the sheer, utter disbelief of what she was hearing settled into her mind. "Did you not hear yourself a few seconds ago? He sounds like a real piece of work."

"After his brother died of an overdose, Spender began a vendetta against the pushers and dealers in the Seattle-Vancouver corridor and the Da Nang Cartel was the largest single source of drugs in that area. All the charges he racked up were against them."

"What about the charge of Manslaughter?"

"Two guys armed with knives jumped out of a van and attacked him," Malcolm said. "In the melee, one of the attackers swung a knife at him and Spender deflected the blow and the knife ended up in the chest of the second attacker. It's not like he intended to kill either of his attackers or anything, and the Cartel plays for keeps. Spender tied up the guys and tossed them into the back of the van, which was full of drugs and weapons. He was on his way to turn everything over to the cops but he got pulled over before he could get there. The van was stolen property so most of the charges I mentioned to you came out of him being in possession of the van and its contents."

"That information improves things a little but I still see so many red flags. How long did he serve in prison?"

"Three months."

"Only three months for all that?"

"Yeah, he was such a help putting away the Cartel he was able to cut a sweet plea deal," Malcolm was trying to read Mary's facial expression to see if she was softening, but all signs were pointing to no. "He spent six times as long in the trial than he did in prison. He says he got out this past January, arranged for a long and convincing backstory for himself, and he's been getting on with his life. Anything else?"

"Yes, one more thing," Mary's sigh was loud. "How can you be so sure about him?"

"You should have seen how solid he was during the entire Da Nang trial," Malcolm drank the last of the coffee and put the cup into the recycling container beside the sidewalk. "The opposing counsel threw everything they could at him to attack his credibility and to make his testimony inadmissible, but he remained calm and professional throughout. He didn't crack even under a brutal cross-examination and because of him, the cartel members were extradited back to Vietnam. He wanted to do the right thing and he never wavered. I respect him for that."

"I'm still not sure this is a good idea."

"Listen, we need to stay out of the public eye as much as possible due to the circumstances of our pasts, right? So, having him as our pretend supervisor will accomplish that. You've heard the expression 'if this person didn't exist, we'd need to invent him?' Well, we just invented him."

"A felon with a fake identity, a history of violence, and who is marked for death by a vicious drug cartel is not what that expression was made for," Mary had lost count of how many times she'd sighed in the past two minutes. "As our 'supervisor', he would be the face of our operation so whatever he did would end up reflecting on us. This is something you should have talked to me about before doing it."

"What's the big deal?" Malcolm said. "It's just a trial period and if it doesn't work out then we wish him well and say adios amigo. Look, we've worked with plenty of undercover people before."

"Completely different."

"How?"

"When we've worked with others, it was a short-term arrangement not a potentially long term one, like you're suggesting for him," Mary was doing her best to keep That Tone out of her voice but didn't particularly care that she was failing at it. "Also, they were pros and highly experienced in doing undercover work and they were used to doing this sort of work for prolonged periods of time. This guy has only a few months' worth of experience maintaining a fictitious past. One mistake and he blows all of our covers. We're dealing with lawyers who are used to sizing people up and getting a good reading off them. Add to that the glaring flaw in your plan I mentioned earlier, which is in order to help us avoid potentially dangerous attention, you want to use someone who himself should probably stay hidden from potentially dangerous attention."

"All good points," Malcolm conceded.

"I know and now this is the part where you address those good points."

"The longer Spender is in the role, the better at it he will become," Malcolm said. "The better he becomes, the less pretending he will have to do."

"Can you say that again using different words?"

"Didn't you understand what I said?"

"I understood it," Mary nodded, "but I'd like to see if you can say it in a way where it doesn't sound quite so stupid."

"Why is it stupid?"

"Because if I may summarize your argument," Mary huffed, "he's going to just make it up as he goes along, trust his luck, and simply hope he doesn't get recognized by the wrong people."

"I have to say that I much preferred the way it sounded when I said it," Malcolm felt the sudden urge to get another coffee. This wasn't going at all as he'd hoped it would. "Look, here's the deal. He goes to the crime scene with us, his trusty 'assistants', and he pretends to make notes. He can say 'hmm' and 'interesting' and frown occasionally. While he's doing that, we're doing the real work. Then we can give him a signal and he can then announce that he has what he needs for now and then he'll call for us to follow him out."

"You make it sound easy when it is actually too risky to be considered a sane option. I am so angry with you right now for leaving so much to chance and not getting my feedback on something which will have a direct impact on both of us."

"Sorry," Malcolm didn't know what else to say.

"This will require more than just a 'sorry'. You're not seriously suggesting I should trust this guy, I hope."

"Of course not."

"Do you trust him?"

"Hell no," Malcolm scoffed. "He has to earn my trust like he had to earn my respect. I'm only giving him this chance because I respect him."

"He was at the crime scene when Janine Andrews was killed in the stairwell. That makes him a suspect."

"Yeah, I know it does," Malcolm nodded. "But remember, Janine had been dead for less than two minutes when we found her and Spender was making an evacuation announcement from the security desk three floors down and across the lobby. It's not impossible for him to have committed the murder, but it would have been damned difficult."

"He was huffing and puffing when he arrived on the scene in the exit stairwell."

"True, but he's a heavy smoker and he ran from the security desk carrying a heavy bag and then sprinted up two flights of stairs. Most people would be breathing heavily after that."

"I still think this is a terrible idea," Mary muttered as they crossed Granville Street.

"You can tell him that when you see him," Malcolm gestured ahead with his hand. "We're just a couple of blocks away now."

Mary and Malcolm walked south along Seymour Street and then turned left into the alley beside the Starbucks. Adam Spender was there, cigarette in hand, waiting for them.

"Mary, this is Devon Whitlock, who you know by another name."

"Hi," had Mary's tone been any colder it could have solidified antifreeze.

"Nice to meet you," Devon Whitlock held out his hand and Mary, with reluctance, shook it. "This is going to sound odd, but I wasn't convinced you really existed until now. I thought Malcolm was making up being married in order to convince me he had a life and wasn't some sad, pathetic loser."

"I'm for real, regardless of what that says about me," Mary looked sidelong at Malcolm. "What about you? Are you married?"

"I was," Whitlock took a drag on his cigarette. "She passed away."

"I'm sorry," Mary felt wretched for her uncivil mood. Her annoyance had been replaced immediately with guilt and sympathy.

"Thanks," Spender said. "But she died doing what she loved while on vacation in a tropical paradise. I comfort myself knowing that she died quickly with no pain."

"Were you with her at the time?" Mary asked.

"No, I was in the early stages of the Da Nang trial so I was stuck here," Spender looked off into the distance and then sighed. "You know, it's a bit ironic. I sent her away on a vacation so she'd be safe during the trial. I was testifying against some nasty people and knew she'd be used as leverage against me if she was around."

"Was there any sign of foul play?" Mary asked.

"No, but the Da Nang Cartel were great at making things look like accidents, so I'll never know for sure," Spender sighed. "It's been a stressful few years, which is why I haven't yet managed to give these damned things up."

He looked with contempt at the cigarette between his fingers and then dropped it onto the pavement. He stepped on it to extinguish it. "Anyway, I'll play whatever role you need me to but I'd like to avoid telling any lies."

"I won't be asking you to lie," Malcolm said, "but to succeed in the role, I'll need you to stretch the truth to a place just short of where a lie would begin."

"I'm not exactly sure what you mean by that."

"Okay, imagine somebody you care a lot about who is very self-conscious asks you what you think about the outfit they have on," Malcolm said. "Are you going to hurt their feelings by saying you think it looks hideous?"

"No, of course not."

"Right," Malcolm pointed at Spender and nodded. "Instead, you might say something like 'you have a lot of other outfits which suit you so much better'. It's not a lie but it's a stretched version of the truth."

"Oh, okay," Whitlock nodded. "I got you."

"Wait," Mary glared at Malcolm. "You've said that to me when I've asked you about my outfits."

"Let's not dwell on the past."

"It was *three days ago*."

"It's still the past," Malcolm wondered who had turned up the thermostat in the alleyway. "We need to be looking ahead."

"I will be," Mary huffed. "To the next time I ask you about one of my outfits."

"Ugh," Malcolm muttered under his breath. "This day is really starting to suck."

"I have to go," Mary said. "I've still got to pack the rest of our stuff."

"We'd better get going too, Malcolm," Spender looked at the time on his phone. "I've arranged for us to meet the managing partner at the pub on Water Street. Nice meeting you, Mary."

Friday, 4:52pm:

Malcolm and Spender sat side-by-side in a secluded booth at the back corner of the pub. Flat screen television sets adorned the brick and teakwood walls and were each tuned to a different sporting event. The dim, ambient lighting and the general noise of sports and conversation ensured they'd be able to talk freely when the managing partner arrived.

Malcolm had a large glass of Coke while Spender had opted for a pint of dark beer.

"We have to be on that ship," Malcolm took a sip of his drink.

"I know," Spender said, patting Malcolm's shoulder. "I won't let you down, buddy."

"I'd feel more comfortable if I were doing the talking."

"If you do the talking, we won't get hired," Spender cast a sidelong glance at Malcolm. "Trust me, I know how to work lawyers."

"Alright, we'll try it your way but if I jump in, go with it."

"Sure thing," Spender took a drink of beer. "Hey, listen, if we're going to be doing some sleuthing in this case, are you looking for me to be like Conan Doyle's Sherlock Holmes or more like Agatha Christie's Hercule Poirot?"

"I'm thinking more like Rudolph Valentino."

"Never heard of him."

"Are you serious?" Malcolm gave him an incredulous look. "He was a huge silent movie star."

"I'm not into movies," Spender said. "Can't be bothered with that sort of thing."

"How can I work with someone who doesn't like movies?"

"I'm sure you'll manage," Spender smirked. "What's the connection between that Valentino fellow and the type of character you want me to play?"

"He was among the greatest silent film stars in history, so I want you to be the strong, silent, charismatic type. I want you to be the silent centre of attention. I want all eyes on you, so play up the silent charm. All you need to do is silently observe people, take notes, and occasionally nod your head silently while doing either. Have I used the word 'silent' enough for you to get the picture?"

"Yes, okay, I get it," Spender chuckled. "You never were the subtle type, were you?"

"To be subtle is to be unclear and I prefer clarity any day."

"Okay, so if I'm supposed to be Mr. Quiet, what do you expect me to do if they ask me a lot of questions?"

"I expect you to give them a lot of one or two word answers. Appear to be in deep thought about what they asked. Whenever you feel lost or don't know what to do, you say 'I have to think about how all these pieces fit together' or tell them you'd delegated that part of the job to me. Otherwise, stay silent and mysterious. As I said, I want everyone watching you and not Mary and me."

"She doesn't like me, does she?" Spender sighed. "Mary, I mean."

"She's unhappy with me, not you, so don't worry about it."

"We'll be working as a team so I have to worry about it," Spender glanced over at Malcolm. "Without trust, we put one another at risk."

"I know. Look, just do what she asks and keep her safe. That's what I do."

"And that's enough to win her over?"

"I sure as hell hope so," Malcolm sipped his Coke. "That's all I've got to offer her. Oh, hey, check it out. That's Bill Sutherland coming in. We're on."

A tall and stocky man entered the pub and Malcolm recognized him from his picture on the firm's website. Bill's cherubic face was adorned with horn-rimmed glasses and wisps of dark hair stuck out from under the brim of his cowboy hat. He wore a bright white dress shirt with no tie and a pair of faded blue jeans.

"Who's that with him?" Spender asked Maclolm as he waved to Bill. Malcolm saw the short Asian woman walking behind Bill. She was in a smart navy-blue suit and had her black hair in a pony tail. She was carrying a laptop and a fat file folder.

"I recognize her from the website as well," Malcolm said as he motioned for them to come over. "That's his assistant Kira."

Bill Sutherland swirled the ice in his glass. Malcolm barely had a chance to see the scotch before Bill chugged it down in two gulps.

"Look, the thing is, Mr. Whitlock," Sutherland sighed, "we don't want to involve the police just yet which is why I appreciate the discrete way you reached out to me."

"I completely understand, Mr. Sutherland," Spender said. "Corporate clients can be a nervous and skittish bunch so you need to keep these incidents as quiet and low-key as possible for the sake of your reputation."

"Absolutely," Bill signalled to the waitress a few tables away that he'd really like another. She nodded. Bill resumed his conversation with the two men across from him. "We recognize the seriousness of the situation but at the same time we're not quite ready to be contacting the police or hiring private security for the cruise. Either may be viewed as an over-reaction."

"Right now," Kira said, "we still consider this to be a private matter and the firm will handle it internally."

"Your credentials, Mr. Whitlock, are impressive," Bill handed the CV back to Spender. "So in the unlikely event any of the recent deaths are confirmed to be the result of foul play, then we'll certainly consider you as a candidate to look into it for us. My first choice will always be people who understand the importance of professional discretion."

Kira looked down at her buzzing phone.

"Sorry, everyone I have to take this." She stepped out of the booth and stood a few feet away.

"Our discretion is not just assured it's guaranteed," Adam Spender continued. "I've worked at your building for a while now and I've gotten to know many of you there. Your colleagues deserve top-tier protection. At the same time, your brand and image must be maintained and protected, of course."

"I'm delighted you understand the firm's priorities so well."

"Oh my God, no," Kira's face bore a contorted expression of shock and pain.

"What is it, Kira?" Bill asked.

"It's Grant McKenzie," Kira said, eyes now watering. "He's passed away."

"Grant's dead?" Bill stepped out of the booth and stood up. "Where did this happen?"

"At his cabin," Kira said. "He was found dead on his boat on the lake this morning by his neighbour."

"This is getting completely out of hand," Sutherland said, slumping back down into the booth seat and burying his face in his hands.

"Mr. Sutherland," Spender said in a calm yet insistent voice. "I'm sorry for your loss but if I may be blunt, one death can be an accident and two *might* be a coincidence. This latest death brings the total up to five lawyers passing away in four days. I'll leave you my fee schedule and you can decide whether you'd like some professional last-minute security for your cruise or not."

"No need," Bill sighed. "You're hired. I'll get Kira to write up the paperwork on her laptop and we'll sign off on it right here, right now."

Adam Spender glanced over at Malcolm who gave him an appreciative nod and a thumbs-up sign.

Friday, 5:23pm:

"For our team-building event Saturday night," Bill downed his third drink, "we were originally going to do a murder mystery game but in light of the deaths of our colleagues, we figure it would be viewed as being in poor taste."

"Agreed," Spender said.

"So we were thinking about maybe bringing a bunch of material, masks, and clothing and make it an impromptu costume party," Bill grin was broad. "People could craft their own costumes and it would be a fun activity."

"From bad taste to bad planning," Malcolm said.

"How so?" Kira asked.

"We would be trying to keep everyone safe from harm on board a boat that's filled with people in disguises," Malcolm said.

"Ah, yes, I see your point," Sutherland nodded, seemingly deep in thought. "Then we should cancel the party."

"No, go ahead with the party, just cancel the costume part of it," Malcolm drank down the last of his Coke. "Make it a cocktail evening or something. Either way, we'll have to try to keep Stacy away from it."

"She's not likely to attend any of the social aspects of the cruise," Bill said. "Knowing her as well as I do, I bet she'll be in her cabin working for the entire weekend."

Kira nodded emphatically.

"Would we be able to get the details of the lawyer deaths?" Spender asked. "I know it's a delicate topic, but in the off-chance there's malicious intent behind their tragic passing, it would be a great help to us if we had some of the details."

Bill turned to his assistant. "Kira, could you send that file to Mr. Whitlock and his assistant before you head home?"

"Sure thing," she said.

"Thank you," Spender said.

"Let me ask you something," Malcolm said. "In light of all that's happened lately, why would you not postpone or cancel the cruise?"

"It's a fair question," Bill glanced to the distance to see if his next drink was soon to arrive. "Frankly, cancelling the cruise won't bring any of our colleagues back from the dead so there's no point in doing so. The lawyers we lost were all of the mind that we needed to do these quadri-annual retreats no matter what. We'll do the event in their honour and hold a moment of silence or something for them on the first night. Plus FIRST is our largest client and we have so much strategic planning to do for the next four years."

"Life goes on, in other words," Spender said.

Silence descended upon the table as their server arrived. She put down a bottle of beer in front of Bill, a mug of Guinness in front of Spender, a spritzer for Kira, and another Coke for Malcolm. She picked up the empty glasses and retreated.

"That's it exactly, Mr. Whitlock," Bill said as he took a swig from the bottle. "Life goes on indeed. It also should be mentioned that the cruise costs were non-refundable so it was better to go than to lose the money."

Bill looked at his watch. "We'd better get moving. The ship sails at six-thirty. I'll meet you there."

"Sure," Spender said.

"Before you go, I know a guy who can discretely look into the scene at Mr. McKenzie's cabin," Malcolm offered. "He can let us know what he finds."

"He's not a cop, is he?" Sutherland stood up out of the booth.

"No, he's a private detective I trust," Malcolm replied. "He's damned good at his job, and he understands the finer points of discretion. So where's the cabin located?"

Friday, 6:22pm:

Malcolm and Mary stepped out of the taxi and Malcolm handed the driver some money and waved him away. They were standing at the address of a private dock located three miles south of the main ferry terminal in West Vancouver. The dense cluster of trees and bushes obstructed the view of the sea but the distinctive smell of the ocean enveloped them. There was an opening in the foliage and they walked along the path which took them into it.

"Kira sent Spender and I the files on the first three dead lawyers," Malcolm said. "The first death was Ben Shapner, who jumped off the balcony of his fifteenth-floor apartment. He left a typed suicide note on his computer screen. The second was Eliza Borwith, who was killed crossing the street when she was struck by a hit-and-run driver."

"Any witnesses?" Mary asked.

"No, it was a quiet street near her home," Malcolm replied. "The third lawyer was Charles Lautzen who lost control of his vehicle and crashed through the guardrail on a bridge and crashed into the rocks below. Each death was a day apart."

"That would have to be one heck of a coincidence," Mary nodded. "And I suppose it's too soon to find out what the firm is saying about Janine Andrews and Grant McKenzie, right?"

"Yeah, though I already know Janine didn't die from slipping on water," Malcolm pointed to the 'welcome to The North Star Express – private property' sign ahead of them. "Looks like we're here."

They continued along the path until they came across the wooden pier.

"I've got Sammy Mendoza on the way up to Grant McKenzie's cabin for us," Malcolm said. "He'll check it out and see if he can find any traces of foul play, and then..."

They both stopped and looked at the ship in front of them. It was neither the large luxury ship nor the yacht Malcolm had been expecting to see.

"It's a damned passenger ferry," he said, bewildered. "Is this for real? That thing's got to be at least fifty years old. They probably bought an old ferry, put a fresh coat of paint over the rust, and then called it a cruise ship."

"Then it's still a cruise ship," Mary said. "It's a ship and we'll be cruising on it."

"I can manage to call it a large floating object, but I'm a long way from being able to call it a cruise ship."

"You're not seeing the positive here," Mary said.

"And what is the positive thing I'm missing?"

"Think about it: right about now we would have been in Baneridge to begin a week of analyzing patient files at the Miralinda Mental Health Hospital," Mary looped her arm through Malcolm's. "Instead here we are, together, about to go on a cruise up the coast."

"Yeah, there's nothing as romantic as being trapped on a floating tin can with the knowledge that there might be a killer in the same confined space," he looked at Mary and winked. "By the way, did you contact Tamara to let her know we couldn't make it?"

"She wasn't there, but I spoke with one of the RN's and told her we would reschedule the patient interviews when we got back."

"Good," Malcolm nodded.

"Let's get on board," Mary said. "It's due to pull out any minute."

"Spender messaged me to say he's already on the ship," Malcolm said. "He's also made note for me of what cabins Stacy and Amy are staying in."

They stepped onto the gangplank and walked up to where three uniformed crew members were standing. They had been greeting everyone as they came on board.

"Welcome," one of them said. "May I see your invitations, please?"

"I'm Malcolm Mercer and this is my colleague Mary Bristol. We've been hired to be security for the cruise. I have a letter here from Bill Sutherland. I hope you got the message from him that we'd be coming."

"Just what we need," another officer said with neither enthusiasm nor sincerity. He was a tall, imposing figure with a mostly-bald head and grey sideburns. "One minimum wage rent-a-cop was bad enough and now we have two more. Fine. Welcome aboard, and all that, but make sure you stay the hell out of our way."

"What's your name, officer?" Malcolm asked.

"Mitch Jorgensen," Mitch looked at Mary then looked back to Malcolm. "She sure as hell doesn't look like a security guard."

"And you don't look like a human being," Malcolm said, "but at least I was willing to give you the benefit of the doubt."

"Security or not, I don't want you interfering with ship operations," Mitch scowled.

"No need for the abruptness, Mitch, they're our guests," the first officer said, grinning. He was an older thin man with a weathered face adorned with a salt-and-pepper moustache and matching beard. "Delighted to have you on board. I'm Wes. Wes Oliphant."

Oliphant held out his hand and Malcolm shook it. Despite Wes appearing beyond retirement age and looking somewhat gaunt, he had a firm handshake.

"Nice to meet you," Malcolm said.

"And I'm Captain Farrell," the third officer said. "Welcome aboard. I've been expecting you. Mr. Sutherland told me about the arrangement earlier today."

"I hope our being here won't be an inconvenience," Mary said.

"Not at all," Farrell smiled. He had close-cropped hair, thick eyebrows, and an impish grin. "Mr. Sutherland's paying the bills for this cruise, so we'll accommodate him any way we can. We still have several unoccupied cabins left, so it's not a problem. Your colleague Mr. Whitlock arrived a few minutes ago. How may I be the most help to you?"

"I'll leave this part to you," Mary said to Malcolm. "What room are we in?"

"I've got you in cabin twenty-four," Farrell pointed at a door with the word 'stairs' stenciled on it. "Go down the stairs and continue on to the end of the corridor."

"Thank you," Mary said. "Nice to meet you all. I'm going to head down and unpack. Could I get a copy of the ship's safety procedures?"

"I'll have one sent down to you," Wes said.

Mary walked to the stairwell door, opened it, and walked through.

"Is she for real?" Mitch gestured towards Mary with a nod of his head.

"Yeah, she can never get enough technical manuals," Malcolm said. "If she asks you to join a book club, say no. So, including you three, how many crew members are on board?"

"There's nine of us who work this ship every sailing," Oliphant said. "The rest of the staff are provided to us by the temp agency we use. They specialize in workers for cruise ships and hotels so we always have a talented pool to choose from."

"And no doubt the turnover rate at a temp agency would be high, so they wouldn't think twice about any eager last-minute applicants with unconfirmed backgrounds," Malcolm nodded. "How many temps do you have on board for this event?"

"Thirty."

"Thirty?" Malcolm's eyebrows shot toward his hairline. "Are you saying it takes nearly forty people including your crew of nine to run this ship?"

"Yes, that's what it takes," Mitch said. "We need prep cooks, servers, room service, maids, janitors, event planners, bartenders, and so on."

"And the nine of you do what jobs?"

"Captain," Farrell pointed to himself, "Wes is First Mate, Mitch is Second Mate, and we also have a navigator, two mechanical engineers, a liaison officer, and two deck crew."

"How far is it to Prince Rupert?" Malcolm asked. "And how long will it take to get there?"

"It's around four-hundred nautical miles point-to-point," Oliphant said. "The ship's capable of thirty-two knots, but we usually run twenty-five. If we traveled at that speed, we'd be done the journey in a little over sixteen hours and we'd be in by ten, ten-thirty tomorrow morning."

"But...?" Malcolm prompted.

"But the lawyer paying the bills wanted to make sure they all had a Saturday night at sea for a party, so we'll be going only twenty-knots through the Strait of Georgia and up to our first stop."

"I didn't realize there were any stops scheduled."

"Just the one," Mitch said. "We'll be dropping anchor between Calvert Island and Hunter Island around eleven."

"And we'll be running the pontoon boat to take passengers ashore for some sightseeing, hiking, and fishing in the afternoon," Oliphant added. "Then back on board for dinner and we'll resume the trip north overnight. We'll be in Prince Rupert between ten and eleven on Sunday morning."

"Thanks guys," Malcolm said. "I'll let you know if I need anything. Oh, speaking of that, where can I guy get some coffee on board?"

"The galley," Farrell pointed toward the stern. "This deck, aft."

"Thanks," Malcolm walked toward the galley.

Mitch and Wes both glanced at Farrell and exchanged weary looks.

Friday, 7:02pm:

Mary stood outside the cabin door and raised her fist to knock but then lowered it. She took a deep breath and then let it out slowly, but it didn't help to relieve the rapid pulse she could feel keeping time inside her head. She raised her fist again and this time managed a quick polite knock.

The door opened after a moment and Amy looked at Mary and froze. The look on her face morphed from surprise to disgust in record time. She rolled her eyes. "Just what I needed," Amy groaned. "You know, it's so aggravating that you have to be here."

"Sorry," Mary said, "but it's my job to keep you safe."

"Seriously?" Amy scoffed. "On a cruise ship? Mom's worried for nothing. I'll be fine without you."

"You're probably right about that," Mary gave a slight nod. "I'm just here in the off-chance you're wrong. May I come in?"

"If you feel it's necessary."

Mary stepped inside. "I know you don't like being on a ship with me but that's the reality we're dealing with. So why don't you accept it and talk to me?"

"Talk to you?" Amy screwed up her face in horror. "Are you serious? I thought you were dead for years, you know. I agonized over your death and it took me a very long time to get over it. Then around two years ago, mom told me you were alive, married to the thug, and that I had a newborn niece. I hate you for what you put me through."

"I put several people through it," Mary's looked down at the floor. She wasn't sure what else she could say. "I'm sorry."

"You owe us all an explanation, and not the 'miraculous cure from amnesia' crap you got Mom to believe."

"I'm afraid the amnesia crap is going to have to suffice, and I'm not even sure Mom believes it."

"You were involved in something awful, weren't you?"

"I can't answer that."

"You don't have to," Amy said, contempt oozing from her voice. "I already know it was because of the criminal you ran off with."

"No it wasn't and you're wrong about him on several levels. I know you want to believe the worst because it would make it easier for you to feel justified in hating me. The truth is, though, over the past five years Malcolm and I have helped hundreds of people and we've saved dozens of lives. We've really made a positive difference in the world. We even helped solve a murder case a few months ago."

"Yes, I know, Mom told me about that," Amy crossed her arms. "She also told me you got attacked twice and were nearly killed in both incidents. I also heard your literal partner in crime was shot and that the idiot nearly bled to death. Even if I can pretend you were doing noble things, it doesn't change the fact that you nearly left your daughter – *my two-year-old niece* – an orphan due to your terrible life choices. Who would have looked after her if you'd both died?"

"Mom said she would make arrangements if something like that happened."

"Making Mom clean up after you. Some solution that is. Making a difference is a nice idea and a lofty ambition, but at what cost? The pain and grief of those you love and your responsibilities as a mother? I will never forgive you."

"I really want to help you," Mary said, her voice soft. "Maybe you can't forgive me, but for now could we at least have a truce?"

"*This is the truce.* Don't expect anything more. Do you think I'd be talking to you at all if Mom hadn't guilted me into it?"

"She's always had a way with guilt. I wish I could explain everything to you but even if I tried, you'd never believe it. Just trust me when I say that amnesia is a far more believable story."

"I'm stuck with you two 'protecting' me, but don't talk to me. I have nothing to say to you. As far as I'm concerned, you're still as dead as you deserve to be."

Mary nodded, not wanting to speak out of worry that her voice would crack. She felt the dampness forming in her eyes so she turned around and walked out of the cabin without another sound. She passed by Malcolm in the hallway as the tears began to flow.

"Hey, what's wrong?"

"I just need a moment," Mary said, walking a brisk pace down the hallway. "Sorry."

Malcolm opened the door and stepped inside. He glared at Amy.

"Oh great," Amy shook her head. "Now the criminal is here."

"What the hell is your problem, lady?" Malcolm snapped. "I don't give a rat's ass if you're angry, you don't get to stomp on Mary's heart like that. I'll only ask this once nicely: try to behave like a human being, alright?"

"Oh, look who's talking," Amy's sarcastic laugh was accompanied by a sneer. "You're a two-bit murdering psycho, so how about you try acting human first?"

"You're not hurting my feelings, you know. It just makes me look at you with more contempt and pity. You're a pathetic, self-centered, rage-machine."

"You don't get to judge me. Not a man with your history."

"I wouldn't waste my time judging you," Malcolm scoffed. "You're not worth the effort. I will tell you this, though. Treat Mary with respect and try to be civilized or you'll experience some enhanced unpleasantness."

"Will you at least do me the courtesy of explaining what it is you and Mary do for a living?"

"We're private-sector analysts and we investigate cases that have unusual angles to them."

"You almost make criminality sound respectable," Amy folded her arms. "Can you tell me what kinds of cases you work on?"

"Hell no. But on a semi-related note, let me ask you something. Do you believe in the supernatural?"

"Of course not," Amy huffed. "I'm an old-fashioned, God-fearing Christian."

"You're old-fashioned, but I'm not convinced you're either of the other two and that's the main reason why I can't tell you about what we do."

"I stopped listening as soon as you used the word 'supernatural'. I don't believe in silly superstitions."

"No, but you believe a flaming bush handed ten rules to a crazy old man on a mountain. It's good to know there's no room for silly stories in your belief system."

"Why do I bother talking to you?" Amy groaned in disgust. "You can't comprehend how faith works; you're just a murdering ignoramus."

"Maybe, but I make a damned good spinach dip so it all kind of balances out."

"Fine, you go on making jokes," Amy snapped. "I'm going to pray for your soul."

"I'm getting the better end of that deal, if you ask me."

"Then at least answer me this: what does Mary want from me?"

"She wants you to be part of her life again and she wants your acceptance."

"I can't give her either of those things."

"I know," Malcolm glared. "You're incapable of letting go of a grudge. It takes a big person to forgive and forget but you're too small to do that. Hell, I told Mary to walk away and cut your judgemental and spiteful ass out of her life but she didn't want to. Frankly, if you're not willing to accept us in your life, then there's no point in Mary hitting her head against the wall over it. For some inexplicable reason, she cares a lot about you even though you don't deserve it. You're a toxic weight that drags her down and I hate it. She deserves so much better than you."

"If you despise me that much, then you must be happy knowing I won't be a part of your lives."

"I only despise you because you're the sort of person who thinks it would make me happy. What I want is for Mary to be happy and you're a big part of why she isn't. If you upset her again, you'll deal with me and you won't enjoy it."

He slammed her cabin door shut as he left.

Friday, 8:05pm:

The ship's lounge was a large, rectangular room on the main deck. It was referred to as a lounge but it was more a sizable, multi-purpose room. There were dozens of people milling about.

There were three bar stations set up at the back of the room, with a small line-up in front of each. The starboard side of the room was lined with folding tables, upon which was an impressive assortment of snacks, soups, food, desserts, and several coffee and tea carafes. No effort had been made to decorate the room, instead the staff used the age-old ambiance trick of simply dimming the lights.

The people in the room had broken into small social clusters and the sound of the various conversations was greater than the background music playing through a sound system at the front of the room beside the small, portable stage.

Mary was standing on the stage in the corner on the port side, scanning the room to look for threats or 'persons of interest'. She preferred to immerse herself in work when she was upset and she was still reeling from Amy's harsh words. Whenever she felt as though her life was falling apart she found strength and solace through her work, so she continued observing the crowd.

It had been easy for her to visually differentiate between the lawyers and the FIRST staff, as the latter were dressed casually while the former had simply made the attempt to look casual. To a certain breed of lawyers, the term 'casual' means leaving their suit jackets behind and, in a few cases, finding the reckless courage to leave their ties in their rooms.

With only a few exceptions, the lawyers in each social circle were the ones doing the talking. 'Client development,' it's often called, though Mary was unclear as to where 'client development' ended and 'talking their poor ears off' began.

The side door opened and Bill Sutherland walked in. More accurately, Mary noted, it was more of a swagger or a strut than a walk. He was still wearing the white dress shirt, blue jeans, and cowboy hat with matching boots that Malcolm had described to her earlier, but it did little to lessen the impact of seeing him for the first time. Mary couldn't help but watch him as he went from one social cluster to the next, shaking hands, making good eye contact with each person, and patting the occasional shoulder. She was in awe of how effortlessly he worked the room. As a life-long introvert, she viewed outgoing, socially-savvy people as having super-human abilities.

Although most people were clearly delighted to see Bill, Mary noticed a number of the lawyers had tensed up when he came around and some of their facial expressions had changed for the worse. Mary decided to try to discretely see which lawyers were exhibiting which behaviours.

With a wineglass in his hand, Sutherland made his way to the front of the room, took the one step up onto the makeshift stage, and then stood behind the microphone stand. He nodded to a ship staff member who flipped a switch to activate the microphone.

"May I have everyone's attention, please?" he said.

Conversations died down and then halted as people turned to look in Bill's direction.

"Thank you all for being here this evening," Sutherland said, "even though it's probably just because the ship's Wi-Fi went down a short while ago. For some of you, this means you'll now be forced to interact with your fellow human beings."

There were a few half-hearted chuckles in the sombre crowd, but the comment was, overall, met with silence.

"A toast to our beloved colleagues who couldn't join us tonight," Bill raised his glass. "Here's to them."

"Cheers," said some in the crowd, "Hear, hear," said a few others.

Bill took a sip and then held up his glass again.

"A warm welcome to our valued clients at Fully Integrated Robotics and Software Technology," Bill said. "When you have a client named FIRST, you know they won't settle for second-best, so at McKenzie Ferguson, we all work hard to give you the top-notch services you expect. We're all so glad you could join us for this magnificent event. So, get some food, have some drinks, and we'll crank the music later for those who want to dance. Enjoy the evening social, everyone."

Bill waved and then stepped off the stage to polite yet scattered applause. Mary saw that Bill was immediately approached by a lawyer and she was close enough to hear the conversation that ensued.

"You've got a lot of nerve toasting the dead, Bill," the man said. "They most likely died because of the way you've handled this."

"I didn't cause their deaths, Ian, but as Managing Partner the buck stops with me," Bill said in what he hoped was a reassuring tone of voice. "I'm going to make everything right."

"This should be good," Ian said. "And how *exactly* are you planning on doing that?"

"I'll tell everyone at the two o'clock meeting tomorrow."

"Why wait?" the lawyer persisted. "Why not get back on that stage and tell us all right now?"

"Because," Bill said. "I have an announcement to make and it's more appropriate for our private meeting than here in front of our clients and the ship's staff."

"What's the announcement?"

"Just a little something I'm working on, that's all," Bill smiled and began to turn away. "I'll explain everything tomorrow."

"I don't think that's good enough," Ian stepped in front of Sutherland. "It might smooth things over with some people if you offered to resign."

"We'll be voting on a Managing Partner when we get in to Prince Rupert," Bill tried to grin, but his face wasn't bothering to make it convincing. "Tonight is about FIRST, not you, or me, or anyone else. Now go and pretend there's nothing you'd rather be doing than hanging out with your clients."

"It's rather convenient that Charles died the day after announcing he would be challenging you for the position," Ian's acidic tone drew the attention of three nearby lawyers who decided to become spectators. "There's no love lost between you two."

"Lautzen may have been an impetuous loose cannon but I wished him no harm."

"Bill, there's something I should tell you as a courtesy," Ian said. "At the meeting tomorrow, I'm also going to put my name into the mix to become the next Managing Partner. We need to steer the firm in a new and different direction."

"That's terrific, Ian," Bill said with a knowing smile. "I wish you luck."

Ian scoffed and walked away. The three spectating lawyers looked at Bill and he looked back at them, shrugged theatrically, and then walked to the side doors and opened one. Sutherland exited the room.

Friday, 8:09pm:

Malcolm went into the galley and saw a woman with a clipboard giving instructions to a staff member. He was able to hear what she was saying.

"If you can't find him, then go tell Segovia to take care of it for now."

Malcolm approached her as soon as the brief conversation had ended. "Excuse me. Are you in charge of the staff on board?"

"Yes, I'm Leah," she offered her hand and Malcolm shook it. "I'm the Catering Supervisor and I look after everyone *The Temp Factory* sent to work on this cruise."

"I'm Malcolm. Ship security."

"Nice to meet you. Is there something I can help you with?"

"No, Leah, I just wanted to introduce myself. However, if you don't mind me saying, you look a bit tense."

"No, not really," Leah smiled. "As a perfectionist, I'm always a bit nervous when I've got a lot of new staff. Communication can be a bit rough on the first day and there's a cleaner I've lost track of, but I'll sort it out. The temp agency always sends us good workers, but I'm a bit of a mother hen so I can't help but worry anyway."

"It must be difficult when you're relying on so many people you can't personally vouch for."

Malcolm caught it. The woman's eyes darted and she took in a quick nervous breath before she recovered and smiled an ersatz smile.

"Oh, it will all work out. It always does."

"Of course it will. Nice meeting you."

Friday, 8:10pm:

Mary stepped off the stage and approached the lawyer who had confronted Bill. "Excuse me, sir."

"Oh, hi," he smiled amiably. "What can I do for you?"

"I'm sorry, but I couldn't help but overhear part of your conversation with Mr. Sutherland."

"If you did, then I'm the one who's sorry," the lawyer said. "I'm Ian Gagnon."

He held out his hand and Mary shook it.

"Nice to meet you, Mr. Gagnon."

"Please call me Ian."

"Thanks, Ian. I'm Mary."

"Nice to meet you as well, Mary," Ian took a sip of his drink. "Listen, don't read too much into the little exchange you witnessed. When you've worked with someone as long as I have with Bill you think of them as part of your family. Families sometimes bicker and say unpleasant things in the heat of the moment and to an outsider it can sound worse than it really is."

"So you're not angry with him?"

"I'm not angry, I'm *furious* with him," Ian said. "I passed angry at some point early yesterday. Look, Bill's like a brother to me. A wrong-headed, misguided, and careless brother, and certainly not a *favourite* brother, but a brother nonetheless. I'd like to get back to my clients, so is there anything else I can help you with?"

"No, but thank you for taking the time to speak with me. Enjoy your evening." Mary went back to her spot at the side of the stage. She noticed Malcolm had just entered the room. He scanned the lounge and when he noticed Mary, he walked over to her and stood at her side.

"Hey," Malcolm said. "How are you holding up?"

"Much better, thank you."

"As long as you're not still upset about Amy."

"I'll be fine," Mary said. "There's a small but decent exercise room downstairs so I took my frustrations out on the punching bag for twenty minutes. Not as good as my normal workout, but I'll take it."

Mary enjoyed attending martial arts classes as a means of staying in shape, but it also had the added benefit of being a way to blow off steam and frustrations. Regular workouts helped her to manage her self-control and discipline, and there was something particularly satisfying to her about punching her worries away. Due to her experience in the field over the years, her fighting style had evolved into more street-scrap than sport. Due to potential liability issues, she was not allowed to spar with other students in the class. Even the instructor wouldn't spar with her, especially after one memorable incident where he delivered a blow to her head and then woke up four hours later in the hospital with a dislocated shoulder and his forearm in a cast.

Mary could only spar against the instructor's roommate who was a two-hundred pound semi-pro mixed-martial arts fighter with an impressive win record. She had yet to defeat him in a match, but the roommate did thank Mary for helping him stay on top of his game.

"I'm glad to hear you're okay," Malcolm said, "because we've got more problems than a possible killer on the loose."

"Great," Mary did an eyeroll. "Just the news we needed to hear."

"I was speaking to Leah who's the supervisor of the temp staff. She's really on edge. There's at least one person on her team she was forced to take on."

"What does that mean?"

"It could mean a cop, a spy, a mobster, who knows?" Malcolm shrugged. "No matter which one it is, though, it's bad news because it's another variable I'll have to keep in mind. She also said a cleaner is missing, but that may or may not mean anything. So, have you seen anything…," he left his words hanging. He saw Mary's glance moving from him to the crowd and then back again. "What? Did something happen before I came in?"

"Yes," Mary said. "Sorry if I seem distracted, but I think something important happened and I'm still trying to figure out what it means."

"Tell me."

"I overheard a particularly interesting conversation," Mary said. "A lawyer named Ian Gagnon was in a heated conversation with Bill Sutherland. I spoke to Gagnon and he likened it to a family squabble and nothing more."

"Weird," Malcolm's brow furrowed. "Aside from Gagnon and Sutherland, have you spotted any other suspicious characters in here?"

"Yes, there's one more I need you to investigate."

"Show me."

"Do you see the lawyer in the red tie standing over there near the bar?"

"The one at my nine o'clock?" he saw Mary nod. "What about him?"

"He's been staring at me and it's more than a casual glance," Mary whispered. "Do you think he's a potential threat?"

"No, I saw him staring at you earlier as well," Malcolm grinned. "He was just checking you out, that's all."

"He was?" Mary glanced in the direction at the man then looked back to Malcolm. "Whenever someone looks at me like that, my first thought is that I have a rip in my pants or have some toilet paper stuck to my heel."

"You do know you're not the only person who feels self-conscious and who assumes the whole world exists just to point out anything that isn't perfect with you, right?"

"I know, but I can't help it."

"Just keep watching everyone," Malcolm yawned. "Are you tired?"

"No, I'm not tired at all."

"Good," Malcolm nodded. "In that case, I'm going to try to have a short nap. I'll check back with you again later."

"Okay."

Malcolm stepped off the portable stage and walked to the side doors and exited while Mary resumed scanning the room. She couldn't help but notice the lawyer in the red tie was now walking toward her. As he approached, his gaze remained fixed upon her. He stepped up onto the stage and stood in front of her.

"Hello, pretty lady," he winked. "My name is Brian. What's yours?"

"It's Mary."

"Well, Mary," Brain said, leaning against the wall beside her. "I have to say that I could easily get lost in those lovely eyes of yours."

"As long as you get lost, I'm okay with that."

"That seemed unnecessarily abrupt," Brian hesitated for a moment, replaying her comment back inside his head to make sure he'd heard it correctly. "You know, I didn't catch your last name."

"You can't catch what I don't throw," Mary managed to force a smile. "It's safer for me if I just go by a first name. Look, I'm sorry if I was rude, but I'm working right now and I would like to concentrate on what I'm doing if you don't mind."

"I understand completely," Brian took a half-step back and put his hands up in a conciliatory gesture. "You're on duty and I need to respect that. So, when are you off duty?"

"In an hour or so."

"When you're off duty," Brian quickly raised and lowered his eyebrows, "do you want to go back to your cabin?"

"Yes, more than anything."

"Great, I'll wait for you."

"Oh, you meant with you?" Mary said. "In that case, no thanks."

"Uh…"

"What?" Mary feigned innocence. "Was I misinterpreting your intentions?"

"Uh, yes, of course," Brian tried to laugh it off. "Hey, I'm as innocent as a newborn baby."

"I see, so you're screaming, demanding food, and wondering where your clothes are," Mary nodded. "Sorry, but I need to get back to monitoring the party. Have fun and good luck with that cheesy line you're using."

Friday, 10:18pm:

"Did you sleep at all?"

Malcolm and Mary walked together along the main deck. They decided they'd do a walkaround of the entire ship in the hopes of finding a clue or seeing something that put them on the right track.

"A little," Malcolm said. He was carrying a thermos of coffee with him and was sipping from the cup. "Every time I started to nod off I was woken up by weird dreams."

"That sounds better than the nightmares you usually get."

"The jury's out on that," Malcolm said. "I kept hearing a woman's voice murmuring and it prevented me from getting any real sleep."

"Strange."

"No, people who wear their hats backwards then shade their eyes with their hands are strange," Malcolm said. "This was beyond strange. It felt like someone was in my room and the voice sounded like a young person. A teenager."

"That still qualifies as strange in my books," Mary glanced to her right and admired the beautiful way in which the moonlight was reflecting off the rolling ocean waves. "What was she saying to you?"

"It was probably just typical dream gibberish but I couldn't make it out anyway."

"Too bad," Mary said. "It sounds intriguing. Anyway, let's finish our rounds of the ship so I can get to bed. So far, I haven't seen anything odd or out of place."

"Odd and out of place?" Malcolm sipped. "I see that in the mirror every day."

"I'm looking forward to getting some sleep once we're done," Mary yawned. "It's been a long day and this sea air is making me tired."

"We only have the upstairs Observation Room left and then you can turn in," Malcolm said as they ascended the external metal stairs. "You can grab a few hours while I keep snooping around."

Malcolm opened the door and walked through with Mary behind him. They both stopped suddenly and Mary gasped.

They saw a man's body lying on the floor of the room. He was on his back and his white dress shirt had a hole in it which was surrounded by blood. The man's head was only half intact. The rest of it was scattered across the floor and the far wall.

"Oh my God," Mary gasped. "Who is it?"

"Stay here while I check it out."

Malcolm went over and knelt down beside the body. He put the back of his hand against the prone man's neck. It was cool to the touch.

"This is what's left of First Mate Wes Oliphant," Malcom said. "He's been shot, and by someone who wanted to make sure the job was done properly."

"What do you mean by properly?"

"He was double-tapped, one to the chest and one to the head, like any professional killer would do," Malcolm explained. "The shots were perfectly aimed and executed. Looks like Oliphant's been dead for two to three hours. And check this out. He's got a clip on his belt to hold keys, but there's no keys attached to it. Can you see his belt clip from there?"

"Yes. So if the killer took them, then he or she would be able to pass through any door or passageway on the ship."

"Exactly. And if he has been dead for two to three hours, then his killer is that much ahead of us."

Malcolm pulled out his phone and took pictures of the crime scene from several angles and perspectives.

"Can we leave now?" Mary pleaded. "I don't want to look at him any longer."

"Come off it," Malcolm shook his head. "You've seen a dead body before.

"Yes, but I haven't seen one where the head wasn't all in one piece."

"Yeah, okay, that's a fair comment," Malcolm admitted. "This is pretty messy."

"Oh Lord above, and the smell is making me nauseous."

"Yeah," Malcolm stood up. "I should have told you to hold your nose as well."

"I've heard people talk about the smell of death but I always thought it was just a metaphor."

"It is just a metaphor," Malcolm walked over to Mary. "Death itself has no smell. On the other hand, rot, decay, and – in this case – various scattered flesh and head parts… with those you've hit the stink motherlode."

"I can't look at him anymore."

"It's just as well you stay back here anyway," Malcolm said. "The last thing we want to do is to leave DNA or fingerprints at a crime scene."

"And yet here we are."

"As usual, we're accidentally doing all the wrong things."

"So what do we do now?"

"We walk away," Malcolm said. "Briskly."

Malcolm and Mary left the Observation Room and shut the door behind them.

"We can't just leave him there," Mary said as she descended the outside stairs.

"Yes we can," Malcolm took the stairs two at a time until he got down to the main deck. "And that's exactly what we're going to do."

"Then we have to tell somebody about what we found."

"Yeah, that's the plan," Malcolm pointed to the ship's bridge. "Let's go and report this to whoever's on duty."

The door of the bridge was locked. Malcolm knocked and Mitch opened the door.

"What do you two want?" he demanded.

"Can we have a word with you all?" Malcolm asked in a somber tone.

"Well, you two are up late," Farrell said. "Sure thing. Come in."

"I was just heading to my cabin for some shut-eye," Mitch grumped. "So whatever this is about make it fast."

"There's no delicate way to say this so brace yourself," Mary said. "We found Wes Oliphant's body in the Observation Room."

"What?" Farrell staggered back a step. "His body? You mean he's dead?"

"Yeah," Malcolm said. "He was shot. We need the room locked and sealed off so it'll be useful to a forensic unit when we dock."

"Wes is dead?" Mitch raised his voice. "What are you playing at? I don't believe you."

"Do you want to see the pictures I took for evidence?" Malcolm offered. "They're pretty gory."

"I don't care," Mitch held out his hand. "Show me anyway."

Malcolm pulled out his phone and tapped the screen a few times. He then stood beside Mitch and flipped through the gruesome crime scene photos.

"Goddamn it," Mitch's voice carried a slight tremor. "Alright, I've seen enough."

"There's one more you should probably see," Mary said.

"Why?"

"Look at the picture of his belt," Malcolm said, pointing to the image on his phone screen.

"What am I looking for?"

"You're looking for what's not there," Malcolm said. "Whoever killed him this evening took his keys. There's the belt clip with no keys attached. He did have a set of keys, right?"

"Yes, he did," Mitch said. "A full set. Now somebody has access to every damned room on board. Wait a minute, how do you know the killing happened two to three hours ago?"

"The state of the congealed blood was a strong indication, plus his body was cool but not cold. My guess is that it happened between eight and nine."

"You seem pretty certain of that," Farrell said.

"I am."

"Then where were you between eight and nine?" Mitch demanded.

"Third grade, I imagine," Malcolm gave Mitch a pained look.

"Smart ass."

"I'm trying to solve a murder, not participate in one."

Mitch looked again at the photo and then waved at Malcolm to put his phone away.

"This is a lot for me to take in right now," Mitch Jorgensen faced the window and looked toward the horizon, staring at the half moon in the clear night sky. "I've been sailing with Wes for fifteen years so this all comes as one hell of a shock."

"I'm sure it does," Malcolm soothed. "Can we get the key to the Observation Room so we can lock it to prevent anyone – including you two – from accessing it?"

"I'm his best friend, damn it," Mitch roared as he turned around and clenched his fists. "Why would you suspect me?"

"Mary," Malcolm said without looking at her, "would you care to answer that question for him?"

"Because you're on the same ship as the victim and you're a human being and Malcolm believes everyone is guilty of something," Mary said as if by rote.

"Here," Captain Farrell pulled a key off his key ring and handed it to Mary. "Lock it up. I'll get out the hazard tape and flag the stairwells leading to the Observation Room as out of bounds."

"Mind if I leave my coffee here while we lock up the room?" Malcolm said, holding up his thermos. "We'll be right back and then we can discuss this in more detail."

"Sure, go ahead," Farrell said.

"Thanks," Malcolm said, setting the thermos down. "Back shortly."

Malcolm and Mary left the room and walked down the stairs to the main deck. They each inserted a wireless earpiece and adjusted the volume.

"And you thought a listening device built into a thermos was stupid," Malcolm said.

"It is stupid," Mary said. "You could have picked something smaller and less conspicuous and then hidden it somewhere inside the room."

"The big ugly thermos is so conspicuous that it's inconspicuous. Nobody in their right mind would think such a big clunky object contained a high-tech listening device."

"Being in one's right mind is not a prerequisite for this job," Mary looked at him sidelong. "If the thermos works, then I'll take it back."

"Shh," Malcolm whispered. "They're talking."

"We'd better call this in," Mitch said.

"I still can't believe this happened," Farrell's voice sounded uncertain.

"No signal," Mitch said. "That's strange. Attention, this is *The North Star Express* requesting contact with anyone on this channel. Acknowledge."

Malcolm and Mary heard silence for a few moments. They went up the stairs toward the Observation Room and locked the door leading into it. They heard more talking through their earpieces.

"The unit's switched on but there's no signal," Mitch grumbled. "Look. Nothing on the interface shows a signal, either incoming our outgoing. Huh. No power to the unit either."

"So what happened?" Farrell asked. "Did we blow a breaker?"

"If we blew a breaker then the radar and navigation systems would be down and both are fully functional," Mitch said. "I don't know what happened so I'll get engineering on it." Malcolm and Mary heard some footsteps and then Mitch spoke again. "This is Mitch. Can you hear me okay?"

"Loud and clear," a voice said over a speaker. "What's up?"

"Go wake up Brian and tell him our comms are down," Mitch said. "He knows the ship systems best so have him find out why the hell our communication systems aren't working. We can't operate without comms."

"Yes sir."

"No comms and no internet access," Farrell sighed. "At least the intercom still works."

"With Wes dead and communications out, regulations state we have to head to the nearest port," Mitch Jorgensen said to Farrell. "We've got to turn this bucket of bolts around now."

"No, Transport Canada regulations only state that there must be at least two people on board at all times who are capable of piloting the ship."

"Right and one of those two is dead."

"There's still me and you."

"Who the hell are you trying to kid here?" the contempt in Mitch's voice was anything but subtle. "You're not qualified to handle a gravy boat let alone a ship like this and you know it. If you don't turn this ship around, I'll make sure it's on the record that you did this all by yourself against my advice."

"Then go ahead and log your objections," Farrell sounded irritated. "I'm sorry that your friend is dead but if we pull in early, this will all be for nothing. As long as you play along and don't blow my cover, I'll take any of the fallout afterwards."

Malcolm looked at Mary and raised his eyebrows.

"Wes is dead," Mitch scoffed. "Do you think I give a damn about what you want at the moment?"

"What about the security guards?"

"What about them?" Mitch said. "Security guards are all the same. They weren't good enough to be cops so they're uptight and bitter while they run around playing pretend. I never met a security guard who wasn't a pain in the ass."

"These two seem… a bit different," Farrell sighed. "I don't know if they're killers, but they're certainly not the usual guard-types."

"Either way, I don't like them. They're oing to get in the way."

"They're coming back."

"This is all your fault, you goddamned bureaucrat," Jorgensen growled. "You know every rule from behind a desk but you're dumb as a bag of hammers when you set foot on an actual ship. Idiot."

"Is he police?" Mary whispered into Malcolm's ear.

"Maybe, but it doesn't seem right," Malcolm whispered back. "They'd have no jurisdiction at sea like this. He's something else, though I'm not sure what." He pocketed the earpieces and began to climb the stairs up to the bridge. He knocked and then he and Mary entered the room.

"Thanks," Mary said, handing the key back to Farrell.

"I'll need you guys to change course," Malcolm said.

"What heading?" Farrell asked, clearly confused.

"I don't know the heading, I'm not a nautical guy," Malcolm said as he picked up his thermos. "I just need you to get us into international waters."

"And why the hell should we do that?" Jorgensen challenged.

"Because," Malcolm met Mitch's glare. "I'm pretty sure somebody else on board is going to die and if I end up having to kill the assailant then I'd rather not get arrested by the Canadian authorities because I did it within their territorial waters."

Farrell turned and looked at Jorgensen. "What's your assessment of that request, Mitch?"

"There's not a hope in hell of that happening, so don't bother asking us again."

"Why can't you do it?" Mary asked.

"Because this ship is nothing more than a converted passenger ferry, that's why," Mitch said. "It's tough enough for these coastal waters but it wasn't built for the open sea. It would be unsafe, especially with that squall coming in."

"How bad is the storm?" Mary automatically looked at the weather image on a nearby computer screen.

"At our current course and speed, we'll miss the worst of it," Jorgensen admitted. "The sea will still be a bit choppy and we'll get some wind and rain. Out here by the coast, we'll have a bumpy ride but out there in the ocean, we'd get tossed around like nobody's business and the ship would probably break up."

"And the weather system that's coming in," Malcolm's face was showing his deep concentration. "It would make it difficult for somebody to escape in a life raft on their own, right?"

"You bet your ass it would," Mitch gave a quick nod. "An inflatable raft is fine with a lot of people in it, because the weight distribution would stabilize it. However, with only one or two people it would flip around like a gymnast on crack. It would get swamped or capsize in two minutes or less, I guarantee it. They'd have to use one of the actual lifeboats in order to stand any chance, and even then there'd be no place for them to go. There's no settlements within range."

"I concur with Mitch's assessment," Farrell nodded.

"Then the only option is to head to the nearest port," Jorgensen insisted.

"If you pull into port, then you're giving his killer a chance to escape," Malcolm tapped his finger on the desk beside him. "We have to stay at sea to keep them trapped on board."

"Upon further reflection, I now say that Mitch is probably right," Captain Farrell said. "We're going to head to the nearest port."

"But we need more time to look into this," Malcolm protested.

"Easy, now, you're all worked up over nothing," Farrell shook his head. "You've still got some time. Even though we have to head to the nearest commercial port, it's almost as close to continue on to Prince Rupert as it is to turn around and go to Port Hardy now that I see our current position on the chart. At twenty knots, you've still got more than nine hours to look into things."

"This is the Baneridge Murders all over again," Malcolm said to Mary. "Everyone's a suspect and there's not enough time to narrow it down."

"Captain," Mary turned to Farrell. "Is there any way you could slow the ship's speed so it takes even longer to get there?"

"What do you think, Mitch?"

"It's do-able but not advisable. I could get our speed down to ten knots and then you'd have nearly sixteen hours. I's reduce the speed gradually so nobody noticed us slowing down."

"We'd really appreciate it if you would," Mary said. "Thank you."

"Yeah, thanks," Malcolm agreed. "But you said it wasn't advisable. How come?"

"Because reducing our speed means we're not going to be far enough ahead of the storm. At ten knots, we'll still catch the tail end of it. Any slower than that and the damned squall will be right over top of us."

"Can the ship take it?" asked Farrell.

"Hell yes, as long as we stay close to shore. I can make a few adjustments to minimize the worst of the effects but it could still be a bit unpleasant for anyone prone to seasickness. Aside from that, though, it shouldn't be too bad."

Malcolm walked over to a wall-mounted schematic of the ship. "How many entrances are there to the observation deck?"

"There's two stairwells," Farrell replied. "One fore and one aft."

"And you've got cameras that would show everyone who went up to that deck during this entire voyage, right?"

"Of course."

"I'll need you to queue it up then," Malcolm said. "I want to see as much as we can before, during, and after your colleague's death."

Friday, 10:50pm:

Malcolm and Mary were huddled around a computer screen, along with Mitch Jorgensen and Captain Farrell.

"There's Wes," Mitch said, pointing at the screen.

Mary felt a chill run up her spine as she watched the ill-fated Wes walking so casually toward his impending demise.

"So according to the timestamp on the camera, First Mate Oliphant headed up to the Observation Deck at 8:37pm this evening," Malcolm said. "Any idea why he went there in the first place?"

"He does a stem-to-stern inspection every morning and every evening," Mitch said. "He was damned thorough and always wanted to make sure everything was in perfect order."

"And when it wasn't it cost him his life," Malcolm muttered.

"From the footage, it's clear he was the only person to access that stairwell since we set sail," Farrell said. "What alarms me is that the camera in the aft stairwell was deactivated, along with a half dozen others."

"That would point to a crew member," Malcolm said.

"Not really, the key to the locked electrical room was stolen, remember?" Mary added.

"Regardless, we know it was someone who knew where the cameras were and where the electrical room was," Malcolm said. "We also know the killer used the aft stairwell to access the room, because the next people to access the fore stairwell are Mary and I two hours later."

"So it would seem," Captain Farrell nodded. "Did either of you see anything unusual while you were in the Observation Room, apart from Wes?"

"I didn't see anything else," Malcolm said, "but in fairness I was somewhat distracted by the Oliphant in the room."

"I should go up there and check it out," Farrell sighed.

"No, it's locked up tight and it should stay that way," Malcolm said. "We don't want to mess up anything that would interfere with a full forensic inspection. We'll look around the ship and see if we can find any clues as to who did this and why. If we find anything, we'll let you know right away. In the meantime, just carry on as though nothing has happened."

"That's not going to be possible," Mitch said.

"All we ask is that you do your best," Mary replied.

"See if you can get someone to fix the security cameras," Malcolm added. "Every extra set of eyes we have helping us will make this that much less difficult."

Malcolm and Mary left the ship's bridge and made their way down the stairs to the main deck. Mary scoffed.

"What?" Malcolm asked.

"You were distracted by the Oliphant in the room," Mary exhaled loudly. "Was it really necessary for you to say that?"

"Sorry, I just blurt things out no matter how inappropriate it is, you know that," Malcolm shrugged. "Listen, can you do an internet search on Wes Oliphant?"

"There's no internet service here and the Wi-Fi went out when the comms were disabled, remember?"

"Use the satellite service on your phone."

"That's only for official ARIES missions," Mary gave Malcolm a grave look. "Waterman won't just look the other way when she finds out. Remember her speech about there being serious career implications for any unauthorized usage no matter what the reason?"

"I know and I'll take the heat for it."

"If we're going to break the rules and use the Sat Phone, then why not use it to call the police?"

"Not yet," Malcolm said. "Right now, I just want to know if my hunch is correct."

"Fine, I'll look up Wes Oliphant. What's your hunch?"

"Either Oliphant or our Captain aren't who they say they are."

"That's an easy one," Mary said as her thumbs typed. "I'm already certain Captain Farrell is a phony."

"What makes you so sure?"

"He's never standing at the helm and he keeps deferring to Mitch when we ask him questions. If he's really the captain of this ship, then why does he always follow Mitch's lead?"

"Good observations," Malcolm wanted to kick himself for not picking up on those details himself. "I want to know more about his comment, the one where he said something about not having his cover blown. I want to know who he works for and why he's here."

"Here we go," Mary held up the screen. "This website says that Wes Oliphant is Captain of *The North Star Express*, a ship that specializes in parties and cruises for corporate and high-end customers. Based on that information, it's obvious he was the real captain and not the first mate."

"Just to be sure, let's look up our illustrious Captain Farrell and see his deal."

Mary's thumbs typed quickly and when the results came back, she nodded.

"Exactly the same as Wes Oliphant, word for word, except this entry has his name on it instead of Wes's."

"Which one is the most recent?"

"Wes Oliphant's page was last updated over four years ago. Captain Farrell's page was only created two days ago."

"The day before the ship sailed," Malcolm sighed. "Convenient. I think it's safe to say we've confirmed he's an imposter. What we need to find out next is what his agenda is."

"The bigger question is why did the killer leave the body there?"

"What do you mean?"

"The observation deck has a door on both the port and starboard side, and both lead out onto a balcony that overlooks the water," Mary said as she switched off the satellite phone and put it back in her pocket. "Why leave the body there when they could have dumped it overboard during the night and let the ocean do the rest?"

"Good point."

"Then again, it's possible they were in a hurry or maybe they weren't strong enough to lift the body."

"They weren't in too much of a hurry to take his keys," Malcolm said. "Also, Oliphant was shot from the front and there's no sign of struggle, meaning Oliphant knew he had no chance from the start. Our killer knew what he was doing so that means this body was left so it would be discovered."

"But why? What message are they sending and what does the killer want everyone to see?"

"Maybe it's meant to instill a sense of fear into everyone else," Malcolm shrugged. "Maybe the message is that if our killer doesn't get what he wants, he can do the same to whomever, whenever, and wherever he pleases."

"I can't even think straight, I'm so tired," Mary said. "Do you mind if I get a few hours sleep?"

"Go ahead," Malcolm put his arm around her and gave her a squeeze. "I'll go get more coffee and then I'll tell Spender what we've discovered."

Malcolm leaned against the rail on the main deck and watched the waves go by.

"Double-tapped?" Adam Spender was leaning beside him, and he couldn't contain his surprise. "In your opinion, then, was this a professional hit?"

"Hell yeah," Malcolm stared at the steam coming from his coffee. "Our killer's been trained, either by military, paramilitary, mercenaries, insurgent units, or they play a lot of 'Call of Duty'."

"If he was murdered for his keys, then it rules out the captain and second mate because they have keys of their own, right?"

"No," Malcolm shook his head. "It doesn't rule them out at all. Maybe they simply wanted to make sure the keys didn't get taken by whoever discovered the body."

"I guess that's true enough."

"I hate ships," Malcolm took a large drink of his coffee. "There's no escape routes so I always feel like I'm trapped."

"Look on the bright side," Spender said, lighting a cigarette. "If there's a killer on board, then they're trapped too. That works in our favour if we need to find someone. There's a limited area in which to look for them and they can't exactly flee the scene."

"I'd feel a lot better if I knew who we were looking for."

"With thirty-nine staff and crew on board, it could be any one of them," Spender exhaled smoke into the wind.

"Thirty-eight now," Malcolm said. "And for all we know, it could also easily be one of the lawyers or admin staff."

"So we're a dozen shy of having a hundred suspects."

"Yeah, that's about the size of it," Malcolm rubbed his eyes. He really wished he could sleep. Sometimes there didn't seem to be enough coffee in the world to take the edge off. "No matter who it is, if they're planning a hit at sea – and I believe they are – then they must have a plan to accomplish the task and get away."

"That stands to reason."

"To go unnoticed, they have to either have a terrific hiding spot or they're hiding in plain sight as a cook, a cleaner, or a server," Malcolm remembered his conversation with the catering supervisor, Leah. She had said one of her cleaners was missing. Was he dead? Or a killer? There was also Malcolm's belief that she had been forced to take on someone she wasn't comfortable with. "We need to start interviewing the crew and temp workers right away."

"So you no longer want me to be the strong silent type?" Spender winked.

"No, not any more. Ask lots of questions and see if you can find anyone who looks, seems, or acts suspicious. I need to go and see the Captain."

Saturday, 5:17am:

Malcolm entered his cabin and closed the door.

"Any luck?" Mary asked from the bathroom as she put her toothbrush away.

"A little bit," Malcolm held up a clipboard with several sheets on it. "Captain Farrell gave me a list of names of the crew, staff, and guests. Between Spender and myself, we've already interviewed the entire night shift and I've drawn up a list of suspects."

"And?" Mary walked out of the bathroom and toward Malcolm.

"It's basically the entire list of names."

"Not helpful."

"It is, in a way, because thanks to the captain, I now have everyone's name, including the temp workers on board."

"Slightly helpful," Mary nodded.

"Our suspects include the boat's crew, the catering staff, the support staff, and everyone at the firm who's on board this ship."

"It would have been easier to say that you suspect everyone except you and me."

"Good point," Malcolm grinned. "Pretend that's what I said. I didn't find the missing cleaner and I also can't believe how many people on board are acting suspiciously. Every single person I've spoken to looks so tense and guilty it reminds me of the last time I was on a business trip at the White House."

"Whatever we do, we'd better do it quickly," Mary said while looking at the sheets on the clipboard Malcolm was holding. "The itinerary said we'd be dropping anchor by eleven o'clock for shore excursions and people are going to notice when it we don't."

"I'll talk to the Captain and have him update the itinerary," Malcolm said. "The shore excursions will need to be cancelled in case our killer was planning to use that stop to slip away. Good catch. By the way, did you sleep at all?"

"Yes, I needed the four hours I got," Mary said. "So, where are we at this point in the investigation?"

"We know we have a killer on board and they have to have an escape plan of some sort. I mean, you don't kill someone on board and then sit around waiting to get caught. How do you slip away from a ship? It would have to be something nobody would give a second look to, so it wouldn't be a helicopter dramatically plucking them off the deck or anything flashy like that."

"The lifeboat or the pontoon?"

"It's possible, but not likely as there are no towns nearby they could try to steer towards. The pontoon and lifeboats aren't equipped for long journeys, especially in ocean waters like these. Besides, someone would be bound to notice a lifeboat being lowered by a crane into the water. What else could they be planning?"

"The boats were all I had."

"If it's not a lifeboat, then I can only think of three alternatives. One, they're going to hide on board until we make port. That's risky because there are only a finite number of places to hide on the ship if things go sideways or if they get found out. Two, they're arrogant enough to believe they won't get caught so they'll be walking around in plain sight, probably in the uniform of a temp worker or crew member. Three, they're planning on hijacking the ship and forcing it to drop them off somewhere between here and our destination."

"What do you suggest we do?"

"I have an idea but you'll hate it."

"Based on your recent track record, I agree I probably will," Mary sighed. "What is it?"

"Perhaps we should beat them to it and hijack the ship ourselves."

"Yup," Mary put her face into her hands. "I hate it."

"But at least we'd have control of the ship and the lifeboat controls."

"How about we make acts of piracy our last resort instead of our first, okay?"

"Fine, be that way."

"Let's look at what we have at this point," Mary began a slow pace in the room. "There's at least one but possibly two killers on board this ship. There's thirty-six lawyers, fifteen people from FIRST, and thirty-nine catering staff and crew members."

"Thirty-eight now, but you're otherwise right. And any one – or more – of those eighty-nine people could be the killer and, including Spender, there's only three of us to find out who it is before they strike again. And I'm not ruling out Spender as a suspect either at this point, so it's an even worse ratio."

"This is the proverbial needle in a haystack."

"No, that would be a preferable scenario because we could take our time finding the needle without worrying about how much hay it would kill before we found it."

"If what you're telling me is true, then there's too many potential targets for us to protect all of them."

"That's where we're at, yeah," Malcolm sighed in frustration.

"For all we know, every single lawyer on board could have a death mark on them."

"It's a reasonable assumption to make."

"It's so inefficient for a killer to be murdering all these targets one at a time like this," Mary said, shaking her head. "It's a lot of risk each time someone is killed and it will take them far too long to get the job done."

"Maybe they're planning to hit several of them at the two o'clock meeting."

"Then why kill any of them at all before then? Honestly, if they wanted to eliminate so many people, it would be so much easier to just…"

Mary froze, a look of horror spreading across her face.

"To just what?"

"To just sink the whole ship."

"As much as I hate to say it, you may be right about that. At this point, we have to accept that as another possible theory. We're in need of leads, so we'll follow up on everything. That means I'll have to search the entire ship at some point to see if there's something that may point towards a planned sinking."

"And you said you interviewed the entire night shift?"

"Yeah, Spender interviewed all the cleaners except the missing one and I took care of everyone else."

"Show me the list of names," Mary held out her hand and Malcolm handed the clipboard to her. "The day shift will be starting soon so we'll also need to speak to as many of them as we can. Tell me what you learned from the night staff."

Saturday, 6:01am:

"I can't interview anyone else until I eat something," Mary said. "I'm famished,"

"The galley is right through here," Malcolm pointed at the double doors ahead of where they were walking. "If you're hungry, let's go and check out the menu and place an order. I hear they make great burgers."

"Burgers?" Mary's mouth hung open for a moment. *"At six in the morning?"*

"Time is relative when you don't sleep," Malcolm looked at his watch. "For me, it's still late at night, no matter what the clock says."

"On a semi-related topic, I'm worried you're not getting enough vegetables in your diet."

"You complained about me eating fried foods, right?" Malcolm held the door open for Mary. "You said grilled food was healthier than deep-fried, so I switched to grilled burgers."

"Which proves that you have, as usual, completely missed the point I was trying to make," Mary stepped inside the galley and Malcolm followed her. "What did you eat last night?"

"I had a salad," Malcolm said.

"There's no way I'll believe you ate a salad."

"Okay, it wasn't an actual salad *per se*, but I did have lettuce."

Mary raised a sceptical eyebrow.

"Okay, I had *one piece* of lettuce. On a cheeseburger."

"You're completely hopeless sometimes."

"Oh, come on. I tried to eat salads, but I gave it up. It wasn't satisfying for me and I'm pretty sure it was also causing alarm and undue stress to our houseplants who probably thought they were next on the menu."

"You don't have to eat salads all the time, just improve some of your other choices. Start by having chicken or fish instead of red meat, and we'll go from there."

"So if at lunch time I have the calamari instead of the burger, you'll be okay with me not eating a salad?"

"Yes, I could agree to that kind of deal, sure."

"So, then ordering the calamari would be considered a squid-pro-quo?"

"Oh dear lord no…what is it with you and puns?"

"It's a seafood joke," Malcolm winked at her. "Not sharing it would be a shellfish act."

"Why are you my husband? I hate you."

"Don't leave me floundering like that."

"Ugh."

"Here, take a look," Malcolm handed Mary a paper menu. "There's lots to choose from so I'm sure you'll find something you like."

"I'm sure I will too," Mary looked over the one-page menu. "I like pretty much everything."

"What you mean is once you add your favourite flavourings and spices to whatever you're eating, it all tastes like the flavourings and spices and not at all like it did originally."

"One of these days I'm going to wind up and punch you right in the nose. You know that, right?"

"Promises, promises."

"Good morning," the young man behind the counter flashed a megawatt smile as they approached. "Are you ready to submit your breakfast order?"

"Yeah, I'll have a coffee and the egg sandwich thing."

"Great choice, sir. You want that with hash browns or fruit?"

"Hash browns."

"No," Mary interrupted. "He wants the fruit."

"But hash browns are made from potatoes," Malcolm said. "Potatoes are healthy."

"Hash browns are fried in oil, and usually not the healthy kind," Mary then turned to the server. "Fruit for him, please."

"Uh, do you two need another minute?"

"No, he's having coffee, the egg sandwich, and a side of fruit. I'll have an Earl Grey tea and the egg sandwich with no yolk on whole-wheat toast. Can I get the toppings for the sandwich on the side, please?"

"Sure thing. We're not busy at the moment, so I'll bring your orders out to you."

"Thanks."

Malcolm and Mary walked over to the seating area and Malcolm sat at a table with his back to the wall. Mary took the seat opposite him.

"I'm going to need to make some time to search the ship," Malcolm said. "The more I think about your sinking comment, the more it makes sense."

"We don't want to start a panic, so be discreet in your search."

"Of course," he smiled. "You know I'm good at discretion."

"Yes, and I don't know how you do it," Mary slowly shook her head. "I've seen you walk into a room and have all heads turn towards you, and yet I've also seen you walk into a room and go completely unnoticed."

"It's how I dress, how I present myself, my posture, body language, whether or not I make eye contact, and how I act in general. You adapt to the group of people you're with based on the reaction you want to get from them."

"I find it all it fascinating and I wish I could do that," Mary said. "I'm getting better at forcing myself to talk to people, but I'm still too introverted to feel comfortable doing it. When I talk to people, I can appear confident for a short while, but when it's done, I need to go away and be alone and decompress. If I made all heads turn in my direction, it would only be because I spilled my drink on the mayor and then knocked over the dessert tray while reaching for some napkins. I associate peoples' attention with embarrassment."

"That's just basic insecur... wait, did you really spill a drink on the mayor?"

"No, that was just an example of the sort of thing that would happen to me."

"Too bad," Malcolm hoped his coffee would be ready soon. "I thought this would lead to something more interesting to talk about."

"Don't belittle my insecurities like that. My fears hold me back."

"Fear of what?"

"I'm always afraid of embarrassing myself."

"Embarrassing things happen to everyone, but only some people make the effort to get embarrassed over them. If something happens, roll with it instead of feeling self-conscious about it. Picture success in your mind and it'll happen. It's like baseball. When the ball is coming at you, if you imagine yourself dropping the ball then you'll drop it. If you instead imagine the ball falling perfectly into your glove, then you'll catch the ball every time. Your brain is wired to achieve what you believe."

"I'm not so sure about that."

"I know you're not, and that is the single biggest difference between your personality and mine."

Malcolm looked up as their server arrived.

"Here you go," the man said as he set down a large platter. He set down Mary's tea and Malcom's coffee. He then slid their two plates off and set them into place. "Enjoy your breakfasts."

Malcolm stretched his arms and yawned. "After breakfast, I'm going to have a short nap. Then I'll get back to interviewing people."

"Sounds good," Mary said. "I'll pick up where I left off with the day shift staff and see if I can get anything we can use."

Saturday, 8:12am:

Malcolm rubbed his eyes as he walked through the ship's interior. Before his nightmare jolted him awake, he had managed between twenty and thirty minutes' sleep. It was at least ten hours less than what his body was demanding, however, and he was feeling the fatigue, particularly inside his head.

He stopped himself as he was passing the bar, surprised as he was to see Mitch Jorgensen sitting on a stool with a bottle in front of him. Malcolm approached him.

"Hey, Mr. Jorgensen. A liquid breakfast for you?"

"And just when I thought I'd get a few moments of peace," Mitch muttered. "I couldn't sleep last night and I feel like hell right now. What do you want?"

"Nothing, really," Malcolm drew nearer. "I just didn't expect to see anyone in the bar at this hour. Especially you."

"And why the hell not?"

"Your shipmate has been killed, somebody with knowledge of your systems has disabled the ship's communications, and a master-set of keys to the ship has been stolen."

"You just described *exactly* why I'm here."

"Maybe I can't relate because I wouldn't be able to sit still with all that happening."

"What exactly do you think I can do about any of that?" Mitch scoffed. "Besides, Wes wasn't just my shipmate; he was my friend of fifteen years. Would it make you feel better if I got all weepy and fell to pieces? People deal with grief in their own way and I don't give a damn if my way isn't yours."

"I don't care how you grieve," Malcolm sat down on the stool beside Mitch. "How did you two meet up?"

"I served with him on one of the local ferry runs," Mitch took a drink. "He's sailed tugs, ferries, and a couple of cruise ships. He was a sailor's sailor. He deserved better than running this old clunker."

"Then why did he take the job?" Malcolm kept his eyes on Mitch and not the bottle. He had not had a drink in a few years, but the cravings were always fresh and at the forefront of his brain.

"The ferry company laid him off when he turned sixty. Wes hated the idea of retiring so he worked on whatever ships he could in the private sector."

"What about you? What's an experienced salt like you doing on, to use your term, 'an old clunker' like this?"

"I was in the Navy for a while," Mitch drank down the last mouthful from his glass and then refilled it. "I left for personal reasons but loved the sea too much to leave it. I was working harbor tugs and whatnot until Wes told me a few years back over drinks he was buying a retired ferry and converting it into a cruise ship. I jumped at the chance to work with him again. A year later, he made me a partner in his business."

"And how long have you known Farrell?"

"I only met him a day or two ago. He's new to this ship."

"I overheard you calling him a desk-based bureaucrat."

"Oh you heard that, did you?" Mitch smirked. "Forget what I said earlier. I was just blowing off steam and I tend to mouth off when I get angry, that's all."

"I'm not much of a people person and I can tell you're not either."

"Wes was the outgoing one. He would deal with the contractors, staff, and clients while I did the heavy lifting in operations."

"So did he do all the people stuff?"

"I do the people stuff when we have to call someone who owes us money. I'm good at that because I can be my blunt, authentic self. What you see is what you get and I always speak my mind."

"Yeah, that little detail didn't escape my attention," Malcolm said with a nod. "You like people being direct and to the point so that's what I'll do. With Wes gone, do you end up in sole possession of this ship?"

"I don't like much what you're suggesting."

"You might as well practice answering it because I'm sure the cops and insurance company will ask you the same thing."

"The ship can rot in a scrapyard for all I care about it. I was here for my best friend, not because I wanted or liked the rust bucket. When all is said and done, yes, I'll probably end up with sole possession. Well, hang on; it will be either the bank or me. We make good money with each booking but these ships are expensive as hell to operate."

"I imagine it's difficult to keep a venture like this afloat."

"Great," Mitch scoffed. "You're a wannabe cop *and* a wannabe comedian."

"The only thing I 'wannabe' is informed. I'm looking to narrow down my list of suspects."

"Here, let me help you reduce it. I sure as hell didn't kill Wes, so there's one off your list."

"I believe you," Malcolm said.

"I thought you mistrusted anything human within a certain radius of any given crime scene, or whatever the hell it was."

"I do mistrust everyone," Malcolm nodded. "You're right. Humanity is responsible for all the world's problems. You, however, aren't responsible for this particular murder even though you technically had opportunity and an arguable motive. If you wanted Wes dead, you could have easily made it look like an accident at some point over the last fifteen years. His violent death means a long, drawn-out investigation and a delayed transfer of ownership. His death hurts you, so you don't benefit one bit."

"Even if you did suspect me, I know I'm innocent so it wouldn't bother me."

"The only thing that bothers me is there's a killer on your ship and we don't know when they'll strike next."

"Well now, look at you and how skilled you are at stating the damned obvious," Mitch shook his head and scoffed. "No offense here or anything but leave me the hell alone. I'm off-duty and I'd like to have my drink in peace."

"I'll leave you to it after one final question. This is your ship, isn't it? You and Wes ran it together, right? And Farrell isn't a business partner or even a real captain, correct?"

"That's more than one question."

"Yeah, but they all require only one single answer."

"You're not wrong about any of it. Now kindly piss off, will ya?"

"Enjoy your drink," Malcolm stood up and left the bar.

Saturday, 9:03am:

After a quick knock, Malcolm entered Stacy Metzner's cabin. She looked up from her laptop and groaned with disgust while shaking her head. "What do you want?"

"I'm interviewing everyone about the deaths at the firm."

"You don't need my permission," she snapped. "Go ahead and do it."

"I'm glad you feel that way," Malcolm said. "Because you're the next one I need to interview."

Stacy stopped typing and looked over her glasses at him. She was silent for a moment before speaking. "Let's state the obvious, shall we? You're nothing more than an amateur bodyguard for Amy, and not a very good one at that. To be even more blunt, I don't believe you're qualified to play the board game 'Clue' let alone investigate an actual homicide. I see no logical or compelling reason why I should waste my valuable time with your little game of make-believe."

"I'm only here to protect Amy, you're right about that. However, in order for me to do that effectively, I need to get to the source of the potential threats. Identifying possible suspects through targeted questioning will improve my ability to keep her safe."

"Okay," Metzner nodded. "You're being proactive." She drummed her fingers on the small table, deep in thought. "Alright, I can respect that. Fine, I'll indulge you. You have five minutes. Go."

"Who stands to gain from these lawyers getting killed?"

"Nobody gains. Everyone loses."

"No, I don't buy that. People don't plot murders in a zero-sum gain situation. Your colleague in the stairwell was killed at the top of the stairs and then thrown down to the landing. That wasn't done by someone who happened to be bored and needed a sick thrill. So, again, I ask you who stands to benefit."

"If you're going to ask the same question twice then this five minutes is going to get even more tedious than it already is."

"When you give me a non-answer to my question, you should be expecting me to ask the same question again, so you're inviting the tedium."

"I already answered you," Stacy leaned back in the chair and folded her arms. "Nobody benefits. Everyone loses. I don't know who is behind this. Period."

"What is your personal and professional opinion of the deceased lawyers?"

"I respected Shapner's legal expertise but I loathed and despised him as a human being. Grant McKenzie was the sweetest and kindest man you could ever meet and Janine Andrews was a brilliant rising star in the firm. Eliza Borwith was a complete and utter dolt whose only purpose in life was to be a walking waste of oxygen. Charles Lautzen was a vile and deplorable human being who would have made an excellent poster child for contraception. Next question."

"Where were you between eight and nine last night?"

"In my cabin," Stacy replied. "I was finishing up a file before I went to bed. The documents are all time-stamped if you need proof."

"No need for that. Have you seen anything out of place or suspicious since you came on board?"

"Aside from you, no, but then again I haven't left the cabin so I'm the wrong person for you to be asking."

"I take it Amy brings you your meals?"

"Yes, she's been taking good care to ensure I am at my most productive and that my time isn't wasted," Metzner glared at Malcolm.

"And you have no clients on board to schmooze with?"

"None that I have any interest in interacting with."

"Then why did you come on the cruise?"

"We have a business meeting at two tomorrow," she said. "Then there's a half-day meeting when we arrive in Prince Rupert where we'll be voting on who's the next Managing Partner."

"Are you running for the position?"

"No, there's no point in me bothering."

"Why not?"

"Personal reasons which have no bearing whatsoever on your investigation."

"Would anyone be so keen on being Managing Partner that they'd harm their competitors or try to strong-arm them out?"

"Only Lautzen but he's dead."

"Did Lautzen discourage you from climbing the corporate ladder?"

"Yes, but he was not successful."

"You know," Malcolm folded his arms, "I can tell when someone is withholding information from me."

"And I can tell when someone's five minutes are up and – oh, look at that – yours are. Goodbye."

"I'm sure I'll have more questions for you later."

"If you do, then I'll have to see if I have any time to indulge you," Stacy then pointed to her door. "Out."

Saturday, 11:10am:

Malcolm walked into the galley where Mary had been observing the day shift and making notes. There was a lot of activity, as tables were set, chairs were wiped down, and sounds of clattering came from the nearby kitchen. He approached Mary.

"See anything I need to look into?"

"Yes," Mary said with an almost imperceptible nod. "I've got someone really interesting for you to check out."

"Who?"

"See the Asian woman dressed as a bartender standing in the corner to my left?"

"Yeah, I see her," Malcolm's subtle peripheral glance was all he needed. "Aside from being the only person not rushing around and aside from being dressed like a bartender yet not tending bar, what makes her appear on your radar?"

"A few things. She's wearing the same uniform as the other staff but her long sleeves are disproportionately bulkier than anyone else's. It's not the standard-issue uniform everyone else is wearing so it may have been custom-made to blend in with the other workers while still concealing something. In addition, she's the only staff member carrying a purse. She's also darting her eyes a lot as well and she's studying every face as though she's looking for someone. And she keeps going from this room to the hallway and then back again."

"Yeah, she definitely looks out of place," Malcolm said. "Well-spotted. I'll check her out."

The woman walked through the swinging doors which led into the hallway. As she walked past the open doorway of a supply room, Malcolm grabbed her right wrist and pulled her inside the door. He spun her around and she collided with the metal shelf unit which extended along the rear wall of the small room. As she spun, her purse dropped and Malcolm scooped it up with one hand while pointing his gun at her with the other.

He closed the door and leaned against it. The woman was against the opposite wall, just four feet from him. Behind her, the shelves were laden with bar towels, cleaning supplies, and plastic tubs and containers of varying sizes.

Malcolm kept his weapon aimed at her while he inspected her purse.

"Oh look, your purse has a lens on it," Malcolm said to the woman. "I think I read somewhere that camera purses were all the rage on the runways of Paris and Milan this year. A real must-have for the peeping tom in your life."

His grin was met with a glare from her. "Your words are completely nonsensical to me."

Malcolm shrugged, then held her purse at an angle and took a quick look inside.

"You know, in this light, that massive nail file sure looks a lot like a throwing dagger," Malcolm said with mock sweetness. "I can't help but wonder why a member of the wait staff would consider it necessary to carry a potentially lethal projectile in her purse."

"Put your gun away," the woman replied. Malcolm thought the expression upon her face was oddly serene and unconcerned, though her eyes were filled with contempt and fury.

"If you don't mind the unsolicited advice, most real wait staff would be surprised if they saw a gun aimed at them so if you want anyone to believe you're a bartender, you need to at least pretend to be afraid."

"I know about you, Agent Malcolm," she said. "I would be a fool if I was surprised to see you with a weapon. You use a handgun the way another person would wear a hat or carry a purse. You take it everywhere so I do not see why I should be surprised you have it, yes?"

"I'm not an agent anymore," Malcolm said. "I'll only ask one time nicely. Who are…?"

Before he could finish his question, the woman's right hand sprung out with surprising speed and precision, sweeping Malcolm's gun-holding arm aside. She came in for an attack with her left hand but Malcolm used his other arm to deflect the blow. As she came out of a spin, a snub-nosed revolver came out of her sleeve and into her right hand. She had it pointed at him just as he got his own gun re-aimed at her. The two figures stood motionless for a moment, each sizing up the other.

"Why are you armed?" Malcolm nodded toward her gun. "Did someone leave you a bad tip in the past or something?"

"Your droll humour is in your file, Agent Malcolm," the woman's furious stare belied her calm tone of voice. "It is neither amusing nor becoming. My reason for being here is none of your concern."

"If you know who I am, then how do I know you're not going to kill me if I let you go?"

"Because if I wanted you dead then I would not be standing here, yes?" she raised an eyebrow. "By now, I would be disposing of your body. You are not why I am here but I have been observing you."

"Why?"

"There are a number of... *curiosities* I need to figure out and you seem to be at the centre of some of them. Perhaps we can talk about them, yes?"

"What curiosities are you referring to?"

"What is the US Government's interest in this matter?"

"None, as far as I know. If you assume they do because I'm here, then don't. As I said, I'm not an agent and I don't do that kind of work anymore."

"Then what government are you working for?"

"I'm not working for *any* government. I'm a private contractor and my current role is that of bodyguard and that's it."

"Are you now a mercenary, Agent Malcolm?"

"No, you're not understanding the situation. Look, this is going to sound strange but I'm not employed by anyone at all on this voyage. I'm only here as a favour to a family member."

"Hmm. I thought I would have fewer questions after talking to you," she shook her head. "Now I somehow have even more than when we started."

"I have that effect on people. Just know I'm telling you the truth when I say I'm not here on behalf of any government or paid employer. What about you? Who do you work for?"

"I am a member of the Vietnam People's Security."

"Huh," Malcolm nodded. "I have to admit I didn't see that answer coming. How does anything on this cruise ship pique the national security interests of Vietnam? It must be something big if they took the time, expense, and effort to send you to look into it. And for that matter, why does Vietnam have a file on me?"

"I will not say at this time," she said. "Not until you have answered some questions first."

"Such as?"

"I want to know why you are here, why Adam Spender is here pretending to be somebody named Devon Whitlock, who the other guard is you are working with, and why it is lawyers are getting killed."

"The answer to every one of your questions is 'none of your damned business' if that helps."

"I am going to need better answers than that."

"Too bad because you're not getting them and this conversation is over," Malcolm snapped. "Let's do the math together, shall we? You're from Vietnam, you know me, and you know Adam Spender, so it all adds up to you working for the Da Nang Cartel. My guess is you're here to settle a few scores but that's not going to happen on my watch. Even if I believed you're a federal cop, you're at least five thousand miles outside of your jurisdiction. I'll give you three seconds to say something that catches my attention or else I'm taking my chances and pulling this trigger."

"You got played."

"I'll need more from you than three words."

"Then I will need more from you than three seconds, yes?"

"I'll give you as much time as you need as long as you put your weapon down."

"I shall comply when you have lowered yours."

Malcolm's mind raced as he weighed the pros and cons of compliance. He ultimately realized her earlier statement had been correct: if she had wanted to kill him, there had been ample opportunities prior to that moment. He slowly lowered his weapon and put it back inside his shoulder holster. "Your turn."

She nodded and with a quick motion of her wrist, the gun retracted up into her sleeve.

"I am not part of the Da Nang Cartel," she said. "My name is Duyen Trinh and I really am a federal officer from the Socialist Republic of Vietnam."

"For now, I'll believe you, Officer Trinh. So talk to me."

"The Cartel," she said. "They were sent back to Vietnam after their trial in Canada, yes?"

"Yeah. And?"

"Not all of them were on board when the plane landed in Hanoi."

"What do you mean?"

"The plane carrying the cartel members was forced to land in China," Trinh said. "The aircraft crew were told to land or an anti-aircraft missile would destroy the plane. The charter airline later stated it was a routine refuelling stop, but no stops had been scheduled for that flight. When the aircraft was finally allowed to leave China, it did so with two of the cartel members no longer on board. Our security team on the plane said six men in Chinese military uniforms came on board and removed them from the aircraft."

"Are we talking actual Chinese soldiers or fake ones?"

"Unknown at this time, but all evidence and logic points to them being fake."

"And am I to understand the security team just let these guys walk on board and take them off the plane?"

"It was either that or get taken themselves," Trinh said. "Easy choice for them, yes?"

"I guess that's true enough," Malcolm conceded. "But what would someone in China want with a couple of Vietnamese drug smugglers?"

"Our theory is they probably wanted their own back."

"Meaning…?"

"The Cartel was based in Da Nang but it was being run out of Guangzhou, China, by a crime syndicate."

"So the Da Nang Cartel was Chinese and not Vietnamese?"

"No, the Da Nang Cartel was Chinese *and* Vietnamese. It was run by criminal elements in both countries. The drugs financed their operations while industrial espionage gave them some prestige and influence over local governments. The syndicate paid off mayors and governors with business secrets which could be easily sold for cash and special favours. This allowed the syndicate to import and export drugs without interference."

"And Adam Spender disrupted that."

"No," she said. "You did."

"The only thing I did was keep Spender alive long enough to testify."

"If the report I read was accurate," Trinh raised an eyebrow, "you also shot Ki-Liu."

"He tried to ambush us on the bridge," Malcolm shrugged. "If he wanted to live longer, he shouldn't have picked 'assassin for hire' as his career choice."

"I see," Trinh nodded, not taking her eyes off Malcolm. "So, you are saying Ki-Liu is dead, yes?"

"Well, my shot hit him in the face, which caused him to fall backwards off the Fremont Bridge, plummet thirty feet, and land in the river. I didn't see him surface, so yes, I figured that probably did the trick. Why? Do you suspect he's alive?"

"I *know* he is alive," she corrected. "I *suspect* he is on this ship."

"How did he survive?"

"All I know is he was rushed back to China and spent quite some time in a non-governmental hospital. I can confirm with one-hundred percent certainty he is back doing missions for the crime syndicate again."

"And you think he might be looking for Spender?"

"It is possible. Or he could be looking for you. Or perhaps he could be here for something else entirely."

"It has to be something else, then. I've heard a lot about Ki-Liu and petty revenge would be beneath a man of his professional reputation. He's motivated only by money and I've never heard of him letting his emotions get in the way of a mission. Why would he suddenly let pride affect his judgement like that, unless my shot damaged his brain? It doesn't fit."

"I agree it does not fit. Whatever he is doing, it is not likely to be revenge. Or, perhaps I should say it would not *only* be about revenge. That is why we are having this conversation. What is it he seeks? If he wanted to kill you an attempt would have already taken place, yes?"

"I'm still trying to figure all of this out myself."

"It would appear that in this game you are too many moves behind to be of any use to me."

"And yet I have the answers to some of your questions."

"And yet you have told me none of them."

"Alright, then let me offer you a little carrot."

"I do not want a carrot," Trinh said. "I want information."

"I didn't mean an actual carrot."

"We were discussing matters of great importance and now you wish to speak about vegetables?"

"No, it's a figure of speech which means I am offering an incentive to you. What I can tell you is you're right: I am working with Adam Spender, known these days as Devon Whitlock. We are trying to find out who is killing lawyers and making sure each death looks like a freak accident. We're only here to protect someone who we feel might be somewhere on the hit list. That's it. We're not even remotely here for anything involving the Da Nang Cartel."

"If both Adam Spender and Ki-Liu are here, then I am most certain *you are* involved in it, whether you intend to be or not."

"Look, I'm sure I've seen everyone who's on board this vessel and I didn't see anyone resembling Ki-Liu. I think you're worried for nothing."

"I have it on good authority that while he was in the hospital, he underwent extensive facial reconstructive surgery to repair the damage you did to him. My sources tell me Ki-Liu no longer looks like the man we both remember."

"I don't suppose you have a recent picture of him, do you?"

"No. We are both traversing this pathway blindly."

"I see," Malcolm sighed and leaned against the rack of shelves beside him. "In other words, on board this ship right now we have someone who likes killing lawyers, a bunch of lawyers who may themselves be killed, and a high-level criminal-assassin from China here on behalf of a violent drug cartel I've pissed off."

"I would say that is a satisfactory summary of things."

"How the hell am I supposed to solve a murder mystery while I have armed spies on the ship ready to kill? How am I going to keep track of which dead people are tied to which event?"

"I have never understood Americans. You are always stating the obvious and doing your thinking with your mouths instead of with your heads. It is amazing your country has made it this far, yes?"

"If you're looking to endear yourself to me that is not the way to do it. The other thing about Americans is we're imaginative problem-solvers. I'll figure this out."

"How do you know the two sets of events are separate and that Ki-Liu did not kill all of the victims?"

"Because some of the killings have been smooth and professional while others were clearly done by a panicked moron who didn't know what he or she was doing. The sabotaged vehicle was done by a professional who planned it out meticulously and knew exactly what to do, whereas the murder of the lawyer who was killed in the stairwell was done by someone who threw a plan together and hoped for the best. We definitely have at least two killers in play, and they may or may not be even after the same things."

"This is all so… what is the word which means too much is happening and you cannot take it all in?"

"Saturday?"

"No, *overwhelmed*." Trinh said. "I am currently *overwhelmed* by what is happening on this ship. Why did you say Saturday?"

"Because you described every day of my life just then and today is Saturday."

"The dialect of English you speak is both unconventional and irregular."

"I'm both of those things, so it makes sense. What does Vietnam want with Ki-Liu?"

"That is not your concern. It is mine."

"Ah, but you're wrong because it is very much my concern. If it comes down to a life or death decision, I will shoot him without hesitation. If you want to capture him yourself, then you'll have to tell me why your country sent you all the way here to do it."

"Ki-Liu is wanted in connection to three murders in Hanoi in June of last year."

"Ki-Liu doesn't kill randomly, he kills only when he's paid to do so. Who were the three?"

"If I tell you, then you must swear upon your life and your honour you will not interfere with my arrest."

"As long as it doesn't get in the way of what I'm here for and you're telling me the truth, then sure."

"Two drug distributors closely connected the Da Nang Cartel surrendered themselves to my colleagues. They had secrets to sell and wanted to act as informants against the syndicate."

"And they wanted to sell their information to Vietnam's police force in exchange for immunity?"

"Yes," Trinh nodded. "A government minister from Hanoi was sent to do the initial briefing and to decide if their information was worth paying for."

"I see. Go on."

"The distributors were taken to a secure location in Hanoi and the minister went to interview them."

"Was this sanctioned by the Vietnamese government?"

"No, they had no idea any of this was happening at the time. I was told this was to avoid any information being leaked back to the syndicate, as we have reason to suspect there are government ministers on the Cartel's payroll. The minister who was sent was trusted and he was put in charge of their safety until other arrangements could be made. Ki-Liu must have followed him. He murdered the government minister and the two distributors."

"And?"

"And what?"

"There's something missing from your story," Malcolm folded his arms.

"The government minister was my father."

"There it is."

"There is what?"

"The missing piece to the puzzle. Vietnam doesn't send cops halfway around the world to arrest a murder suspect. That's what INTERPOL is for."

"I do not care to hear your opinion on this matter," Trinh's tone was testy. "I have told you what I must. From this point forward, this is no longer your concern."

"You're here as a rogue element, aren't you? Does your government even know you're here doing this?"

"You have asked enough questions. I will be watching you and Adam Spender closely. You must believe me when I say I will not hesitate to shoot either of you if you get in my way."

"I believe you. I hope you believe me when I say I don't trust you or your story."

"What you believe is not my concern," Trinh walked past Malcolm and opened the door. "Leave Ki-Liu to me and there will be no need for anything unpleasant."

She exited the storage room and Malcolm watched the door slowly close.

Malcolm retrieved Mary from the bustling, crowded galley and the two walked outside and made their way to the back of the boat. They leaned on the railing and watched the churning water below.

"People seem to believe I still work for the US Government," Malcolm said. "I guess they didn't get the memo stating I'm out of that business."

"I don't think they would care even if they did get it," Mary said. "While you were working for the government, you upset a number of your foreign counterparts."

"Just Russia's and North Korea's."

"And China's."

"No, the explosion on the island of Hainan was not my fault. Mine just happened to be the only face which showed up on the one camera that was still working afterwards."

"And you're banned from India's Punjab province."

"That was also not my fault," Malcolm said. "The Minister of Tourism pulled a knife on me, so what else was I supposed to do?"

"It was a ceremonial Kirpan and he was just taking it out to show it to you."

"He over-reacted."

"*He* over-reacted?"

"Yeah," Malcolm was matter-of-fact in his response. "His arm wasn't even broken."

"And you're also banned from entering France."

"Okay, that one *was* my fault, but you're missing the point. My security guard cover is essentially blown. If Officer Trinh knows who I really am then others may know as well."

"How does this Trinh person affect things?"

"I don't know, it could be a little or a lot," Malcolm shrugged as he gazed to the horizon. "It depends if Ki-Liu is here like she says he is."

The gentle mist kicked up by the plowed waves sprayed against their faces. The droplets were cool and invigorating. The sea wind rushed through their hair and the sound of the engine and churning water below created a wall of sound to mask their conversation.

"And if Ki-Liu is here?" Mary said eventually. "What then?"

"Then we're in a hell of a lot of danger. I'd better go and update Spender about this."

"Fine," Mary said. "I'm going to continue observing the day shift and see if I can find anything else we can use. If Trinh was disguised as a temp worker, then Ki-Liu could be as well. And there may be more than just the two them."

"With my luck, there will be."

"It's hard for me to believe Ki-Liu could be back from the dead," Spender said as he walked with Malcolm below deck along the corridor. "You shot him. I saw him fall backwards over a bridge and he hit the water hard."

"I agree that he *should* be dead," Malcolm said, "but I'm not one to take chances. If there's even the slightest of chances he's alive then I have to be prepared for that contingency."

"Alright then, let's assume Ki-Liu is alive. What do we do if he's on board? I've got a chill just thinking about that possibility."

"I don't know what to do yet, to be honest," Malcolm said. "Ki-Liu and Officer Trinh are additional complications I don't need in an already-complicated scenario."

"Listen, Malcolm, if Ki-Liu is alive then you're going to need all the help you can get. I really want to prove myself and be useful to you and there's more I can do aside from interviewing people and playing pretend. Give me a real job so I can help you with this."

"I don't know if I'm ready to do that."

"You don't trust me, is that it?"

"No, I don't, but don't take it personally," Malcolm patted Adam on the shoulder. "I don't trust many bipedal life forms. A few people have earned my trust but they're as rare as whales in Idaho. If there was some magical way I could know who was safe to trust then it would be a whole lot easier for me."

"I suppose it makes sense that a man with your experience and history is going to be more suspicious than most people. Okay, then tell me how I can prove myself to you and I'll do it."

"Just keep working hard and coming up with new ideas," Malcolm said. "That's how you'll prove yourself. Keep doing what you're doing."

"What about Officer Trinh? Do you believe her story?"

"I don't know. If she's telling the truth then I have more questions than answers, which is pretty much what she said to me as well. None of this adds up."

"Give it time, buddy. You'll figure it out and I know you'll make the right choice."

Saturday, 1:09pm:

Mary continued sauntering around the galley, studying faces and reading body language as she went along. The galley was a large room with ample seating and it was currently a hive of activity. Lunch was winding down and there were several people collecting plates and cutlery, wiping down tables, sweeping the floor, and more. This was exactly the situation Mary had been hoping for, as it put the bulk of the day shift in one spot where she could carefully yet discretely observe them and take notes.

Aside from herself and the day shift, the only other people in the galley were a half-dozen lawyers who were seated around a table. Mary figured them all to be between twenty-five and thirty years old. The young men were talking in raucous tones interspersed with even louder laughter. Out of the corner of her eye, Mary noticed one of the lawyers from the group looking at her. Even though he was only in her peripheral vision, she recognized him as the lawyer in the red tie who had tried the pickup line on her the previous evening. He then got the attention of his colleagues, leaned in closer to them, and began speaking in hushed tones. Occasionally, one of the lawyers would look at her with a sidelong glance. Their huddle broke and the men stood up and assumed what they mistakenly believed were nonchalant poses.

One of them began walking towards Mary and she could feel herself tensing up.

"Good afternoon," he said.

"I hope it is," Mary stood with her feet slightly apart, arms at her side, ready for whatever this was about to become. "What do you want?"

"Relax; I only want to ask you a question."

"Go ahead," Mary locked eyes with him.

"Are you religious?" he asked. "Because you're the woman I've been praying for."

"I doubt that," Mary replied. "I'm not inflatable."

"Oh come on," the man chuckled. "There aren't any windows in this room and yet with you here, it's like we have our own private sunshine."

"And there aren't any dogs on board and yet something must have dropped you," the annoyance in her voice would have been difficult to miss. "Please leave me alone."

The man scoffed. "It's your loss."

"I'll do my best to somehow get over it."

He want back to the group and began speaking to the rest of his group. When he'd finished, the group laughed loudly.

Mary shook her head, deciding then and there that she would never truly understand the male brain. She began to walk closer to the kitchen where the majority of the day shift were now working.

She saw a different lawyer from the group now approaching her. She sighed.

The man was quite tall with close-cropped blonde hair. He flashed what he thought would be a disarming grin but rather than feeling disarmed, Mary was wanting to head to the armory.

"Hello, pretty lady," he said. "Do you know what my shirt is made of? Boyfriend material."

"And mine's supposed to be made out of pest repellant," she said, "but it's clearly not working."

"Let me ask you a question," he pointed at her. "Do you think you have what it takes to be with me?"

"My vaccinations are up to date and I have access to penicillin if that's what you mean."

"Come on," he chuckled. "Give me a break here. I'm offering to give you the best night of your life."

"Really?" Mary said in mock surprise. "You mean you're offering to hire me a sitter, a maid, a personal chef, and a masseuse while you stay far away from me? That's a tempting offer."

The man smiled and then turned and walked back to the group of men he had come from. The group were then chatting and laughing.

Malcolm entered the room and walked over to Mary.

"Spender and I have... what's wrong?"

Mary summarized the past five minutes to Malcolm.

"Why are so many of those idiots hitting on you?"

"I have no idea, but it's annoying."

"I can only imagine," Malcolm patted her arm. "Want me to go bust some heads?"

"No, but thanks for asking," Mary smiled at him. "I can handle it myself."

"Alright," Malcolm said. "Seen anything?"

"Not yet, but I haven't yet had enough uninterrupted time to properly observe everyone. I'll start interviewing the staff when they're less busy with the cleanup."

"Alright. I'll help you observe the staff from the other side of the room."

"Thanks."

As Malcolm walked across the galley to the opposite wall where he would have a good view of the kitchen, Mary noticed a third lawyer in a crisp business suit approaching her.

"Good evening, lovely lady," the man said with a wink. "My name's Keith. And who might you be?"

"I might be someone getting annoyed by you and your colleagues," Mary replied.

"Don't mind them, they're harmless."

"I would disagree with that assessment," Mary said. "Your little group over there is bothering me and I don't appreciate it. What do you want?"

"I just wanted to pay you a simple compliment, that's all."

"If you must," Mary exhaled. "Get it over with."

"You look like you're in good shape," Keith said, looking her up and down. "Do you work out?"

"Yes, I do."

"Then how about we work out together?" he winked. "You know, two people having sex can easily burn a thousand calories."

"Then it looks like tonight you'll only be burning five hundred."

"Meow," Keith laughed. He then turned around and found himself face-to-face with Malcolm.

"Hey, buddy," Malcolm growled. "Do you mind coming into the hallway with me for a second?"

Keith turned to his group, made an exaggerated face of surprise, and then followed Malcolm through the inner doors into a hallway.

"What do you want?" Keith looked down his nose at him.

"The woman you're bothering is a security guard," Malcolm said. "She and I are here to see if we can minimize the amount of funerals you and your colleagues need to attend."

"I know that," the man scoffed.

"No, I'm not convinced you do," Malcolm took a small step closer so their faces were less than two inches apart. "Have you noticed the attrition rate in your department has been a bit higher than usual this past week? I hope it doesn't come as a surprise to you that none of the recent departures from the firm have been voluntary, though all have been permanent."

"Yes, I'm aware of that," the man took a step backwards. "So?"

"So, we don't know which one of you jackasses might be next in line for an unscheduled departure from the airport of life. If you guys keep on distracting her, that's one less set of eyes we have to make sure everyone else stays alive. Are you following me?"

"Yes."

"Good," Malcolm said. "So then how about leaving her alone, alright?"

"Sure, but…"

"But what?"

"The guys and I… we kind of have a bet going."

"How about enlightening me with the particulars."

"Brian tried to pick her up last night and she just roasted him with her rejection," Keith smirked. "So today, he bet us a hundred bucks nobody could get burned worse than he did. We've each been taking turns trying different corny lines on her to provoke a reaction, that's all. I'll have to go tell them about the burn she gave me. I'll probably win the hundred."

"She's trying to do her job," Malcolm could feel the pulse in his forehead sounding the war drums. "The last thing she needs is a group of hormonal morons acting like creeps and distracting her. She's not a plaything for your wagering amusement; she's a professional trying to keep everyone alive."

"We all know that," Keith's voice oozed with contempt. "Look, be a good sport and don't tell her what's going on, okay? We're just having a little fun and we could all use some levity right now."

"I'm not getting through to you, am I?" Malcolm raised his voice. "Has it crossed any of your minds that she might find the harassment uncomfortable?"

"It's not harassment, pinhead," Keith's ability to sound patronizing would have won him the gold if there were an Olympics for it. "We don't touch her and when she says no we walk away."

"Harassment is in the eye of the beholder," Malcolm was making an effort to control his temper. "Women have to deal with this crap from men all the time and it's not happening on my watch. I thought a lawyer would be better versed on what constitutes harassment."

"I know what harassment is and I certainly don't need to have it explained to me by someone whose career path led him to be a security guard."

"The bet's off and your 'fun' is over," Malcolm said. "Lives are at stake, alright? She and I may be your best shot at getting off this ship alive."

"You don't get to tell me what I can and can't do," Keith put his fists on his hips. "Maybe you didn't know who I am. I'm Keith Jasek, the senior Tech Lawyer."

"I don't know *who* you are, Keith, but I know *what* you are and I usually flush such things away."

"You insolent little prick."

"Don't do anything you'll end up regretting once you sober up."

Keith swung a punch, but Malcolm swept his right arm up to deflect the swing and then spun Keith around, which was easy to do with momentum on his side. Malcolm grabbed Keith from behind and put him into a chokehold.

"Let me go," Keith gasped.

"No, I'm quite happy with things the way they are at the moment," Malcolm squeezed tighter, causing Keith to cough and gag. Keith tried to reach behind and grab Malcolm but his flailing hands couldn't grab hold of anything. He tapped Malcolm's forearm with his hand.

"This isn't wrestling, you idiot, you can't tap out," Malcolm shook his head in pity. "Hey, Keith, while we're here hanging out like two guys just having a little fun and enjoying some needed levity, let me ask you a few questions. Let's start with an easy one. You and your buddies... what kind of law do you practice?"

Malcolm loosened his hold and Keith gasped and wheezed. "Let me go. This isn't the best time to be making small talk."

"It's the perfect time because I know I'll have the maximum amount of your attention while at the same time being guaranteed the minimum amount of bad attitude in your answers."

"Okay, okay. We specialize in Tech Law."

"Yes, I know that part already, but what kinds of things do you do in that area of law?"

"Our clients specialize in information technology, artificial intelligence, video games and design, entertainment, media, and that kind of thing," Keith gasped another breath into his lungs. "We give them advice, help them with patents and intellectual property laws, and so on."

"So FIRST is your biggest client and they're also a high-tech company, right?"

"Yes, yes, they are."

"Tell me about them."

"They're on the cutting edge of robotics, AI, software, game development, and programming."

"Thank you for your cooperation."

Malcolm released his grip on Keith and pushed him away.

"You could have killed me, you putz. I demand to speak to your supervisor."

"You're in luck, he's on board," Malcolm flashed a manic smile. "I'll make sure he gives you a customer satisfaction card to fill out."

"That was assault and battery, my friend, and as soon as the phones come back on, I'll be calling the cops and pressing charges. I'll sue you and then see to it you get thrown in jail. You'll never work in this town again."

"This town? We're on a ship at sea, far from any towns, you know."

"It doesn't matter," Keith shouted. "I'll ruin you anyway."

"I'll be sure to start caring about your feelings as soon as I'm done finding out who's killing your colleagues."

Saturday, 1:49pm:

Malcolm approached a young man sitting alone in the galley. He was in jeans and a golf shirt and was wearing ear buds and typing on a laptop.

"I'm with security," Malcolm said. "Can I get your name, please?"

"Kevin Denbigh," the young man glanced up. "What's going on?"

"You're not one of the suits at FIRST, are you?"

"No. I'm one of the three heads of R&D at the company."

"Okay," Malcolm said. "Listen, I need to ask you a few questions."

Kevin removed the ear buds. "What about?"

"Dead lawyers, mostly." Malcolm noticed Kevin tensing up.

"I don't see how I can help with that."

"Maybe you can't, but can you think of any hypothetical reasons why anyone would want to bump off the lawyers who are assigned to your company's account?"

"Maybe a rival firm is looking to scoop up our business and they're taking some drastic initiative," Kevin shrugged. "I don't know and I don't care, either. I hate lawyers. If they die, it's not as if there's not thousands more of those bloodsuckers to take their place."

Kevin lifted his plastic cup to his lips and took a drink.

"You've got a tensor bandage around your right wrist," Malcolm gestured toward Kevin's hand. "How did you injure it?"

"I spend all day on the computer. My wrist gets sore from time to time with all the typing and mouse work I do."

"Your hand was also shaking when you lifted your cup," Malcolm said. "That's not caused by repetitive strain injury. So, just to be clear, you're not at all concerned about lawyers being murdered?"

"No, I'm not, okay? And why should I be? Dead lawyers are a tragedy but that's McKenzie Ferguson's problem. There's no loyalty in the corporate world anymore so if they can no longer represent us, the suits on the top floor will send a sympathy bouquet and then find a new firm to work with."

"What are you hiding, Kevin?"

"Hiding?"

"Your body has tensed up, the pitch and cadence of your voice has changed, and you look as though you're about to burst. And now that I've mentioned all that, you look as though someone just walked over your grave."

"I'm under a lot of pressure at work that's all."

"If you're going with that ridiculous story, then you'll understand if I decide to make you my main suspect. That's a lot of homicide charges and a lot of life sentences to go with it, but it's your decision."

"I didn't do anything, okay? I just don't want to answer any more of your questions right now, that's all."

"Just one last thing. You said you're in Research and Development, right?"

"What about it?"

"You said you were one of three. Who are the other two who work with you?"

"Sita Sharma, who's the girl in the wheelchair at the soda station getting a refill, and David Chow is the Chinese guy over there eating lunch by himself."

"Thanks."

"Talk to David first," Kevin said. "He's from mainland China but his English is perfect. He's our main programmer."

"Got it, thanks," Malcolm started to leave.

"Wait, I have a question for you," Kevin called out. "Have you guys managed to find anything useful yet?"

"We're following up on several leads but that's all I can tell you at this time."

"You're piss-poor security guards. You're out looking for clues and meanwhile someone's been killed right under your noses."

"And nice to meet you as well," Malcolm said as he walked away and headed over to where David was seated. David was wearing a white t-shirt under a faded denim jacket. He had short, black hair and his thin face seemed engrossed in whatever he was reading on a tablet.

"Hey," Malcolm said as he drew up to him. "Are you David Chow?"

The young man nodded.

"I'm with security and I need to ask you a few questions."

Another nod in response.

"You've heard about lawyers being killed, right? I'm hoping you can help me to discover why."

David shrugged and looked away.

"Sorry, but I was led to believe you were a programmer and not a mime. Let's change things up. How about I ask you questions and then you do something crazy like give me audible answers."

"But I have nothing to tell you."

"You have no clue, no guess, or no theory at all as to why lawyers would be targeted?"

"None at all," David shifted in his seat.

"I heard you're from China. How long have you lived in Canada?"

"Ten years."

"And how long have you known Kevin and Sita?"

Malcolm perceived a slight change in David's facial expression at the mention of his colleagues. He knew something had just happened, but he wasn't sure what it was. He only knew that was feeling very uncomfortable.

"Seven years."

"What can you tell me about Kevin?"

David glanced over at Kevin across the room and shrugged. "He's clever and he works hard."

"That's it?"

"What else do you want me to say?" David ate a French fry. "He's the first one in at work and he's the last one to leave. He pretends to be a tough guy full of attitude but he has a generous heart and he's a good and kind friend."

"And what about Sita?"

David shrugged again and shook his head.

"Oh, I'm sorry but if you recall, this is the audible answer segment of our show. Please try your answer again. What about Sita?"

"She is brilliant. I deeply admire her imagination. Everything we work on starts out with her asking 'what if?' Her creativity is incredible and her work ethic is admirable."

"Okay, thanks. Tell me about how the three of you work together in terms of the roles you play at FIRST."

"What does this have to do with lawyers?"

"Just humour me, okay?"

"Sita comes up with most of the initial ideas, then Kevin takes her ideas to his team and they map them out structurally into logical sections. They work out how the idea will actually function, what features should be emphasized, and what it should look like to the end user. Then I do the bulk of the software coding with my team to bring it to life."

"The three of you make quite the talented team."

"No. The three of us are quite the talented *individuals*, but together as a team, we are much greater than the sum of our parts. Collectively we are capable of anything."

Something happened again and I'm still missing it, Malcolm thought.

"Anything?" Malcolm raised an eyebrow.

"Anything that is robotic and requires software. If Sita can imagine it, then Kevin can structure it and I can code it. We each have our own support teams which we lead and what the three of us come up with, our teams make happen."

"So it all starts with Sita, does it?"

"Why did you say that so ominously?"

"It wasn't meant to be ominous, I simply found it intriguing," Malcolm said. "I'll be speaking with her next."

"Why? She didn't kill anyone, you know," David said.

"I didn't ask you if she did. She's as valid a suspect as anyone else on board."

"She shouldn't be a suspect. None of us should be suspects."

"Oh, but she is a suspect, David," Malcolm's grin was deliberately menacing. "You all are. And the three of you are getting more and more interesting by the minute."

"We didn't do anything wrong," David leapt to his feet. His face was red and his fists were clenched.

"I didn't say you did," Malcolm said. "Is there something about the three of you I should know about?"

"No, leave us alone," David stormed out of the room.

"An interesting and unexpected reaction," Malcolm said under his breath. "I just wish I knew what it meant."

Saturday, 2:00pm:

Mary walked over to the part of the galley where Malcolm was. "How are the interviews going?"

"Not great, to be honest. I've spoken to every executive and suit at FIRST about the lawyer deaths and all I'm getting are variations of 'such a tragedy' and 'quite a shock'."

"Not terribly helpful."

"No, but I just spoke with two of the three members of FIRST's R&D team. At first, I thought some of the lawyers brought their grown kids on board, to be honest, because they're so young. Regardless, so far they're both showing up on my radar as people I need to get to know better."

"Who's the third person?"

"That young woman over there," Malcolm gave a subtle nod.

"The one in the wheelchair? I see her."

"Yeah, her name's Sita Sharma."

"What's wrong?" Mary put her hand on his shoulder. "You look a bit flustered."

"I'm not getting the answers I need."

"That happens."

"No, it doesn't happen if I'm doing things properly," Malcolm said. "I'm not getting the right answers so it means I'm not yet asking the right questions. I need to figure out what the questions are before I'll get anywhere."

"Remember we're not really detectives," Mary smiled. "We come at things differently. Despite our efforts to be logical and methodical, it's been our more chaotic approaches that have yielded the best results. Maybe stop trying to ask conventional questions and zig-zag a little. Put people off their guard. Be unconventional."

"You're right," Malcolm said. "I can do that."

"Yes you can," she smiled. "Better than anyone I know. I have to get back, but let me know how it goes."

Malcolm watched Mary leave and did not break his gaze until the door had completely closed.

"Chaotic," Malcolm said under his breath. "Unconventional."

Malcolm then made his way toward where Sita was reading a book. She was a twenty-something young woman who had black hair with magenta highlights. She was dressed in clothes, which could best be described as 'goth meets grunge'.

"Hey," Malcolm said with a nod. "I'm Malcolm and I'm part of the security detail on board."

"Hey," she nodded back. "Sita Sharma."

"Good to meet you, Sita. You're part of FIRST's R&D team, right?"

"Yeah, why?"

"If you have a moment, I'd like to talk to you about the unfortunate deaths of some of the lawyers at McKenzie Ferguson."

"Yeah, sure," she shrugged. "What do you want to ask me?"

"First, how long have you lived in Vancouver?"

"I was born there, dude," Sita looked indignant. "Are you just asking me that question because I'm brown?"

"No, I'm asking because Vancouver's a technology hub and people come from all over the place, that's all," Malcolm shrugged. "How long have you been at FIRST?"

"We all started together, around three years ago."

"And what's your role over at FIRST? You're with the R&D team, right?"

"Yes, I'm one of three heads of the team," Sita said. "We're inventors, really."

"What do you invent?"

"Mostly toys and gadgets. I come up with things that help businesses and people."

"I was hoping for you to be a little more specific," Malcolm admitted. "For example, imagine I came to you and told you I had a business idea. For the sake of argument, pretend my idea is an ice cream truck, but instead it sells tacos and margaritas. I'm thinking a second truck can follow it that sells antacids. What could you do for me?"

"I certainly wouldn't invest in your idea for starters," Sita shook her head. "It doesn't work anything like that. Half the time we don't even wait for people to come to us with a need. Often times, we invent the toys first and then our Marketing Department finds the most likely way our toys can fit the needs and best benefit our customers. Then our Sales team formulates a strategy and a pitch they can use to approach them. With a little creativity, any of our inventions has a profit potential and business use. Any and all of our creations involve robotics, software, or both and we try to make our creations as innovative and intelligent as possible."

"Like self-aware intelligent?"

"We haven't gotten that far yet, but that's the Holy Grail of our industry."

"How did the three of you meet?"

"We all went to high school and then college together. Our first project as a group was to try to develop a chess game where the computer got to know a certain person's style and adapted its moves accordingly. It would get smarter after each game, making the challenge to the user even greater. We didn't quite accomplish that goal, but we still made some amazing breakthroughs, which we've since incorporated into other projects. If we had access to today's AI tech back in high school, I think we would have succeeded."

"I'm not a big techno-nerd, so what's so special about artificial intelligence?"

"Seriously dude? Imagine a computer that has the ability to learn, to think, and to adapt. Think of the problems it could solve in the world. It's exciting."

"I consider that kind of thing terrifying but maybe it's just me," Malcolm sat in the chair beside Sita. "Listen… as I said, some of the lawyers who represent your employer have passed away, right?"

"Yes, and I was like, 'Whoa! What's going on?' It's scary."

"All but one of the deaths have occurred in the Tech Law department. The deaths were all made to look like accidents but they weren't. I don't think that's news to you, is it?"

"No, and it's pretty freaky, to be honest."

"Okay, so then help me out. Why would that group of lawyers be specifically targeted? If they represent your company, what would somebody want so badly they'd kill for it?"

"Sorry, dude. I don't even have a guess."

"Alright, then let's try this from a different angle. Once you have a toy that's fully-tested and market-ready, what do you do with it?"

"FIRST finds an investor or a buyer, sells the patent, and then each of us goes home with a pretty awesome bonus cheque."

"What projects have you guys been working on lately?"

"We always have so many projects on the go at any given time, so it's hard to say."

"Then only focus on the ones that are ready to ship or are at least in the advanced testing stage. Now, what do you got?"

"We have a few phone games ready for testing, such as poker, blackjack, and other casino games. Unlike your usual software, though, we've used the AI to allow your computer opponents to have personalities so that you can observe them for tells. The AI also studies you through your camera to determine whether or not you're bluffing."

"You can do that?"

"Almost," Sita smiled. "At this point, we're still fixing the bugs but it's coming along. We're maybe a year or so away from perfecting the AI. We've made so much progress and last month we won an award at a global tech fair and it put FIRST on everyone's radar."

"I dare say it did," Malcolm muttered. "What was the award for?"

"Our advances in software and robotics."

"What other projects do you have on the go?"

"We're working on a robotic bird toy. It flies, flaps its wings, and uses AI to navigate itself so that it avoids tree branches, power lines, and so on. It also remembers where it was launched from so it can always return. It even folds its wings when it lands."

"Is it like a homing pigeon then?"

"Only kind of. It might be more accurate to think of it as one of those trained falcons you see on nature shows. Right now, we only have a seagull prototype but we're planning on developing an eagle, a hawk, a vulture, and other birds as well."

"And what else?"

"Uh… let's see… there's an emergency app that's still in beta testing."

"What does it do?"

"It lets you find a person or pet if they get lost. It's like a tracking device. There's a GPS but there's also a two-way communication tool that even works in remote areas. You can activate it via satellite link and it opens audio and video so you can see and hear what's happening in the vicinity. If you need to, you can push a button and connect to 9-1-1 and it can direct any emergency responders in the area to their location."

"What would tech like that be worth on the open market?"

"I don't know. Depending on the customer, it could be six or seven figures."

"That's a lot of zeroes," Malcolm nodded. "Could any of this stuff get weaponized?"

"Weaponized?"

"Yeah. Look, take off your nerd hat for a moment and pretend you're a military person looking to blow stuff up. How could you use any of this tech to help your allies or kill your enemies?"

"I suppose you could weaponize the tech if you adapted the programming."

"Okay, so with that in mind, which of your little toys would be the most sought-after by bad guys?"

"All of them, though I'm not sure exactly how," Sita lifted her head and began scanning the galley. "Let me get Kevin over here. He knows more about alternative applications of tech."

"Sure."

"Kev! Yo, dude, come here for a sec."

"Yo, Sita," Kevin said as he approached. "What's up, girl?"

"This guard is looking for information that might help prevent more killings of lawyers."

"Yeah, I know," Kevin shot a contemptuous glance at Malcolm. "He needs all the help he can get. So what do you need now?"

"She says you're developing casino games, a robotic bird, and a GPS-driven child locator. I was asking if maybe any of this technology could get weaponized."

"Why?" Kevin shot a dirty look at Sita and Malcolm noticed it. "Do you think lawyers are getting killed because of our tech?"

"I'm not sure, but I can't rule it out yet," Malcolm said. "So if you were the evil dictator of your own regime, how could you weaponize your casino games?"

"You can't really," Kevin shrugged. "I mean it's just a card game, right?"

"Oh, hey, Kev, what about using the camera tech itself?" Sita's eyes widened. "I mean, if you were some evil despotic ruler, it could come in handy. Once we got the final bugs worked out of the cameras, you could, like, put them all over the place. The facial recognition software could compile a database of everyone and then you could monitor everyone who comes and goes. You'd know their every move."

"I guess," Kevin said, "but…"

"And don't forget: by then it will be able to look for tells."

"How would that help?" Malcolm asked.

"It would help because you could then also use the camera software to interrogate people," Sita said. "The program should be able to learn enough to know when they were lying."

"And, if I understand you correctly," Malcolm said, "the more they lied, the better the software would learn, right?"

"Right."

"Interesting," Malcolm nodded. "And what about the robot birds?"

"Forget it," Kevin's hand waved as though he was shooing away a fly. "There's nothing our birds can do that a military drone can't do already."

"Most military drones need someone back at base piloting it, don't they?" Sita asked.

"I think so."

"So then what if a military drone could fly and navigate on its own?" Sita asked. "Then it could get to and from any target on its own too, couldn't it?"

"In theory, sure," Kevin's face was reddening.

"That would make sense," Malcolm nodded. "When it flew around, it wouldn't stand out like a drone would, and it would be small enough to still look like just another large-ish bird on radar. Could it carry a bomb or a warhead?"

"No way, the bird's too small and the wings don't have enough lift for anything large," Kevin's voice had gotten noticeably louder. "As it is, we had to increase the wingspan of the prototype in order for it to carry anything at all. At best you could fit a small hand grenade or something even smaller like that as its payload."

"Still," Malcolm said, "it would be a hell of a way to assassinate a single target."

"Maybe, but it would be an expensive one," Kevin shot back. "It would only be worth it if the target was worth spending a hundred grand to kill; otherwise, it's too expensive to be practical."

"Every air strike or cruise missile attack the US carries out costs tens of millions, so don't be so sure about your math on the risk-reward ratio," Malcolm then turned back to Sita. "What if you used plastic explosives and a detonator? It would be lighter than a warhead."

"As long as the entire device weighed four pounds or less, then sure," she said. "Anything like that could work."

"What about the GPS person-tracking thing?" Malcolm spoke faster as his curiosity became more and more piqued.

"You could use it to track a target," Sita nodded.

"No," Kevin shook his head. "You'd have to physically plant it on them."

"True, but if I understand you right, it could still work," Malcolm said. "I mean, if you knew where the target hung out, the bird could plant the device there and you'd get real-time alerts whenever he or she was on-site and you could see and hear everything nearby."

"And then you could fire a missile at the GPS coordinates and take out the target or detonate the bird," Sita said. "That would work."

"Thanks, guys," Malcolm stood up. "You've been a big help. These are all interesting ideas and I can certainly see why nefarious people would want to get their hands on them. I'm still not sure why anyone would kill so many people over it, but..."

"Oh my God, you guys," Sita said, wide-eyed. "I just thought of the most epic thing."

"What?"

"I was thinking... you combined two of our ideas, but what if we combined all three of those techs into one?"

"How would that work?" Malcolm sat back down.

"Sita," Kevin's brow furrowed and his tone was grave. "Don't."

"No, listen... a robotic bird with AI, loaded with facial recognition software... able to carry and drop a lightweight explosive device... with a GPS system... you'd have a device that could fly over anywhere looking like just another bird, right?" Sita spoke in a rapid and excited tone. "Meanwhile, the bird is out there collecting faces, voices, conversations, locations... And if we took out one of the heavy batteries and added camouflaged solar cells to keep the other battery charged, it could stay out in the field for weeks at a time."

"Interesting," Malcolm nodded. "So they could compile a database of known associates and then detonate the explosive when it saw the right target."

"Exactly," Sita's eyes lit up. "We should make that our next project and we could sell it to the Pentagon and retire."

"Shut up, Sita," Kevin snapped. "We don't discuss ideas when other people are around."

"What's the big deal?"

"Intellectual property, that's what the big deal is," Kevin said. "If you know what's good for you, you'll stop talking right now. He's already told me I'm his main suspect., so we're all done with his questions. Ask any of us anything else and I'll consider it harassment and I'll get you fired. Sita, don't open your mouth to this loser again or he'll get all psycho on us."

Kevin stormed out of the galley.

"Awkward," Sita said in a singsong voice. "I guess I should go. I have some ideas I want to write down anyway."

"What's he so upset about?" Malcolm asked. "What's he hiding?"

"Kevin's a bit intense, but he's cool," Sita began rolling in her chair toward the door. "I'm not saying anything more to you. Sorry."

Saturday, 2:49pm:

Mary stopped by one of the windows in the ship's lounge and looked out at the teeming rain. It was almost mesmerizing the way it bounced off the glass and sent droplets slithering down the pane.

"Excuse me," a voice said from behind her.

Mary turned and saw Ian Gagnon standing nearby. "What can I do for you, Ian?"

"Have you seen Bill Sutherland by any chance? He didn't show up for the two o-clock meeting."

"No, I haven't seen him," Mary said. "Is it unusual for him to be late?"

"Bill's never late for meetings, especially when he's the one who set it up," Ian said. "It ended up being a very short session because most of the agenda items were things he was bringing forward. He also said he had something important to discuss with us this afternoon, so yes, it's very unusual that he'd miss this."

"Did you check his cabin?" Mary asked.

"Yes, I went to his cabin and knocked, but he didn't answer. The door wasn't locked so I went inside and looked around but he wasn't there."

"Alright, thanks for letting me know," Mary gave a slight nod. "I'll let my colleagues know and we'll start looking for him right away."

"No sign of Bill on this level either," Malcolm said as he met up with Mary by the internal stairwell.

"I hope he's okay," Mary said.

"Every minute that passes without finding him increases the odds he's not."

"By the way, I checked his cabin while I was downstairs, and Ian's right: there's no sign of him," Mary said. "We've covered all the indoor areas, so it's just the outer decks left to check."

"You might want to do up your jacket," Malcolm said as they approached the door leading to the outside. "Look out the window. The rain is even worse now. It would seem we've reached the bad weather Mitch warned us about."

"And you're going to wear that ugly jacket in this storm?"

"Yeah," Malcolm said. "It may be old and tattered, but this leather jacket is good in the wind and rain."

Mary went to the door leading to the outer deck. She pushed it but it wouldn't open. "The wind is so strong I can barely budge it."

"Let me try."

"No, I'll do it, thanks," Mary said. "If I'm not strong enough to subdue a stubborn door, then there's a problem."

Mary put her shoulder into the door and it opened far enough for them to both squeeze out. The door slammed shut behind them. The wind was a constant roar in their ears and it nearly took their breath away. As they inched their way along the deck they were being battered by heavy rain. They held onto the railing to steady themselves.

If this was just the tail end of the storm, then Mary didn't want to know what it would be like in the middle of it. She looked up and saw a shape on the deck ahead of their position and she squinted to make it out. "Look over there," she shouted at Malcolm. "Is that a body under those metal stairs?"

"It sure looks like it," Malcolm yelled. "Let's go check it out."

They pressed forward until they were closer to the shape and it was most definitely a prone body. Malcolm knelt down and undid the zipper of his own jacket.

Mary was bewildered. "Why are you taking your jacket off?"

"Because he's dead," Malcolm shouted his response.

"I can see that," Mary yelled. "But I somehow doubt he's in any condition to care if he gets wet."

"I'm not planning on putting my jacket on him."

"Then put it back on or you'll get soaked and freeze."

"No," Malcolm shouted. "I'll eventually dry out and warm up but the jacket will get ruined."

"I have no idea what you're talking about right now."

"The smell," Malcolm looked at Mary. "The thing about leather is it absorbs smells. I once threw out an expensive jacket because it smelled of dead guy."

"Then you should have taken it to a dry-cleaner."

"I did," Malcolm said. "Somehow it came back smelling even worse."

Malcolm examined the body while Mary watched from a few feet away.

"Is it Bill Sutherland?" she shouted. Even though she could see the distinctive cowboy boots and white shirt she was hoping against hope it wasn't him.

"Yeah, it's definitely him."

"How bad is he?"

"The back of his head is bashed in so I'd say he's fine in the sense that he no longer has a care in the world," Malcolm looked at Mary. "You probably don't want to see this, so stay where you are."

"You're probably right about that," Mary said. "I've decided to take your word that it's Bill Sutherland."

Malcolm stood up, now drenched from the rain. Water teemed down his face and countless fresh droplets relentlessly bounced off him while his white shirt flapped in the gusts of wind. He turned and walked back toward Mary, picking up his jacket along the way. Mary once again struggled with the door against the strong winds but managed to open it just wide enough for them both to squeeze back inside.

"This just got so much worse," Mary said as she stamped the wet off her shoes.

"By the numbers, they got better," Malcolm saw Mary's surprised expression so he continued. "What I mean is, I now have one less suspect."

"Oh great," Mary exhaled and shook her head. "According to your reasoning, if we wait long enough we'll find the killer based on him or her being the only one left alive on the ship. That's not a realistic option."

"I know Bill made a few enemies," Malcolm shivered, "but were things bad enough to kill him?"

"Do you think Ki-Liu did this?"

"No, because this hit was sloppy and not a clean hit like Wes Oliphant. This was the same MO as Janine's death. There's also signs of a struggle and Ki-Liu is a killer, not a fighter."

"I'm not ashamed to admit I'm really scared right now."

"I don't blame you," Malcolm hugged Mary. "People are getting killed and so far we've only accomplished a big fat zero in figuring this out. To be honest, I really did have him as a possible suspect."

"I worry about how Amy and Stacy will take the news."

"So do... wait a minute," Malcolm took a step back and waved his finger, the expression on his face suddenly serious. "Stacy said 'nobody gains, everyone loses' when I asked her about the killings."

"And?"

"And I was so busy trying to find a suspect, I didn't really think about what she said."

"How does her comment help us?"

"She knows a lot more than she's letting on," Malcolm rubbed his soaking wet arms to try to get some warmth into them, but his actions only served to send droplets of water spattering around him and make his hands even wetter. "It's like she expected the deaths. She'd already thought everything through to its logical conclusion: nobody will gain and everyone will end up losing over this. It's safe to assume everyone in the Tech Law section at the firm is either marked for death or already dead, right?"

"Right. And?"

"And there's not many lawyers from that practise area left on board. That creepy lawyer Keith is a tech lawyer and so is Stacy, so there's got to be more we can get from them. Let's get your sister and then head to Stacy's cabin right away and we'll start there."

"First things first," Mary said. "For the sake of your health, we'll stop off at our cabin on the way so we can put on some dry clothes."

Malcolm and Mary approached Amy's cabin door.

"Mary," Malcolm whispered, "in order for me to get the information I need, you have to play along no matter what I say, alright?"

"I'll try," Mary whispered back.

Malcolm knocked on the door.

"Who is it?" Amy called from the other side of the door after a moment.

"It's the criminal thug," Malcolm said.

The door opened and Amy peered out from behind it. "What's going on?"

"Come with us next door to Stacy's cabin," Malcolm said. "You need to hear this too."

Malcolm knocked on Stacy's cabin door and then opened it and walked in, with Mary and Amy behind him.

Stacy Metzner glanced up from her computer, scoffed, and then went back to typing. "I'm too tired and busy for any more of your nonsense, Mercer. Come back some other time."

"No," Malcolm said. "We need to talk. Right now."

"Why?" Amy asked. "What's happened?"

"We located Bill Sutherland," Malcolm said.

"Good for you," Stacy looked over her reading glasses at him. "Did you manage to find out why he scheduled a meeting and then didn't show up for it?"

"Yes," he replied. "Bill couldn't make the meeting because he was too busy being dead."

"If you're joking, it's in terrible taste," Stacy snapped.

"It's no joke," Malcolm said. "He was bludgeoned to death sometime in the past one to two hours."

"Oh my God, no," Amy, eyes wide, covered her mouth with her hands. "Not Bill."

Amy was unable to hold back the tears and she began sobbing. Mary stepped beside Amy and put an arm around her.

"Amy, we all need you to keep it together, okay?" Mary said in a low, soothing voice. "Panic won't be of any help. Can we rely on you to stay centred and calm?"

"No, I'm too scared, okay?" Amy shouted between sobs. "I can't do this," she gasped. "Does it make you happy hearing me say that?"

"Not really," Malcolm said. "I was hoping to hear 'okay I'll hold it together so I can help you' to be honest. Now *that* would have made me very happy."

"I feel sick right now," Stacy said. "This is a real gut-punch. This has all gotten too far out of hand."

"I feel sick too, but mostly because you've been holding out on me," Malcolm folded his arms. "When my life is on the line, I prefer it to be in cases where I have all the information I need."

"What are you saying?" Amy said, a tear rolling down her cheek.

"I'm saying your boss knows more about what's going on and why people are getting killed than she's letting on."

"I can't say anything more than I already have, nor do I want to at the moment," Stacy massaged her temples and exhaled. "Besides, it's strictly need-to-know."

"Then you strictly need to know this: I'm done protecting you both."

"Then good riddance," Stacy said. "I don't want your protection."

"But I do," Amy sobbed. "Stacy, please. I'm scared."

"Don't listen to him," Stacy glared at Malcolm. "He's just trying to get you worked up and terrified."

"It's working."

"Good," Malcolm said, "because I honestly believe within thirty minutes of me walking out this door, you'll both be dead."

"Ridiculous," Stacy stood up and leaned on the small table her laptop was upon. "You wouldn't let Amy or me get murdered."

"Yes, I would. Hell, better you than me. What do you have to live for? A law practice, which is a sad statement on your life's priorities, I have to say. As for me, I've got a young daughter at home so my life is worth more than yours in that equation. I'd risk my life for a worthy cause if necessary, but I'll be damned if I'll die for someone withholding information from me. Besides, these killings have all been targeted. So if you're as innocent and uninvolved as you let on, Ms. Metzner, then you and Amy will have nothing to worry about, right?"

"I can't believe that you…"

"Shouldn't you be spending your last moments alive writing a will or saying your goodbyes?"

"You're being completely…"

"Listen, I have to go now," Malcolm put his hand on the handle of the cabin door. "There are some lawyers on board who seem to have gambling addictions. I want to start a pool with them where we each bet on your time of death and a half hour isn't a lot of time for me to set it all up."

"Stacy, please," Amy's face was tear-stained and her bottom lip was trembling. "If there's something more to say then say it."

"Alright," Stacy said with a sharp, audible groan. "It's true. There really is some danger and I'm not *completely* innocent."

"I already know that, so I'm out of here. I'll see you both in Hell."

"You can knock off the theatrics, alright?" Stacy slammed her laptop lid down. "I'll disclose some additional details if it helps your joke of an investigation."

"Alright. I'm listening."

"There was a meeting in the office a few days ago," Stacy said. "The Tech Law Group and Bill Sutherland were in the boardroom and Bill confronted some of the lawyers about a shady deal he'd learned about. That's it."

"What kind of deal?" Malcolm asked. "Oh, come on, don't give me that look. It's not good enough to call it a shady deal and then give me no details so I can judge for myself just how shady it was."

"A few of the lawyers, most notably the late Charles Lautzen, made a deal with a third party contact who wanted to get copies of some technology files. In exchange, they'd pay a substantial sum of money."

"How much?"

"I wasn't told the amount."

"Who was the third party contact?"

"A contact who claimed to be an executive at a Chinese technology company, though we learned soon afterward he was actually part of some kind of East-Asian crime syndicate. Anyway, apparently the deal fell apart and it caused a lot of panic. Normally grounded, well-respected lawyers were suddenly acting like unhinged lunatics."

"What about Bill Sutherland?" Mary asked. "Was he in favour of the deal?"

"No, Bill was completely against it and he got into a shouting match with Charles. The department was divided into two camps, the would-be sellers and the opposers, and some particularly heated words were exchanged. That night, one of the sellers, Ben Shapner, died. He allegedly jumped off the balcony of his fifteenth-floor apartment. The next night, one of the opposers,

Eliza Borwith, was killed when a hit-and-run vehicle struck her. Then on the third night, Charles Lautzen' car sailed off the edge of a bridge with Charles still inside it."

"So when Sutherland learned of the plan to sell access to the technology," Malcolm folded his arms and leaned against the door, "what did he do?"

"In the meeting, he said he was going to stop any chance of the deal going through to protect the client's intellectual property," Stacy rubbed her face with her now-trembling hands. "I wasn't sure what he meant by that at the time, but he didn't go into the office the next day. The seller faction was livid and began shouting that they couldn't find the files anywhere on the network. They spent the day in boardrooms arguing with opposers with raised voices. It was like everyone had lost their minds."

"And?"

"And then Bill came by my place late that night in secret. He gave me a memory stick and he told me to keep it secure. He told me he'd let me know the password at a later time but for that moment he wanted me to hide the stick in a safe place. He made me swear not to tell anyone about it or where I'd hidden it until he told me otherwise."

"Does anyone else know Bill Sutherland came to see you at your house?" Mary asked.

"Someone must have known because my place was broken into the next morning while I was at work," Stacy tapped her pen on the table for a moment before continuing. "They didn't take anything but they seemed to have looked through everything. Thankfully, I hid the files well."

"So they must suspect you know where the files are," Malcolm rubbed his chin. "What else did Sutherland say to you that night?"

"Nothing. He left quite abruptly after that. Don't even think of asking me where the memory stick is."

"I don't want to know where it is," Malcolm shook his head. "Just tell me it's safe and that nobody has taken it from you."

"Yes, it's safe. I made sure it was hidden where nobody would look for it. I found out from the IT Department that Bill even had the backups wiped so the files couldn't be restored to the server."

"But the files would also be on FIRST's computers," Mary said, "so won't the would-be sellers just get them from there instead?"

"FIRST's servers are our servers," Stacy replied. "They have their own payroll and employee systems but all the intellectual property is stored with us. There's a virtual connection between their office and ours."

Mary nodded. "I think it's safe to assume Bill moved the files of those projects onto the memory stick to keep them out of the hands of the sellers."

"I've been assuming the same," Stacy said, "but I don't know for certain because he didn't send me the password."

"But he implied he was going to send it to you."

"Yes, Mary, I know but I didn't receive anything."

"And being dead, he's in no shape to do it now, nor can he tell you when it's okay to tell anyone about anything," Malcolm tapped his finger against his jaw. "When did he stop by your house?"

"The night before the cruise."

"So it's not as though he didn't have time to send you the password or anything," Malcolm's eyes stared at the ceiling while he tried to think. "Did you receive anything else from him at all since you last spoke? An email, a phone call, or a file? Hell, even a pack of gum?"

"Nothing. The last thing he gave me was the memory stick."

"Ms. Metzner," Mary said softly. "You knew there would be more deaths before we even set sail, didn't you?"

"After the first three killings, it was only logical to anticipate more would follow," Stacy shrugged. "There was no reason whatsoever to believe there'd be any sort of truce on the cruise.

When two factions fight this viciously, it won't stop until the beligerents on one or both sides are killed."

"Which is why you said nobody gains, everyone loses, right?"

"Yes, that's exactly what I meant," Stacy sighed. "I'd like some time alone now, if you don't mind."

"Sure," Malcolm said and he turned and opened the door.

"I'll catch up with you," Mary said to him. She took Amy's arm and led her to the side door, which connected to Amy's cabin. She took her inside and closed the door.

"Hey," Mary said in a soft voice. "Are you okay?"

"No, I don't think I am."

"Why don't you come and sit on the bed here?"

Amy moved over to her bed and sat down. She appeared dazed.

"Hey, Amy," Mary said as she sat down beside her. "Do you remember when we were small and you brought home that wild rabbit you found on our way home from school?"

"Yes," Amy said, a brief smile appeared then disappeared on her face. "I remember naming him Mister Carrots. Why?"

"Remember Mom said we either had to take him to the SPCA or she'd cook it?"

"Oh my goodness, yes."

"We were so scared, so we took Mr. Carrots to the SPCA but forgot to tell Mom where we were going and she thought we ran away."

"We were so grounded after that," Amy sniffed.

"Yes, but we were both okay with the grounding because we believed we'd saved the bunny's life."

"I never forgot that."

"You were fearless, strong-willed, and determined to do what was needed. I need you to have that same strength now."

"This is completely different."

"Not really," Mary took Amy's hand and gave it a gentle squeeze. "I always looked up to you because of your outgoing nature and inner strength. I was jealous because you were so good at everything. I never understood why you just gave it all up."

"I got pregnant, that's why," Amy glanced at Mary. "I was suddenly made aware that I needed to be able to support a child. I married Brett for security – a big mistake, I might add – and then all the things I wanted for myself sort of got put on a shelf for another day. The dreams are still there but they're looking further away instead of closer. I had ambitions to take the world by storm, but so far I've only managed the storm part."

"I'm sorry," Mary pulled a tissue from her pocket and handed it to Amy.

"Don't be," Amy took the tissue and blew her nose. "My kids are the centre of my world and I have no regrets about that. When they're out on their own and living their own lives, I'll still have a chance to fulfil a few of my own dreams."

"That's a good way of looking at things. Keep thinking about your kids and it will help you to get through this."

"You know, twenty years ago when you ran away I thought you'd lost your mind," Amy stared at the floor. "At the same time, though, you were out there living your life. It was an appalling choice of lifestyle, in my opinion, but it was still a choice. I was so envious of you but I comforted myself with the knowledge that at least I had a husband and three great kids and you didn't. Brett and I split and things got rough for five years, but then I remarried."

"You overcame adversity," Mary patted Amy's hand. "You faced the problem and came out victorious. Now you're now in a situation where you need to overcome some more of it. I need you to help me, okay? Keep it together and we'll get out of here alive. Does that sound like a plan?"

Amy sniffled and then sighed. She then nodded, though without any enthusiasm.

"Okay, good," Mary smiled. "Keep your door locked and take care of yourself and Stacy the best you can. I'm going to go and try to find a killer."

Saturday, 4:19pm:

Mary walked at a brisk pace along the wet outer deck until she had caught up to the person she had been following. The wind had died down, though it was still blowing, and the rain had lessened to a light drizzle, making it still unpleasant enough outside that most people were choosing to remain indoors.

"Hello again," Mary said as she got alongside him.

"Oh, hello," Ian Gagnon said. "It's Mary, right?"

"Yes," she smiled. "Nice to see I'm not the only one who's willing to brave a little inclement weather.'

"I grew up in the Vancouver area, so I learned pretty early in my life that if you're not willing to go out in the rain you're not going to get out much at all."

"That's so true," Mary said. "Ian, would it be okay if I asked you a few questions about Bill's sudden death?"

"Why?"

"Because the team I'm working with isn't just here for appearances sake, we're currently investigating the death of a member of the ship's crew."

"Oh, so the rumour mill was right for once," Ian said. "I'd heard whispers about a crew member dying."

"It's true. And he was one of the senior crew members."

"Accidental or... *otherwise*?"

"Very much otherwise."

"Oh, wait, let me guess," Gagnon sighed. "Bill's also dead and because he and I argued, you've got me profiled as some kind of homicidal maniac."

"No, but you did exchange some heated words with Bill just before he died," Mary shivered as a cold gust of wind kicked up unexpectedly. "Plus with Bill gone, you now stand a better chance of being chosen as Managing Partner."

"Yes, but neither of those things make me a killer."

"No, but either one of them would make you a suspect, let alone both of them."

Ian took a few steps in silence before answering. "Thinking about it, I suppose that's not an unreasonable assumption for you to make based on the perspective you're viewing things from. That said, however, anyone at the firm will vouch for me. I have Bill's back and have nothing but the greatest respect for him."

"Had."

"I'll stick with the present tense if you don't mind. Even dead, Bill has more integrity and is a better human being than many of my colleagues."

"What do you mean by that?"

"I'm afraid I can't tell you."

"Why not?"

Ian stopped walking and stared off into the distance for a moment. He then turned to face Mary. "Remember when I told you the firm is like a family? I meant that on several levels. First, the thing about most families is there's a code of silence. Secondly, families are also notorious for fighting amongst themselves until an outsider gets involved, at which point everyone rallies to defend one another against the outsider."

"And I'm the outsider in that scenario," Mary's eyes studied his. "So does that mean you won't cooperate with me?"

"On the contrary, that's not what I'm saying at all," Ian said. "You're trying to find out who's killing members of my work family so I'll give you whatever help I can."

"Look, I'm sorry so many of your colleagues have passed away."

Gagnon scoffed. "Thanks, but 'passed away' isn't a suitable synonym for 'murdered'. We're not idiots. Deep down, we all know these weren't accidental deaths."

"Do the police have any suspects?" Mary asked, feigning innocence.

"They're not involved at this point."

"Dare I ask why?"

"The firm's reputation is the reason people are giving."

"Based on your tone of voice, I can tell you're not a fan of that reasoning."

"When people – *my friends* – die, it's not good enough for me to hear 'it's bad for business to call the police' so you're right, I'm not a fan."

"Is that why you're running for Managing Partner?"

"That's the biggest of several reasons, yes."

"Stacy Metzner said there was a heated discussion in a boardroom meeting just before the first death."

"There was indeed a meeting and an argument took place, sure," Gagnon answered carefully.

"Can you tell me anything about what was discussed in the meeting?"

"What was said in that meeting will forever stay within the four walls of the room," Gagnon said. "Hanging outside the door of Boardroom 205 is a sign listing the strict rules which must be adhered to once inside. Among the rules, there's no cell phones, no video, and no minutes can be taken, and the penalty for violating the rules is immediate on-the-spot dismissal from the firm. The sign has the title 'Staying Alive in 205' to give you a sense of how seriously we take the code of silence."

"Is it possible someone or a group of someones broke the rules and that's why they didn't manage to 'stay alive' afterwards?"

"It's possible, but not likely. There'd be rumours or whispers of something and I've heard nothing."

"Mr. Gagnon, were you present at that meeting?"

"No, nobody from the Finance Department was invited."

"Would you even tell me if you were invited?"

"Yes, of course I would," he said, nodding. "It's no secret if I did or did not attend a meeting. If I did, though, once I walked into that room everything discussed within it would be kept confidential."

"Why weren't you there if you're connected to FIRST through your role in the Finance Department?"

"I didn't even think to ask. We weren't invited so I assumed it was a family-related thing."

"Family as in 'law firm family' right?"

"Yes."

"Was Stacy Metzner in the meeting?"

"No, she was in the meeting prior to that one, which was what caused the second meeting to be called."

"Meetings with no minutes, a code of silence, comparing colleagues to a family… this all sounds a lot like how the mafia operates."

"No, it's just our corporate culture," Gagnon chuckled. "You may not be aware of this, but law firms are notoriously incestuous. People move from firm to firm constantly and turnover is a big budget issue as well as a headache for our HR Department. We're always hunting for top talent and we're not the only ones trying to lure excellent people away from their current firms. In order to minimize turnover, we've tried to create a close-knit family culture so people feel valued thus making them more likely to stay. There's not much loyalty out there anymore so we're trying to build some from within. Trust me: corporate law is nothing like the mob even though there's always a couple of people in any given group who may take things too far."

"With all that's going on, why do you think Bill insisted on the cruise going ahead?"

"We're a resilient bunch. We get things done no matter what the obstacle. However, this… this killing stuff… it's got us all rattled. It just feels wrong to be out here now. I can't concentrate on clients with everything else that's happening."

"I don't understand why your firm spends so much money to show your clients you care. This almost sends a message of 'look what we spend your billings on' or something."

"I don't know if you've noticed, Mary, but a lot of people don't like lawyers," he saw her nod. "Every four years we have a retreat with our top client and we get them to relax with us, have fun, play, and dance and for those few days they forget we're lawyers. They get to see us as just regular human beings who want them to succeed as much as they do."

"Are there any clients you have who weren't happy about being left off the guest list for the cruise?"

"FIRST makes up eighty percent of the Tech Department's billings and seventeen percent of the firm's entire revenue. Our second-biggest client makes up just four percent. Every client we have gets an appreciation event, but only one gets anything on this scale. We want our client events to be memorable."

"This event will definitely be memorable," Mary said. "Though for all the wrong reasons."

"You know, I have to say this: you don't see a husband-wife security team every day."

"What makes you…?"

"Matching bands on your fingers and your body language when you interact with one another."

"Very observant."

"I'm also observant enough to know that a murder investigation would be a better job for the police to handle."

"I agree, but they're not on board so we've taken the lead for the time being."

"And you have the authority and necessary skills to lead a murder investigation, do you?"

"Under the internationally-recognized Incident Command System, the first able person on the scene is authorized to take control of an emergency situation until the authorities arrive, so that's a big yes to your question. We discovered the body so we're in charge until we can dock."

"That's the flimsiest bit of reasoning I've heard today but if you want to take charge of a corpse, then I'm not going to argue with you. Good luck with it all."

"I would appreciate your discretion."

"Discretion comes with an hourly fee attached to it."

"What?"

"It's just an attempt at a joke, relax," Ian sighed. "If we didn't have senses of humour we'd crack under the pressures of the job, especially with Bill's sudden passing and the deaths of my colleagues. Is there anything else you need from me?"

"I don't know at the moment, but can I come to you again if I think of something?"

"Please do," Gagnon headed toward the doors leading back inside. "Listen, I need to go change into some dry clothes but I'd like to know something first. What happened to Bill's body?"

"My colleagues photographed the crime scene and then moved the body to a secure location so it can be looked over by a qualified forensics team when we dock."

"Just tell me he's locked away somewhere out of sight for my own peace of mind."

"Yes, he's locked away in the ship's morgue, such as it is," Mary said, omitting the detail that their yet-unknown suspect had a full set of keys. "Why are you asking?"

"Because if people find out Bill's dead there's going to be panic on board, and I'd rather not have that. Let's keep his death as quiet as we can for the time being."

"Certainly."

Saturday, 4:23pm:

Malcolm jogged to catch up with Kevin, who had exited his cabin and was heading toward the stairs leading up to the main deck.

"Kevin," he called out when he got close enough. "Hold up a second. You and I need to chat."

"I have nothing more to say to you," Kevin continued walking. "I'm pretty sure I made that clear."

"You can talk to me or to the cops," Malcolm said as he got immediately behind him. "Trust me, it's better that you talk to me."

"I'll take my chances," Kevin huffed. "I was serious about there being repercussions if you didn't leave me alone."

"Oh, hey, and speaking of consequences, I know about the crime you committed."

Kevin stopped walking but didn't turn around. "What crime?"

"You're too bright to be playing dumb. Let's start by talking about the sale of FIRST files and how it went bad from there. I know all about it now as well as the role you played in it."

"Look," Kevin turned around to face Malcolm. "I had no choice, so leave me alone. Things just... *happened.*"

"If you want me to leave you alone then I'm going to need you to give me all of the details."

Kevin's eyes darted around and he leaned in and spoke in an urgent whisper. "Look, back off, okay? I didn't know he would die. It was an accident."

Malcolm nodded, but he had no idea which death Kevin was talking about. With all the people who had died lately, Kevin's outburst was too vague to be useful. He knew he needed to probe further, but without giving the game away.

"An accident?" Malcolm scoffed. "A death like *that* couldn't have been an accident."

"What detail did I miss? Every clue pointed to this being a suicide."

Ah, Ben Shapner, Malcolm thought. *The lawyer who 'jumped' to his own death.* "Tell me in your own words what happened."

Kevin made brief eye contact, and then bowed his head. He leaned in closely. "I was originally helping the group of lawyers who wanted to sell access to the tech files in exchange for a cut of the money. Ben had earlier tried to persuade me to switch sides but I refused. I had no idea it was all going to end up so wrong."

"Go on."

"He invited me over to his apartment and he said he'd explain everything," Kevin took a deep breath and closed his eyes for a few seconds. "He said if I allowed him to explain his case, he'd respect whatever answer I gave him."

"And?"

"It sounded like a great way to resolve the problem so I went there," Kevin took another deep breath and let it out slowly before continuing. "A few minutes in, he invited me out to the balcony to check out the great view of the city. When I got to the railing, he pushed me halfway over. He held me there and demanded I stop helping the others. He said it was a betrayal. I panicked, we fought, and that's how I really sprained my wrist. I was only focused on trying to get my feet back on the balcony so I twisted my body and tried to push him away but ended up pushing him over instead. His fall seemed to happen in slow motion but I still remember the sickening thud of his body hitting the ground. I ran out of his suite, took the elevator down to the lobby, and just started running and… I don't know. I tried to pretend I knew nothing about it."

"You took the time to type out a suicide note, so you had some presence of mind."

"I don't know what came over me."

"You should have told somebody."

"How could I have told anyone?" Kevin's voice was breaking. "I didn't know who I could trust and I still don't. Mr. Shapner was one of the most respected lawyers in the firm, so who would believe my version of events over his? Nobody. Once Shapner died, it was the end of my being involved with the selling faction."

"How do I know I can believe you about any of this?"

"Who do you think moved the files onto the memory stick for Sutherland?" Kevin glared at him with tear-filled eyes. "Bill's a good guy – *or he was a good guy* – but he's no computer genius. He can barely type, let alone use a computer. I moved the files for him and it was me who got the offsite backups wiped for him. I was helping him prevent the sale."

"Fair enough," Malcolm softened his tone of voice. "Look, that was a brave confession to make. Let me see what else I can find out about this, alright?"

"Don't tell anyone what I told you, okay?" Kevin wiped his eyes with his shirtsleeve. "The firm is like a cult. If they think I had anything at all to do with Ben Shapner's death, I'll be a marked man."

"Don't worry," Malcolm said. "I'd like you to survive the cruise, so I'll keep your secret safe."

Saturday, 5:20pm:

In the galley, Malcom sat across the table from Mary, looking in horror at what she had ordered for dinner. He knew a comment would start an argument but he ended up blurting it out anyway. "Your salad looks like weeds, seeds, and topsoil."

"It's a delicious quinoa stir fry," Mary looked up at him. "You should try it, it's completely organic."

"Crap's organic too, but that doesn't mean it's good to eat."

Mary rolled her eyes and shook her head. "You eat far too many processed foods and that kind of crap is arguably as bad as the type you just referenced."

"You used to complain when my meals consisted only of coffee," Malcolm held up his cup. "At least now I eat actual food."

"Don't get me wrong, I'm glad about that," she said. "But man-made stuff takes a back seat to what nature provides."

"Nature also provided polio, diphtheria, and measles, yet man-made vaccines and medicines seem to be preferred in polite company," Malcolm said. "Natural doesn't always mean better."

Mary shook her head again. "Look, let's review what we've learned and not talk about food, okay?"

Malcolm nodded. "Well, we know there was a heated argument in the boardroom and that it left some bitter feelings. Later that same night, the first lawyer died after allegedly jumping off the balcony of his fifteenth-floor apartment in an apparent suicide. We've since learned that it may have been an accidental death involving Kevin, more details pending. A second lawyer, Eliza Borwith, was killed the next day thanks to a hit-and-run incident involving a vehicle. Then a third lawyer's car went off a bridge on day three. All were made to look like freak accidents. That's way too much to be a coincidence so that's where we start."

"We need to find out who else knows anything about what went on in that meeting and then interview every last one of them to find out what the argument was about."

"Yeah, and most people aren't even acknowledging there was a meeting, let alone what was discussed in it. We have so many suspects at the moment it isn't funny. Is it too obvious to suspect David, the programmer nerd from China, as being connected to a Chinese crime syndicate and a Chinese assassin?"

"No, he's definitely a valid suspect," Mary said. "But at the same time we can't rule out Kevin, Sita, or any of the other seven dozen people on board either."

"Sita, Kevin, and David are definitely the brains behind the technology," Malcolm said. "But they hardly fit the profile of killers or thieves. The rest of FIRST's people on board are creatives and executives who love the technology but clearly don't understand its full potential."

"Still, we have a lot more questioning to do."

"I'll take care of that," Malcolm took a drink of coffee. "How are you holding up?"

"I'm fine despite the lack of sleep, but by the time we wrap this up I'll be exhausted. When we're done this job I want to go home and read books in bed for a week straight."

"Then on our way home we should stop off at the bookstore and get you something. You said you were interested in trying out a trashy romance novel. Maybe this would be a good time to do that."

"No, I know I said I was interested in trying one out but I'm over it now," Mary took a drink of some sort of thick purple juice. "I'll pass on the trashy romances, thank you."

"What changed your mind?"

"I finally read a few chapters of one."

"Was it that bad?"

"I'm convinced they're all written by men because the women in those stories don't think properly. I can't relate to them at all."

"For example…?"

"In my mind, one particular scene I read should have been more like 'in his passion, he tore at her clothes, popping the buttons off her blouse. She moaned, because she dreaded the thought of having to find beige buttons in the white carpeting. Also, she hated sewing and she hoped her favourite blouse wasn't ruined' or something along those lines."

"When we get home, you really need to write a romance novel. I would totally read something like that. So, you're sure you're not tired?"

"Yes, I'm wide awake."

"In that case, I'd like to go lie down for a while."

"Hopefully you can sleep a little."

"That would be nice but I won't get my hopes up. I just need to clear my head so I can think straight."

Saturday, 7:02pm:

Malcolm woke up with a start, his latest nightmare sending his heart beating at a frenetic pace. He sat up in the bed, breathing heavily and trying to calm his trembling body. He looked over in the near-darkness at the digital clock. He had been in bed for just over an hour and he figured he'd slept somewhere between thirty and forty minutes. Malcolm wiped the sweat from his brow, then took in a deep breath, and then slowly exhaled.

Malcolm had grown accustomed to the sporadic sleep patterns that plagued his life. He managed short naps throughout the day but his nightmares even seeped into those. His lack of sleep affected his long-term concentration, but he had otherwise learned to function with his lack of slumber.

Odd, but despite his lack of regular sleep he rarely felt fatigued. As long as he was busy and as long as his mind was racing, he felt wide-awake. It was when he slowed down or tried to relax that his body began waving around sleep's overdue balance sheet and demanding at least partial payments, to say nothing of the compound interest which had accumulated.

It wasn't only the nightmares that chased away the sandman; it was also the non-stop whirring of his mind, which always seemed primed and ready to recall its choice of traumatic moments from Malcolm's past as he would begin to doze off. He would hear a gunshot or a scream, or the wailing of those mourning the sudden, violent loss of someone close to them. No matter how many years passed by, the sounds remained as vivid as the day they first etched themselves into his brain.

Things he had suppressed or tried to forget came rushing back to his mind whenever he closed his eyes for anything longer than a blink. However, the nightmares he had been having the last three times he fell asleep were something new entirely.

The voice of a young woman kept repeating the same words over and over, and his ability to hear her fluctuated. He felt a severe chill run down his spine as her words continued to echo in his mind.

Putty. Noisy. Cramped. Wires.

He reached over to the bedside lamp and turned it on. Even though there was still daylight in the early evening sky, his cabin was not facing the sun, which left his room dimly lit.

While the spoken words were parading around in his head, Malcolm tried to assign some sort of meaning to them. 'Noisy' and 'cramped' pretty much described most of the apartment complexes in Queens he had seen. What does putty have to do with anything? Noisy putty? Cramped wires?

The things the woman's voice said to him left him feeling unsettled and confused. Most disturbing of all was what she said next…

Malcolm burst into the ship's lounge where the Evening Social was in full swing. He raced around until he was able to find Mary.

"Oh, hey," she smiled as he drew near. "Did you sleep at all?"

"Thirty or so minutes, maybe," Malcolm blurted out. "It'll keep me going."

"It will keep you going the same way making the minimum payment on a maxed-out credit card will 'keep you going' but that doesn't mean it's enough to deal with the problem at hand."

"Can we forget about my sleep issues for a moment?" Malcolm was not aware of how loudly he had said that.

Mary saw the near-frantic look in his eyes and only then noticed his elevated state of agitation. "What's the matter?"

"I have two things on my mind and I need to speak to you about them immediately, outside, and in private," Malcolm walked at a rapid pace to the door. Mary followed behind him, somewhat bewildered.

Once they were outside, they found a secluded spot, alee from the wind.

"What are the couple of things on your mind?"

"One's a puzzle and the other is…" Malcolm hesitated, "…*impossible.*"

"Intriguing," Mary nodded. "Okay, start with the puzzle."

"It's something Kevin told me when he confessed to the accidental death of Ben Shapner. Something about it doesn't make sense to me."

"Tell me."

"Did you see the photo of Shapner they displayed at the Friday Night Social?"

"Yes."

"He was six-four, barrel-chested, had arms bigger around than most peoples' legs, and he probably weighed between two-twenty and two-fifty. He was an avid boxer and he had a lot of other athletic interests."

"Yes, I know. What about it?"

"Kevin, meanwhile, is maybe around five-eight or five-nine and might weigh as much as a hundred thirty if he had on a heavy coat. He's basically a scarecrow in glasses."

"Oh, I think I see where you're going with this," Mary said. "How does a skinny light-weight like Kevin accidentally knock a massive, athletic guy over a railing?"

"Exactly."

"If his balcony railing was the standard forty-two inches in height and assuming Shapner was twice Kevin's weight, then there's no way Kevin twisted around and knocked Shapner over without also going over himself. Either they both fell over or neither of them did."

"Right," Malcolm made an emphatic waving motion with his index finger. "Kevin said he distinctly remembers the sickening thud of the body hitting the ground and that bothers me too."

"Why?"

"I don't care how big and strong you are, if you're falling fifteen floors to your death, you're going to shout or scream."

"Good point," Mary said. "And yet none of the people questioned heard any screaming, even though some of them had their windows open that evening."

"Exactly."

"Which means Shapner was either dead or incapacitated before he fell."

"Yeah, and there's no way Kevin could have lifted that much deadweight and tossed it over."

"Meaning either he had an accomplice or he's protecting somebody."

"Or both," Malcolm shrugged. "There was an accomplice and Kevin's protecting them."

"And Kevin could have put on some rubber gloves and typed the suicide note on the computer and then left the scene."

"My thoughts exactly."

"It's creepy yet completely plausible," Mary then locked eyes with Malcolm. "Now, what's the impossible thing you wanted to discuss?"

"Those thirty-ish minutes of sleep I had ended when I woke up with a start and it all went weird from there."

"For my own understanding, define the term 'went weird' for me".

"I heard a voice in my head and I was awake when I heard it."

"That sounds to me like a by-product of your sleep deprivation," Mary gave him a look. "This just sounds like a vivid dream."

"Believe me, this goes way beyond vivid," Malcolm fidgeted. "At first I heard the woman's voice repeating words to me in my dream but then I woke up with a start. As I was sitting up, I could still hear her voice for a moment until she faded out. And, in case you're wondering, I turned on the bedside lamp and there was nobody in the room with me and the door was still locked."

"I still don't…"

"The nightmare had ended, I was wide awake, sitting up, my feet on the floor, reflecting on what was said, and then the voice continued talking to me," Malcolm paused to let that sentence sink in. "And then the last thing I heard the voice say was 'I have to go but I'll see you in two weeks. Now don't just sit there', and then nothing."

"That's odd."

"Odd? No, that isn't odd at all," Malcolm said. "Wearing socks with sandals is odd. Putting fruit on pizza is odd. This goes way beyond odd and is currently settling into a suburban neighborhood in the District of Impossible."

"Was this, by any chance, the same young woman's voice that has been keeping you awake recently?"

"Yes, it was exactly the same voice."

"So what was this voice telling you?"

They heard a door shut and turned to look. Adam Spender saw them and stopped in his tracks.

"Hey you two," Spender said, throwing his cigarette overboard. "And here I thought I was the only one who was skipping the party."

"Hey, Whitlock," Malcolm then turned to Mary and winked. "I'll tell you more later, Mary. I need to speak with our intrepid detective for a moment, so I'll catch up with you in a little bit."

Mary nodded and then went back inside.

"Come with me a sec," Malcolm said.

Adam Spender walked with Malcolm in silence until they were at the back of the ship.

"I know what we need to do," Malcolm said in a hushed voice.

Spender looked over his shoulder before responding. "You mean you've figured everything out?"

"Not even close," Malcolm admitted, "but I did have a flash of insight which should blow this case wide open."

"That's fantastic," Spender was excited. "Hey, I'll take anything that moves us forward at this point. This is all about those FIRST files, isn't it?"

"Yeah," Malcolm sighed. "That seems to be at the heart of everything else that's happening."

"Just tell me the files are someplace safe for my own peace of mind."

"As far as I know they are."

"It worries me they're out there," Spender frowned and rubbed his chin. "I'd be a lot less nervous if you had them. At least then I wouldn't be worried about the wrong sorts of people forcefully obtaining them."

"I'd prefer it if I had the files as well but people have died because of them," Malcolm said. "The person currently caring for them doesn't know who to trust and I can't blame them. I have to look around the ship for something. I have a new mission for you."

"Great," Spender rubbed his hands together. "I'll make you proud, buddy. So, what do you want me to do?"

"I'm going to lay a trap," Malcolm whispered. "It'll take a bit of work on my end first, but in order for it to work it's critical you be there when it gets sprung."

"You can count on me."

"I know I can," Malcolm nodded. "It came down to whether I trusted Officer Trinh's story or yours. I've finally decided which of you to trust."

"That means everything to me," Spender said. "You won't regret this."

"I sure as hell hope I won't," Malcolm leaned on the rail. "There's still so much to unravel here."

"So what exactly do you want me to do?"

"I want you guarding Stacy Metzner's cabin around the clock," Malcolm said. "I can't search the ship and protect her at the same time. If somebody comes for her, I want you to be there to get in their way and stop them."

"If me guarding her mean she has the files, then I'll gladly do it. Metzner is completely ill-equipped to keep them safe."

"If it makes you feel any better, I could just be getting you to stand guard so that everyone else *thinks* she has them."

"Ah, now that's clever. Nice."

"Maybe, but it's also a gamble," Malcolm exhaled, frustration in his voice. "First I need to do a complete search of this ship to test a theory."

"I won't let you down, buddy," Spender patted Malcolm's shoulder. "I owe you my life. So do you want me to spend the weekend standing outside Metzner's cabin door?"

"No, the cabin beside hers isn't occupied. Move into it. Make Metzner access her cabin only through the connecting door between the suites. That way you can know when she's coming and going and you can monitor her safety that way. She won't like it, but too bad. Be insistent. Amy's cabin is on the other side of Metzner's, so get her to use the connecting door to Stacy's room and make sure they both leave their front doors shut and locked at all times."

"Got it, but I have a question," Spender raised his hand like a classroom pupil. "How can I protect them against an armed assailant? I don't have a weapon so I'd be no more than a brief inconvenience to anyone."

"I anticipated your question which is why I brought my second gun. Here."

Malcolm held out the 9mm Beretta and Adam Spender hesitated before taking the weapon. Once he did, he ejected the clip and saw it was fully loaded. He nodded and reinserted the clip.

"I'll take good care of everything," Spender winked at him. "Don't you worry."

"I know you'll prove me right."

"Count on it," Spender said. "Now, go do your search. I'll guard Metzner with my life."

"You have got to be kidding me," Stacy Metzner glared at Adam Spender. "You're saying you want to monitor our comings and goings constantly?"

"For your safety, yes," he replied. "I want you to keep your cabin door locked at all times. I've taken up the empty cabin beside yours. Use the door that connects to my room and only come and go through there. That way, anyone who wants to get to either of you has to go through me first."

"Mr. Whitlock, I'm only going along with any of this nonsense so that Amy feels at ease and is better able to focus on her work. As it is, she's scared half to death every time she has to step out the door. I don't need these overzealous security protocols of yours and I don't want them, either."

"We believe your life is in danger."

"Yes, it probably is in danger but if I get paranoid about it then I won't have a life worth worrying over, will I?" Metzner challenged. "Either way I'm still in danger, so I'd rather just get on with what I need to do. I only tolerate you and your two colleagues for Amy's sake."

Spender was at a loss for words, so he simply nodded and then went through the connecting door to his own cabin. Once he had shut the door behind him, he went over to his bed, sat himself down, and then exhaled loudly.

"That went well," he said to himself without a trace of sincerity.

There was a knock on the door of his cabin. Spender slowly stood up and shuffled toward the door. He opened it partway and saw a young Asian man at his door.

"Yes?"

"I saw you moving your things inside this cabin. Are you the detective in charge of the murder investigation?"

"Yes, that's me," Spender asked, trying not to let on how puzzled he was. "What can I do for you?"

"My name is David Chow and I'm surrendering to you."

"And why exactly would you be surrendering to me?"

"Because," David said, "I want to confess to the murders."

Saturday, 8:31pm:

Mary entered the galley, which was deserted except for one other person.

"May I join you?" Mary gestured to the padded chair beside where Sita had parked her wheelchair to read a book.

Sita glanced up at Mary with a weary look. "Lady, it's way too late in the day for questioning."

"I'm not here to interrogate you; I was just hoping to have a chat with you for a minute."

"Whatever," Sita nodded toward the chair. "Knock yourself out."

Mary sat down. "So, how long…?"

"Since I was six years old," Sita answered in a singsong voice. "You were about to ask how long I've been in the wheelchair, right?"

"Sorry, but yes I was."

"Here's the abbreviated version: me, small child, no booster seat, car accident, hospital, wheelchair. You're now all caught up."

"Sorry."

"So am I, but my chair doesn't define me. I work hard and I'm now part of a technology team that's made headlines around the world."

"You've got the right attitude."

"If some dude could run the United States from a wheelchair back in the Forties, then there's no reason I can't change the world with my inventions today."

"I'm fascinated by technology myself," Mary said. "I've written code for security companies. I'd sure like to get your take on the software industry."

Saturday, 8:33pm:

Adam Spender led David by the arm until he found where Malcolm was.

"Malcolm," he called out. "Over here."

Malcolm marched over to Spender and was fuming. "Why the hell aren't you guarding Amy and Stacy?"

"I don't think I need to anymore," Spender pointed to David. "Here's the killer we've been looking for."

"David Chow? What makes you think it's him?"

"Well, he confessed to everything, for starters," Spender said. "That's usually a clear indication, if you ask me. What should we do with him?"

"Your cabin's close by, so let's take him there, ask him a lot of questions, and write everything down," Malcolm said. "When we dock, we'll turn him over to the authorities."

"Sounds like a plan to me," Spender began walking with David in tow. They rounded the corner and walked down the passageway. When they arrived at his cabin, he opened the door and stepped inside with David. Malcolm came in last, closing and locking the door once he did.

Spender decided he would stand guard at the cabin door, in case David changed his mind and tried to make a hasty exit.

"Sit down," Malcolm said, pointing to the bed. David nodded and walked over to the bed and sat upon it.

"Now, tell me about what happened."

"No," David said, staring at the floor. "Instead, just ask me questions and I will answer them."

"Okay, then," Malcolm nodded. "Let's start with a big one. Who hired you?"

"I can't tell you. It's not worth my life."

"Then tell me why you did it."

"Money," David shrugged.

Malcolm paused and rubbed his chin before continuing. "How much were they going to pay you?"

"A lot," David had no emotion in his voice. "I can't exactly say how much."

"How about approximately?"

"Can't say that either."

"FIRST already pays you six figures from what I understand," Malcolm leaned against the wall and folded his arms. "What do you need more money for?"

"Whatever I want."

"How many people did you kill?"

"I won't say."

"Then at least tell me how you killed them."

"With a gun, of course," David's response was testy.

"Rifle or handgun?"

"Handgun."

"What kind of gun?"

"I don't know, it's just a gun," David raised his head and looked directly at Malcolm. "You aim it and then you shoot people with it. What difference does it make what kind it was?"

"May I see the gun?"

"No, I threw it overboard," David's gaze returned to the floor.

"Are you good with a gun, skill-wise?"

"I'm obviously good enough. If you want me to sign a confession or something, I'd like Kevin and Sita to act as witnesses."

"No need yet, I still have two questions left," Malcolm unfolded his arms and took two steps toward David. "First, why did you shoot each victim three times?"

"I wanted to make sure they were dead."

"Okay," Malcolm nodded his head. "Now just answer this final question and then you're free to go."

"Free to go?" David stood up and glared at Malcolm. "But I've confessed to the murders."

"You didn't kill anyone and I doubt you even know how to use a gun," Malcolm said. "Hell, I wouldn't even want you on my team in a game of laser tag. None of the victims were shot three times and some weren't shot at all."

"I don't always count, you know. You must believe me. I did it."

"Which leads me to asking the final question I alluded to a few seconds ago," Malcolm stepped even closer to David, locking eyes with him. "You're confessing to something you clearly didn't do. So, who are you trying to protect?"

David broke eye contact and then sat back down on the bed. He lowered his head and resumed his seeming fascination with the carpeting. "Nobody."

"Stay here and continue guarding Stacy and Amy," Malcolm said to Spender. "I'm going to carry on with the rest of my search. I have a feeling things are going to get much worse very soon."

"What about David?" Spender nodded toward the seated man.

"David, you want to be arrested, right?" Malcolm waited for David to nod, which he did after a moment. "Then go to your cabin and let's call it house arrest. One of us will come and get you later."

Saturday, 9:19pm:

"Thanks again for sharing your table with me," Mary said as she walked alongside Sita's wheelchair. "It was fun getting to know you."

"You too," Sita smiled. "I'm now glad I decided to read out there instead of in my cabin."

"The website interface you showed me is excellent," Mary smiled. "I like tight, clean code and it drives me nuts when people write lazy, sloppy code."

"I know, right?" Sita continued her roll along the hallway. "I have to say you're the first interesting person I've met on this stupid cruise. I don't know why you're a security guard, girl; you know a lot about programming."

"I only dabble in it these days. To be honest, I was just seeing if I could somehow determine if there was a connection between your projects and the fatalities."

"I'll help you if I can. There's nothing else to do on board."

"You could consider relaxing and enjoying the cruise."

"I can't. Cruises are boring and I don't see what the big appeal is about them. You're stuck on a boat with people you already see every day at work. Even worse, the Wi-Fi hasn't worked since the day we left port. It's totally lame."

"Then why did you come?"

"It was expected of me. I'm supposed to set an example. Screw that. The only reason any of us came is because there's nothing else we can do at work right now."

"Why?"

"Stacy said the server we work from had to get an emergency upgrade. The hardware and software are in place but we're still waiting for our project files to be put back on. It's been a few days, so like, hello? How long does it take to do a data restore? It could have been done overnight easily."

"You're right. It certainly does seem strange."

"Anyway, it was cool talking to you. I'm going to chill in my cabin for a while."

If you don't mind, I'll walk you the rest of the way there."

"Sure thing."

The two women were silent as Sita rolled up to her cabin door. She opened the door and nodded to Mary, who nodded back. Sita rolled inside and closed the door. Mary turned and began walking down the corridor but stopped when she heard Sita scream.

"What are you doing in my cabin?"

Mary hurried back to Sita's door and ended up colliding with Kevin who was hurrying out of the room. She wanted to chase Kevin but saw Sita's wheelchair overturned and Sita lying motionless on the floor. Mary ran into the room and checked on Sita and was relieved to see she was alive. Mary leaped into the hallway and looked both ways, seeing no sign of Kevin. At the end of the hallway, she saw Malcolm and she called out to him. He was surprised to see her there.

"I was on my way to see you," Malcolm said and he jogged toward her. "I've got some really bad news... wait, what's wrong?"

"Did Kevin just run past you?"

"No, why? What happened?"

"Sita's been attacked," Mary said. "Kevin attacked her and must have run the other way down the hall."

"Is she dead?"

"No, she's just knocked out, but I think she'll be okay," Mary said. "I'll take care of her. You go find Kevin and find out why he attacked her."

"Right, I'm on it," Malcolm turned and broke into a run. He sprinted around the corner at the end of the hallway and ran right into Mitch Jorgensen.

"Watch where you're going, you reckless idiot," Mitch snapped. "What the hell's your hurry anyway?"

"I'm chasing a suspect and I've also discovered four bombs on your ship."

"What?" Mitch roared. "Are you serious? Bombs? Where are they?"

"Lower deck," Malcolm pointed downwards. "There's one in each of the two engine rooms and then two more bombs in the wide crawlspace near the front of the ship where the pumps are."

"Come with me a sec," Mitch led Malcolm further down the corridor to a wall-mounted evacuation diagram of the ship. "Show me on the schematic exactly where you saw the bombs."

"There's a couple here," Malcolm put two of his fingers on the map, "and then one here and the last one's here."

"How the hell did you get into the engine room?"

"My guess is the same person who so inconsiderately killed your shipmate was also inconsiderate enough to leave the engine room doors unlocked when they were done setting up the explosives. Remember, the killer has keys to everywhere."

"What kind of bombs are we talking about?" Mitch's tone became somber. "Are we talking firecrackers or something big enough to worry about?"

"They're definitely the worrying kind," Malcolm said. "I took a picture of one of them."

Malcolm pulled out his phone and showed the photo to Mitch.

"What's that stuff?" Mitch asked, pointing to the screen. "It looks like someone flattened a giant wad of gum and tried to cover the inner hull with it."

"It only looks like gum," Malcolm said. *Or putty,* he remembered the voice he'd heard in his head. *Putty* in a *noisy* engine room. Then a bomb in a *cramped* crawlspace using many *wires*. "It's actually a plastic explosive called C4, and that much of it would be enough to knock out a concrete pillar in a high-rise."

"Then we're in for a hell of a ride," Mitch sighed. "If you're right, then the two aft bombs will not just take out the engines, they'll blow gaping holes in the hull. Those are two big compartments to have flooded. The two in the fore section will take out the main pumps and punch two more massive holes in the hull below the water line and will take out the floor above it, too."

"You need to order an evacuation."

"No, first I've got to ask you something," Mitch folded his arms. "Did you do place these bombs?"

"No, and frankly I was about to ask you the same question."

"If you didn't do this, then how did you know to look in those specific places for the bombs?"

What Malcolm did not say was 'because I was tipped off by a disembodied voice' and instead opted to say, "My searches were thorough."

"When are these bombs rigged to blow?"

"No idea," Malcolm admitted. "Maybe now? When we dock? It could be anytime. My biggest gripe is that real-life bad guys are so inconsiderate by not putting countdown timers on the detonators. That said, we were supposed to dock by ten or so tomorrow morning, so my guess is they'd be set to blow before then."

"Great," Mitch's sarcasm was laid on thick. "That gives us maybe twelve hours. Somebody's going through a hell of a lot of trouble to take this ship out of action."

"I know. Is there a firearms locker on board?"

"No."

"For once, that comes as a relief to me. At least they can't use Wes' keys to arm themselves to the teeth. What about the comms? Are they repaired?"

"Hell no," Mitch said. "Look, I'll level with you, but keep it to yourself. Whoever disabled them didn't just snip a wire, they yanked the entire array out."

"Do you suspect a member of the crew did this?"

"No, the bastard who killed my friend and stole his keys is my suspect. We haven't found the array yet so it was probably thrown overboard."

"We've got to get everyone off this ship."

"I'll make the announcement and get the crew to prepare the main lifeboats."

"There's a small lifeboat near the back of the ship, right?"

"Do you mean the pontoon? It's hardly a lifeboat, it's used to ferry people from ship to shore for small excursions. What about it?"

"How many people does it hold?"

"Up to ten. Why?"

"I have a huge favour to ask."

Saturday, 9:28pm:

A sharp tone sounded from the public address system.

"Attention all passengers, this is Acting Captain Mitch Jorgensen. You all need to make your way towards the main deck to one of the four muster stations. Everyone on board will need to evacuate the ship immediately. I say again, we will be evacuating the ship. This is not a drill. Proceed to one of the muster stations on the main deck and do so in an orderly fashion."

Several people opened the doors of their cabins. Some poked their heads out into the hallway, others stepped out, but all looked bewildered. A member of the crew came down the stairs.

"Alright everyone, you heard the announcement," he said in a loud, clear voice. "Everyone head up these stairs and assemble at one of the muster stations. You will each be given a life jacket and sent into one of the lifeboats. Do not stop to pack, do not delay. You are to exit immediately."

Another announcement came over the PA system: "All crew report to emergency stations." Warning bells sounded for a second, then off for two seconds, then back on for one and the cycle continued.

"Evacuate immediately," the crewmember repeated and walked down toward the end of the hallway. "All room doors must be kept closed so be out of them by the time I get to you."

Passengers began to scurry about and the air became thick with urgent conversations and raised voices. As Malcolm ran, he had to dodge the myriad people in the passageway on his way back to Sita's cabin to retrieve Mary.

"Thank goodness you're here," Mary said. "Why is the ship being evacuated?"

"That's what I was trying to tell you earlier," Malcolm said. "I have bad news, worse news, and then the worst news."

"That's a lot of bad news in one sentence."

"First, how's Sita?"

"She's fine aside from a headache. She's just packing a quick bag to leave with. What's the bad news?"

"I lost track of Kevin," Malcolm sighed. "I wasn't able to find him and I don't know where he got to."

"Oh crud."

"The worse news is there are four bombs on board this ship and that's why the evacuation has been called. We have to get Amy and Stacy on a lifeboat and do so as quickly as possible."

"I was hoping to be wrong about the sinking theory," Mary admitted. "How long do we have before the bombs go off?"

"I don't know but we can't take any chances," Malcolm took Mary's hand and gave it a squeeze while looking deep into her eyes. "Mary, I need you to take Stacy and Amy to the pontoon lifeboat at the back of the ship and protect them both the best you can."

"What?" she pulled her hand away. "Wait a minute, where are you going?"

"That's the worst news," Malcolm took a deep breath before continuing. "I'm staying on board."

"Like heck you are, buster. You're with us."

"I can't," Malcolm realized he had said that louder than he'd intended. "Four of my main suspects – Kevin, Ki-Liu, Officer Trinh, and Captain Farrell – are unaccounted for. I'm not leaving until I find each and every one of them."

"Why?"

"Because if I don't deal with Ki-Liu now, he'll never stop coming after us until we're all dead. I'll have to flush him out and finish this the old fashioned way. When I'm done, I'll launch the last lifeboat and meet up with you. Just stay away until all the action is over."

"But what about the bombs?"

"The bad guys aren't going to detonate them while they're still on board so I'll be fine," Malcolm added the word *hopefully* in his mind. "You have to keep Amy and Stacy safe. Mitch is preparing the pontoon boat as we speak. He's agreed to take you, Stacy, and Amy with him."

"Got it," Mary said, "but if we get out of this in one piece, you and I are going to have a long talk about how you set your priorities."

Mitch's voice once again came over the public address system while Malcolm and Mary picked up Sita and placed her in her wheelchair.

"This is the last call for all passengers to abandon the ship. Proceed immediately to one of the life boats on the main deck. There will be no further announcements. All crew members: do a final sweep, collect passenger names, and then get yourselves off the ship."

They stepped into the corridor, pushing Sita's chair in front of them. Sita was starting to stir and began looking around. People in the hallway were running to and from cabins and the corridor was abuzz with activity. Malcolm saw David Chan running toward them.

"Excuse me," David said as he approached Sita. "I have to get you to a life boat."

"Wait…" Malcolm began, but Mary waved her hand at him, signalling for him to say nothing. David took the wheelchair from Malcolm and he began pushing the chair around people and toward the starboard elevator.

"Uh, Mary," Malcolm said to Mary while gesturing towards Sita. "We just let a confessed murder suspect take away a key witness. Was that really a wise thing to do?"

"Definitely," Mary smiled.

"He's no killer, but he's been acting suspiciously."

"Not really. He's acting exactly how I'd expect a young introvert to behave when he's in love."

"In love?" Malcolm darted his eyes from Mary to David and then back again. "With Sita?"

"I'm only clueless in my own relationships. It's obvious to me that he's head-over-heels for her."

"Huh. How the hell did I miss that?"

"Maybe it's because you assess everyone based solely on their threat potential. I'm more of an empath. I could tell he liked her."

"Makes sense, now that I think of it. He confessed to the murders shortly after I told him Sita was a suspect, so he was protecting her. Now get yourself to the pontoon."

Malcolm ran down the corridor to Mary's right, dodging and weaving through the people in his way, and then disappeared around a corner. Before Mary could do anything, she saw Adam Spender coming down the corridor towards her from the opposite direction.

"What are you doing here?" she asked.

"I'm evacuating with you," Spender said. "I'm supposed to be protecting you, and I don't know where Ki-Liu is. If you think I'm leaving your side until you're all safe, you're crazy."

"That's not what Malcolm said to do."

"I know, but he told me to keep you all safe no matter what," Spender said. "It was the one and only job he gave me, so I'm not going to let him down. There's a lot of panicked people and a lot of confusion right now. This would be an ideal setting for an assassin to strike. Listen, Mary, I'm sorry I haven't earned your trust yet but this is my chance to do that. I know I have a guilty past but that doesn't mean I'm still guilty today or going to be guilty tomorrow. It's going to take a long time for me to atone for everything I've done in my life, but I'd like to do what I can. Besides, Malcolm told me to stick to you, Ms. Metzner, and your sister, so that's exactly what I'm going to do."

"Alright, come on then," Mary said. "We're heading to the pontoon at the back of the ship."

Malcolm ran around the corner at the end of the corridor and was tripped by a leg, which was extended as he went past. He tumbled, but then rolled back up onto his feet.

"Put your weapon down slowly, Agent Malcolm," Officer Trinh said, her gun aimed at him. "There has already been enough death on this ship, yes?"

"Not too many people get the drop on me like that," Malcolm's hands were raised.

"I do not understand the phrase 'get the drop' but do not care enough to," she said. "English is such a ridiculous language; at least it is when you speak it. Now very slowly take out your gun and put it down on the deck."

Malcolm, with great care, retrieved his gun and then lowered himself and placed it on the floor. He stood up with his hands still raised. "So what happens now?"

"Now? You keep your hands up and stop thinking about reaching for your weapon."

"Fine, I know that part. I was really inquiring about after that."

"You have gotten in my way too often," Trinh said. "The time has come for me to remove you from play. This is the final farewell, Agent Malcolm."

"We've managed to get things organized on the ship and the last of the passengers are being loaded onto the lifeboats," Mitch said. "The crew has it under control. Now I can get you all off the ship. I was told, however, there'd be only three passengers on this pontoon with me, not four."

"And I was told to make sure these three stayed safe," Adam Spender said. "So I'm coming with them no matter what."

"Just proceed with the evacuation, Acting Captain Jorgensen," Stacy said. "There's no time to overthink this."

"Very well," he said. "Step inside and I'll activate the crane and get us lowered into the water."

"I've got to admit it, Officer Trinh," Malcolm said, his hands still raised. "You had me fooled. I really believed you were a Vietnamese cop and not Ki-Liu's stooge."

"Stooge?" Trinh wore a puzzled look. "What is that?"

"A person who does what someone else tells them to do, even if it's wrong. They don't question orders."

"Every time I think I have mastered English, you speak," Trinh's frustration was apparent. "I guarded the British embassy in Hanoi for six years and did not have a problem understanding them. Are you accusing me of getting my orders from Ki-Liu?"

"Obviously."

"Do not play the role of the fool, Agent Malcolm," Trinh demanded. "I really am from Vietnam and I really am a cop and I believe you are very aware of this. We have arrived at the time for these silly games to end. I know it is you who is working for Ki-Liu. That makes you a problem I must remove, yes?"

"What?" Malcolm's eyes widened. "I'm not working for Ki-Liu; I'm here to stop him."

"Curious."

"What is?"

"You are either completely stupid or you assume I am."

"The only thing I'm assuming right now is that there must be more than just those two choices."

"I received a message from my government just before we left port," Trinh said. "I asked a colleague with ties to the Chinese embassy to assist me and I have had it confirmed: Adam Spender is working for the Guangzhou Crime Syndicate."

"I know that," Malcolm said. "Or at least, I know that now. I only learned of it around ninety minutes ago, to be honest. What I don't know is why. Ki-Liu wanted Adam Spender dead. He ambushed us in Seattle on the Fremont Bridge. It was only by chance we didn't die and we barely got out of there with our lives. The shot I took that hit Ki-Liu wasn't even aimed; I just pointed the gun in his direction and fired. I got lucky and I know it. Spender then testified against the Da Nang Cartel, so he was working *against* Ki-Liu."

"That answers my curiosity," Duyen Trinh nodded. "You really *are* completely stupid."

"Will you stop dancing around things and tell me what you found out?"

"You said Ki-Liu ambushed you on that bridge, yes?"

"Yeah."

"And you truly believe he was there to kill Adam Spender?"

"Well, of course."

"Then you are as incorrect as you are foolish," Trinh said. "Allow me to offer you an orange vegetable this time. Ki-Liu's main task was to kill you, Agent Malcolm; not Adam Spender."

"Why would he want to kill me?"

"To those who know about you, you are considered a problematic adversary. Once the Syndicate learned of your involvement with Adam Spender, you were a potential threat to their plans. They wanted to fake Spender's death and smuggle him out of the country so the trial would collapse, but with you protecting him it was considered too risky to leave it to a regular member of the Da Nang Cartel so they sent their top assassin after you. They needed to make sure they got the job done."

"And what exactly was their plan?"

"I learned that his orders were to wound you and then pretend to kill Adam Spender. You were supposed to have an injury severe enough to bleed to death from, yet stay alive just long enough to tell everyone that Spender was killed."

"Why not just kill him?"

"Adam Spender stole eight million dollars from the cartel. They wished to interrogate him to locate the money."

"Did they locate it?"

"Spender sent his wife to live in South America with half of the money until the trial was over. Ki-Liu tracked her down and killed her and retrieved the four million. He then tracked down Spender and suggested a deal. Adam Spender could keep the remaining four million as long as he helped Ki-Liu in a job for the Guangzhou Syndicate."

"So that's why he's been working with me yet also against me."

"Correct. It is like I said to you earlier: you got played. You kept Spender alive and he was able to go through the entire trial process and put away the cartel, but you were not able to protect him completely. Because he testified, he still ended up losing everything."

"Somehow, this day manages to get worse and worse. He was playing me for a fool and as I said, I only found out about it very recently. I set a trap for him but I didn't get a chance to spring it properly. I've been so distracted by all the goings-on that I haven't been as vigilant as I should have been and haven't had any time to act on the information."

"It would seem that you are the stooge, then, yes?"

"If what you're saying is true, then I'm Moe, Curly, and Larry all rolled into one."

"I am not sure what dialect of English you speak, but it is not one being taught in south-eastern Asia. Regardless, I must find Ki-Liu."

"I'll help you. Let's split up so we can cover more ground."

Saturday, 9:50pm:

Malcolm, his gun in front of him, walked in a slow, deliberate way in order to be as silent as possible. Even though the ship alarm was still sounding, he was not taking any chances.

He got to the corner at the end of the hallway and peered around. He caught a glimpse of someone running in his direction. Malcolm pressed himself against the wall and waited for the person to run past. As the man rounded the corner, Malcolm grabbed him, spun him around, and pushed him against the wall. "Wait, Keith?"

"You've got to help me," a wide-eyed Keith Jacek said, while grabbing Malcolm's arm. "He's going to kill me."

"Why the hell isn't your stupid ass on one of the lifeboats, you idiot?" Malcolm pushed him away.

"It was too dangerous," Keith wailed. "Help me."

"This ship is likely to blow up and sink," Malcolm said, using his 'talking to idiots' voice. "When it does blow, there will likely be a nasty fire which will only be put out by the rising sea water as the ship sinks. Now call me crazy, but I think all of that is more dangerous than a lifeboat."

"I'll take my chances," Keith said, looking over his shoulder. "Bill's been murdered so that means I'm the only one left who remained in the deal. The rest are all dead. I'm not leaving without protection. You're ship security, so protect me."

"I'm *private* security and I've already been hired to protect somebody else."

"I'll pay you."

"Sorry, can't. Conflict of interest."

"There must be something you want."

"You know, you're right," Malcolm said after a moment's thought. "There actually is something I want. I want some honest information. You tell me what I want to know, including things discussed in Boardroom 205, and I'll keep you safe as long as you do *exactly* what I say."

"Anything, sure."

"This is damned hilarious."

"What is?"

"First you want me fired and ruined and now you want to hire me," Malcolm chuckled. "Nice twist. Okay, let's get you off this ship without any sudden death occurring. I need to get my bag from my cabin, so follow me. Once we're there I'll figure out an escape plan."

"I'm in so much danger," Keith moaned.

"Yes, I believe we've already established that. Let's keep moving. Stay within two feet of me at all times and do not deviate from my instructions."

"Yes, yes."

"Tell me about the argument with Bill Sutherland in the boardroom that day."

"The deal with the buyer was done on the sly and nobody was supposed to know about it but it got leaked to Bill. That's when everything went sour."

"Who leaked it?"

"Stacy Metzner," Keith said. "She was with us at first but then backed out and ratted us out. Then Ben died later that night and nobody will ever convince me he jumped off his balcony."

"Yeah, I don't think he did either," Malcolm peered around the next corner. "You said Metzner backed out of the deal. Something must have caused that to happen because she doesn't seem like the type of person who loses her nerve."

Malcolm motioned for Keith to follow him around the corner.

"Charles Lautzen was what happened," Keith said, mere inches behind Malcolm. "We had a deal to sell access to the technology to an organized crime syndicate in China through a shell company. Everything was perfect until Charles went rogue."

"What did he do?"

"He told our Chinese contact the price had doubled and the contact didn't take that news well. When he balked, Charles said if he didn't come up with the money, he'd take the details of the transaction and leak it to the Chinese embassy and the US State Department which would put a lot of heat on them."

"Bad move," Malcolm said. "Chinese business culture relies on honouring your word. Changing the terms like that is a great way to piss everyone off."

"I know. If Charles wasn't dead, I'd want to kill him myself."

"He sounds like he was a real piece of work," Malcolm glanced back at Keith for a second. "Not that you're Mr. Ethics yourself, mind you."

"Just because I had a few lapses in ethics doesn't mean I deserve to die."

"You're right about that," Malcolm admitted. "But if you knew it wasn't ethical, why did you do it?"

"It was so much money, it seemed risk-free, and it seemed so easy."

"And you seemed to be wrong," Malcolm said. "Then what happened?"

"Our Chinese contact asked Lautzen for a few days to make the arrangements. For a while, we thought maybe Charles wasn't such a dumbass after all and maybe he'd pulled it off. However, we soon realized the 'arrangements' being made were for all traces of the deal to be erased, including the people who were part of it."

"So who's left from the boardroom gang?"

"Just me and Stacy," Keith's voice carried a tremor in it. "But then an associate of our Chinese contact told me if we wanted to live, we were to hand over the tech and to expect no payment in return."

"An associate of your contact? Why didn't you tell me that little detail during our little Q&A session last night?"

"Because they hadn't said it to me yet."

"They're on board?"

"Yes, obviously, or why would I still be on a sinking ship? Well, they've probably evacuated the ship by now, but you tell me. You work with him."

"Devon Whitlock, the security guard from your building, right?"

"Yes."

Malcolm put his finger to his own lips.

"My cabin is right there," he whispered. "Stay silent."

"Hurry up," Keith's loud voice was responded to with a glare from Malcolm. "I feel exposed standing in the hallway like this."

"I said to stay silent," Malcolm hissed. "Alright, now stay here until I've checked the room."

Malcolm slowly turned the handle and eased the door open a crack. Keith pushed past Malcolm, flung the door open, and ran panicked inside the room. Two shots rang out and Malcolm was splattered with blood while Keith's body fell backwards into the hallway, a bloody hole in his forehead and another in his chest.

"Damn it," Malcolm shouted as he fired two shots blindly into the room as he retreated. "Will you stop killing all of my suspects?"

Leaping for cover, Malcolm dove around the corner from the direction he'd come. He had his weapon ready and was peering around the corner when a slender, balding Asian man wearing the uniform of a cleaner fired shots in Malcolm's direction as he burst out of the room. The man began racing down the hallway away from Malcolm.

Malcolm leapt out from around the corner and began to run after the shooter. "At least now I know what Ki-Liu looks like," he said under his breath as he ran. "The idiot rebuilds his whole damned face but doesn't give himself any new hair."

Ki-Liu sprinted toward the stern of the boat and he arrived just as the pontoon was pulling away from the ship. He saw Stacy, Amy, and Mary, so he pulled out his pistol and took aim. Amy was closest to him, and Stacy was directly behind Amy.

"Move," Ki-Liu yelled. Amy, Mary, Stacy, and Mitch all looked up at once, each surprised at the sudden command. Amy screamed, but froze in place. The boat was now far enough away as to be out of firing range.

"Freeze," Malcolm yelled, but Ki-Liu took off, running zigzags until he was around the nearest corner. Malcolm gave chase, and as he followed around the corner, he saw Officer Trinh to his left.

"That's Ki-Liu," Malcolm pointed. "He's the missing cleaner."

Trinh saw Ki-Liu go through a set of double-doors. "He is mine," she shouted as she broke into a run.

Malcolm was about to join Trinh in the chase, but turned just in time to see Kevin. When Kevin saw Malcolm, he swore and ran toward the same double doors Ki-Liu and Trinh had gone through. Kevin was a fast runner and soon overtook Trinh and was now mere steps behind Ki-Liu, unaware of who he was.

Ki-Liu went down the internal stairwell, immediately followed by Kevin, who was himself immediately followed by Officer Trinh and Malcolm.

Ki-Liu ran down the dimly lit lower-deck maintenance corridor, but quickly discovered it was a dead end. He swore in

Mandarin and ducked into a small closet at the end of the hall. Kevin, also upon realizing the lack of exits, took the small storage room on the right. Malcolm and Trinh were running down the hallway toward them when they heard a shot ring out from behind. Both dove to their left into a doorless firefighting supply room. Malcolm's head narrowly missed hitting a glass cabinet containing firefighting equipment.

"Who is shooting at us?" Trinh asked.

"No idea," Malcolm said. "It came as quite a surprise to me as well. We've got Ki-Liu down the hall to our left and an unknown assailant down the hall to our right, and we're stuck in between them."

"How did you find Ki-Liu?"

"He was in my cabin for some reason and he killed a witness."

"He was looking for the files," Trinh said as Malcolm stood up. "Are you alright?"

"Yeah, thanks," Malcolm slowly got to his feet. "Every time I take a case, I either end up shot or shot at. Just once I'd like to be sent to an actual combat zone so I'd feel safer."

"How is it possible that I can always understand your words but never your meaning?"

They heard Ki-Liu begin shouting from the room to their left. "Let me out of here and give me the memory stick and you can all live."

"I don't have it," Malcolm called back. "Why did you have Bill Sutherland killed?"

"I didn't," Ki-Liu responded. "Why are you after me?"

"I'm not after you," Malcolm called out.

"Then why are you on this ship?" Ki-Liu called back.

"I don't know anymore," Malcolm replied. "I only came here to protect someone."

"Then who are you chasing?"

"A completely different someone."

"Give me the files," Ki-Liu shouted.

"I just told you I don't have them," Malcolm called back. "Why do you want them?"

"Why do you care about them?"

"I don't know."

The voice of Captain Farrell called out next. "Everyone drop your weapons and step out into the hallway where I can see you."

"Now we know who shot at us," Trinh whispered to Malcolm.

"Captain, you might not want to be here right now," Malcolm stated in a loud voice. "Not that we believe for a second you're a real captain, of course."

"You are correct, actually," Farrell replied. "I'm a federal agent."

"For what country?" Malcolm asked.

"What do you mean *for what country?*" Farrell's voice was a blend of indignation and bewilderment. "How many governments did you have to choose from?"

"Presently?" Malcolm shrugged. "As many as five, depending on what answer you give me."

"Look, everyone put your weapons down right now and step out into the hallway," Farrell repeated.

"This is your first time doing this, isn't it?" Malcolm called out while shaking his head.

"No, I'm just giving everyone the chance to resolve this peacefully."

"Oh great," Malcolm whispered to Trinh. "He's a damned Canadian."

"How do you know?" Officer Trinh whispered back.

"Did you hear him just now?" Malcolm pinched the bridge of his nose. "The idiot actually believes the only thing we need in order to get out of this mess is a friendly mediator. We need the cavalry and instead we're stuck with Dudley Do-Right."

"Did you pass English classes as a child?" Trinh huffed. "I never seem to understand what you are saying."

"Alright, everyone, listen up," Farrell said. "I'm part of the Canadian Coast Guard's Maritime Security team and I am authorized to arrest anyone who does not comply."

"So you're not with the military or CSIS?" Malcolm did a poor job hiding his contempt. "Damn my luck. Why are you here?"

"We were tipped off that a foreign agent would be on board this ship."

"Which one of the foreign agents were you tipped off about?"

"*Which one?*" Farrell snapped. "How many foreign agents were on board this weekend?"

"I think four, but it's possible I lost count along the way," Malcolm admitted.

"Who do you work for?" Farrell shouted.

"Nobody," Malcolm shouted back. "I'm here on vacation."

"Then fire your travel agent," Farrell said. "Who's the woman with you?"

"I'm Duyen Trinh," she said. "I am here on behalf of the Vietnam People's Security."

"Vietnam?" the pitch of Farrell's voice went up a full half-octave. "What the hell are you doing here?"

"I am here to arrest Ki-Liu," Trinh called back.

"Who's Ki-Liu?"

"Are you seriously that far behind?" disgust mixed with disappointment in Malcolm's voice. "He's an assassin working on behalf of a Chinese crime syndicate and he's here to kill any and all loose ends."

"And are you two the loose ends he's after?"

"We're two of several loose ends," Malcolm replied. "And now that I've answered your questions, you and everyone else within earshot are loose ends as well. So, you've just added to his workload."

"Ah, not good," Farrell said in a softer voice. "Who's the fellow across the hall from you?"

"He's another loose end I'm trying to capture alive," Malcolm was only then realizing how ridiculous his current situation was. "He's a murder suspect."

"And you said you're just here on vacation, am I right?" Farrell was unable to mask the confusion he was feeling.

"Yeah, and I can't wait to get back to work," Malcolm said. "I've come to the conclusion vacations are vastly overrated. Anyone who says they're fun and relaxing is lying to you."

"I didn't want anyone to die," Kevin shouted from his place of refuge.

"We are wasting precious time," Officer Trinh hissed at Malcolm. "This is the most absurd conversation I have ever heard, and if you knew my family you would know I do not say that lightly. Give me cover fire and I will flush out Ki-Liu myself."

"If I poke my head out the door and start shooting, I'll probably get shot by the damned Canadian outside."

"Ki-Liu is the priority," Trinh said. "Nothing else matters right now."

"*My head matters*, so excuse me if I don't want to risk getting shot right now," Malcolm hissed. "And for the record, yes, Ki-Liu is a priority but so is the other guy."

"You cannot get to who you want until we neutralize Ki-Liu," Officer Trinh attempted to muster what little patience she had left. "Help me with him and I will make sure you get who you want as well, yes?"

"By the way," Farrell announced in an almost singsong voice, "which one of you placed those bombs? Whoever it was, I have some really bad news for you. I found them both, neutralized them, removed the remote detonation antenna, and then safely put all the pieces into an evidence bag."

"Did you say *both* bombs?" Malcolm asked.

"Yes, they're both gone so there's nothing left for you to achieve, so it's all over," Farrell proclaimed. "You've lost. Now come out and surrender so nobody else has to die."

"Sorry if I seem hung up on your use of the word 'both' but that usually implies *two*." Malcolm exhaled, aware he was tensing up in anticipation of the coming conversation. "I'm aware of *four* bombs, so which two did you neutralize?"

"The two which were in the aft engine rooms," Farrell's voice became slow and doubtful. "So… where exactly did you see the other two bombs?"

"In the front of the ship below the crew quarters."

"When are they set to detonate?"

"Why do people keep assuming I know that?" Malcolm sounded exasperated. "They're not my bombs and I sure as hell didn't set them so I don't know."

"Most likely, they were set by Ki-Liu," Officer Trinh called out. "If he cannot complete his mission one way then he will blow up the ship to do it another way. We must stop him. Do not let him get past you. Do you understand what I said?"

"Yes, I understand," Agent Farrell said, "but right now all I can think about are those other two bombs."

"Yeah, they're kind of weighing on my mind as well," Malcolm admitted. "How did you disarm the first two?"

"There was no mystery," Farrell said. "There's a simple on-off toggle switch connected to a battery. Flick the switch and you disconnect the power supply leading to the detonator. Then remove the antenna so they can't detonate the bomb remotely."

"That's it?" Malcolm couldn't hide his astonishment. "If I'd known it would be that easy, I'd have disarmed them all myself."

"We need to disarm the other two before they go off."

"Yeah," Malcolm nodded. "Do you think you could find those other two bombs based on what I told you?"

"Yes, I think I know what compartment you're referring to," Farrell called out. "It's the crawlspace where the pumps are, right?"

"Yeah, that's the one. Go and disarm the bombs before it's too late."

"No, I can't leave until you're all…"

The sound of a loud, rumbling explosion filled the air, shaking the floor they were standing upon, and the ensuing shock wave threw everyone to the floor.

From the deck of the pontoon, Mary watched the explosion in horror and saw the smoke begin to billow out of the front of the ship while ghastly orange and black flames licked their way up the side of the ship.

"Oh God, no," Mary whispered. "Please be alive, please."

Amy's hand covered her mouth and her eyes were wide. The seconds ticked by slowly and she watched as the front half of the ship was gradually lowering into the sea. The ship now had about a ten-degree slope. She felt helpless watching from a distance.

"Oh my God," Mitch was slack-jawed at the fiery hell-scape unfolding at the near horizon.

"We have to call for help," Stacy said. "There's people on board that thing."

"The comms are still down but the emergency tracking beacon would have auto-activated as soon as we were lowered into the water," Mitch said as he held the wheel. "All we can do now is wait for the Navy or Coast Guard to come and get us. In the meantime, we have to make sure we don't drift too close to shore in the darkness. It's all rocky fjords along here and we have low visibility in this blasted darkness."

"Can we go and check for survivors?" Stacy asked.

"Lady, the only reason we're even this close is because the damned motor died," Mitch grumbled. "I'll try to repair it once things settle down, but it won't be easy to fix in the dark."

"How long do you think it will it take for a rescue ship to find us?" Mary asked.

"Maybe an hour or two," Mitch replied. "Could be as many as five or six."

"But the ship will probably have sunk by then," Amy said.

"They'd get here a hell of a lot quicker if I had some way to contact them directly."

"Do you have their number?" Mary asked.

"I always keep it with me but there's no cell service out here."

"You could use my emergency satellite phone," Mary pulled the device out of her pocket. "I think this qualifies as an emergency."

"It sure as hell does," Mitch held out his hand.

"No, Mary," Spender said. "Put the phone away."

"But we have to call for help," Mary said.

"We also have to go back and check for survivors," Mitch said. "It's Maritime Law."

"It's too dangerous," Spender said. "Besides, there's no way anyone is going to survive that."

"There's still people on that ship, damn you," Mitch snapped. "I say we go back. I'm the senior officer here so I'm the one in charge, not you."

"And I'm the only person on board with a gun, and I say we don't," Mitch pulled out the Beretta and pointed it at Mitch.

"What the hell are you doing?" Mitch snapped, still gripping the steering wheel. "Put that thing away."

"The files, Ms. Metzner," Spender said, now pointing the gun at her. "Hand them to me. Now."

"Do not shoot," Ki-Liu shouted from the room he was in. "I am ready to surrender."

"Throw your weapon into the hall," Trinh commanded.

A handgun was tossed out into the now-sloping corridor from the room Ki-Liu was in.

"Mr. Farrell, sir," Trinh shouted. "Do not shoot me. I am coming out into the hallway to apprehend the shooter."

"Okay," Farrell called back. "But I'm watching you, so don't do anything crazy."

"Ki-Liu, you must step out into the hallway immediately," Trinh demanded. "Make sure your hands are in the air."

Ki-Liu emerged from the room, hands raised. Officer Trinh stepped behind Ki-Liu and gave him a light push forward.

"Go," she ordered. "Up those stairs."

Ki-Liu nodded and walked along the hallway toward the stairs where Farrell still had his weapon aimed at the approaching figures.

"Mr. Farrell," Trinh looked at him. "This man is an assassin who has killed people on this ship. He must be restrained. Do you have anything I can use to secure his hands?"

"Bring him up to the main deck and I'll see what I can find," Farrell said, lowering his weapon. "Besides, I have a lot of questions."

"What files are you referring to, Mr. Whitlock?" Stacy asked Spender.

"Don't insult my intelligence, Ms. Metzner," Spender said. "I've had ample time to observe you so I already know where the files are."

"That was a terrible bluff," Stacy chuckled. "You don't know anything."

"That's a lovely hair barrette you have," Spender gestured toward Stacy with his gun. "Hand it over."

"Why do you want it?" Stacy glared. "It wouldn't even match your outfit."

"My compliments, by the way," Spender's grin was mirthless. "It was brilliant to disguise the memory stick as a hair accessory. It's pure genius and it took me a long time to figure it out. Those files, however, are worth more to me than to you, so hand them over."

"You're a weak and pathetic man, Whitlock," Stacy's defiant tone blended well with her contempt. "Hiding behind that gun like a coward tells me everything I need to know about you. I won't give it to you."

"I can always take it off your corpse if you don't cooperate," Spender stated, still pointing the gun at Stacy. "Is it worth your life?"

"Yes, it is," she said, standing up and moving to the edge of the boat. "Not that I believe you have the stones to pull the trigger in the first place."

"Bill Sutherland thought that as well," Spender said. "The last thing he learned before he died was how wrong he was. Eliza Borwith didn't take me seriously either, and the last thing she saw before she died was me hitting her with a stolen car. Janine Andrews didn't cooperate either. So don't be the next dead lawyer I had to prove myself to."

"You sick pig," Stacy's voice carried a tremor. "Why? Why did you kill him?"

"He wouldn't tell me where the files were and they weren't in his cabin. He wasn't cooperative, so we had an altercation. I got his phone and saw a picture of you two together. It was obvious he gave them to you, so I just had to figure out what you did with them."

"If you shoot me, then I'll fall overboard along with your precious files," Metzner snapped. "If you want to lose everything, then go ahead and pull the trigger. That is, if you even can, you miserable half-wit."

"You'd really be willing to die for the files?"

"I certainly couldn't live with myself if I gave up the files to Bill's killer," Stacy's voice cracked, "so let's call that a solid yes, shall we?"

"I guess we shall," Adam Spender's left arm shot out and grabbed Amy by the arm and he yanked her towards him. She stumbled, fell, and was kneeling on the deck. He put the barrel of the gun into the top of Amy's head. "Could you live with yourself if it cost your assistant her life?"

"No, please," Amy cried.

"Leave my sister alone," Mary said, stepping forward.

"Step back, Mary," Spender snapped. "I'm really sorry you and Malcolm are involved in this. It's not what I wanted, I promise you, but I don't have any choice in the matter. I don't want to kill you or anyone else, especially with Malcolm's gun."

"Forgive me if I don't believe the sincerity of your concern for my well-being."

"You should believe it," Spender said. "I'm planning on you being my insurance policy against Malcolm. As long as I have you, he won't do anything too... *impulsive*. You're his weakness so I'd definitely prefer it if you remained alive."

"Why are you doing Ki-Liu's work for him?" Mary shifted her weight in a way that allowed her to move forward another couple of inches.

"I'm not here for Ki-Liu. He and I have the same employer at present, but it's a long story and there's no time for it now."

"I don't understand," Mary managed another few inches forward. "You helped put away the Da Nang Cartel."

"Yes, and it cost me everything," Spender shouted, moving his glare from Amy to Mary and back again. "I had a new life waiting for me overseas and your husband ruined it. So now I have a second chance at that life and you're all close to ruining it again. Ms. Metzner, the files, please, or I will gladly kill your assistant right here in front of you."

"Wait," Mary said. "Let Amy go and I'll take her place."

"No, Mary, I like you better at a distance," Spender shook his head slowly. "I know you're a good fighter and I'd rather you not be tempted to try your luck against me while in such close proximity. As I said, I don't want to kill you. These bullets aren't meant for you. Now Amy, on the other hand, I would have no hesitation to kill. I'd just say a quick 'good riddance' and be done with her. The question is whether or not she's worth anything to you."

"Wait," Stacy said. "Okay, fine. If you let Amy go, I'll give the barrette to you."

"No, Stacy," Mary urged, stepping forward. "Don't do it."

"Mary," Spender snapped. "Take one step closer and I swear I'll kill you."

"Let my sister go, right now," Mary took a small step closer and then another.

"I'm sorry Mary, but you've brought this on yourself."

Spender moved the gun with such speed, Mary had no time to react. He aimed the gun at the centre of Mary's chest and pulled the trigger. The shot sounded like a crack of thunder in the night.

"Hey, Kevin," Malcolm called out as he stepped into the hallway. "It's just you and I left down here. Are you really so certain that drowning is your best option?"

There was no answer from across the hall. Out of habit and an abundance of caution, Malcolm took slow, silent steps across the hall toward the small room where Kevin had taken refuge even though the sounds of groaning metal and rushing water would have masked his approach. Malcolm swung gun-first into the room and saw Kevin slumped on the dark, metal floor. He looked broken. Defeated.

"How about coming along with me upstairs to the main deck?" Malcolm suggested as he lowered his gun. "You know, away from the direction the water is coming from?"

"No," Kevin's voice was shaking. "I won't go. I can't."

"Then I sure hope you can swim in cold sea water. If death by hypothermia or drowning was on your bucket list, then I hope it was the last thing on it."

"You'll have to leave eventually to save yourself," Kevin replied after a moment. "I'm willing to wait. Are you?"

"Take your time," Malcolm put his gun into his shoulder holster. "I've got the rest of your life to wait."

"My life is already over so don't bother. You might as well leave and save yourself and leave me here."

"Why did you attack Sita?"

"I didn't attack her."

"I beg to differ."

"No, listen," Kevin sniffed. "I was really pissed off because she was blabbing about our tech capabilities when she knew people were already trying to steal it. After all the recent deaths, I was really worked up. I didn't want Sita ending up dead or blackmailed too. Sita's brilliant but she's also clueless when it comes to danger. She was blurting things out and it was reckless of her to spout off like that."

"So what was your plan?"

"She wasn't there, so I waited in her cabin for her to come back. I was going to tell her off in private. Instead, I must have really startled her because she freaked out and started hitting me. She actually punched me once in the face. I gave her a shove and she fell backwards in her chair and hit her head. I've got to be cursed or something. I'm not a violent person. I've only ever pushed two people in my life and now they're both dead."

"Sita's not dead, she was knocked out," Malcolm said in as patient a voice as he could manage considering he was on a ship that was taking on water. "Mary got her to the life boat and Sita's safe on it with David. When this is all over, Sita will just have one hell of a headache."

"Seriously?"

"Yeah, she's okay."

"Thank God. So, what do I do now?"

"In light of our current situation, might I suggest running away from the rising sea water like a couple of maniacs?"

"Why should I run? I'm already haunted by what I've done. Now you want me to relive everything as I face a possible murder charge in court?"

"You didn't kill him, I know that now," Malcolm stated. "You took a security guard with you to Ben Shapner's apartment, didn't you? Specifically, you took Devon Whitlock to his place, right?"

"Yes, but I didn't know he was going to kill Shapner. I was scared, so Whitlock said he'd come with me to make sure I stayed safe. Then he pulled out that truncheon and bashed Shapner in the back of the head while he was at the balcony."

"You didn't know that was going to happen. You won't face a murder rap."

"I'm pretty sure conspiracy is a felony, even if it was uninetentional. I didn't know I was planning Shapner's death, it was just supposed to be a creative exercise."

"I know, but I don't care right now. Getting you off this ship is all I'm concerned about, okay?"

"I can't clear my head of the memories, even at night. I can't even sleep."

"I completely understand," Malcolm said with absolute sincerity. "But this doesn't have to be the end of everything for you. Come with me and let's try to sort our way through this."

"Will the ship really sink?"

"It's looks highly likely, but if you start singing 'My Heart Will Go On' I swear I'll leave you here to drown. The slope in the floor is getting more pronounced by the minute, so I'll need you to come with me right now. We need to get the hell out of here and we'll worry about what happens next at a later point in time."

Malcolm held out his left hand. Kevin stared at it for a moment and then reached up and grabbed it. Malcolm helped pull him up to his feet.

"That's it," Malcolm encouraged. "Now let's get out of this room."

Malcolm led Kevin out into the hallway.

"Kevin," Malcolm said, pointing down the hall to his right. "Look. There's already water at the end of the hallway and in the two rooms at the end. We need to shut all these doors and latch them to slow down the flooding. The more watertight we can make the ship, the longer it'll stay afloat. Help me."

The two worked together to close and latch the four doors that were in the short hallway. Malcolm then gestured to the stairs and they both took the steps two at a time, racing up to the main deck.

Mary had seen the gun pointed at her and she had heard the shot ring out, so her brain had already calculated the point of impact for the bullet. Out of sheer reflex, her hands flung up to her chest. It was only at that point she realized she had not been hit at all.

Perplexed, Spender fired at her a second time, then raised the gun and fired a third shot, this time at her head. In all three shots, there were no impacts. He quickly ejected the clip out of the gun and he inspected it closely.

Amy took advantage of Spender's distraction and scurried along the deck of the pontoon until she was between Mitch and Stacy over at the front of the boat.

"He gave me a gun filled with blanks," Spender shouted from the stern. "What an untrusting son of a bitch."

Captain Farrell saw Malcolm and Kevin emerge from the stairwell and jogged toward them.

"How bad is the water level down there?" he asked Malcolm.

"The end compartments are flooding, but we've closed and latched all the doors. The water level is still rising but at least it's happening a little slower now."

"Well done," Farrell nodded. "Latching those doors should buy us a little more time, but we still need to get off this ship as soon as we can. First, we need to make our way to the bridge so I can activate the emergency beacon and get the flare gun."

"You're not going to try to arrest me or anything else stupid at this point, right?" Malcolm asked.

"We'll have to sort all that out later," Farrell said. "There's no time to talk about such matters right now."

Malcolm looked to his left and saw Officer Trinh standing beside Ki-Liu near a bulwark. He was on his knees and his hands were on his head.

"Officer Trinh," Malcolm called out to her. "Is Ki-Liu secure?"

"We have not yet found anything we can tie him up with, but yes, he is otherwise secure. Why do you ask?"

"Because he doesn't look like a defeated man."

"I am not defeated," Ki-Liu smiled. "You are."

"How do you figure?" Malcolm took a step toward him.

"Because there are not four bombs," Ki-Liu said, throwing himself to the deck. "There are five."

"Aw, for…"

Malcolm's sentence was cut off by the sound of the blast.

The explosion and resulting fireball on *The North Star Express* startled everyone on board the pontoon. Out of pure reflex, Adam Spender recoiled and turned to look at the source of the noise and Mary took advantage of the distraction and lunged at him. Spender turned in time and tried to punch Mary, but she brushed aside his fist and sent her elbow into the side of his face.

She spun, looking to deliver her other elbow into his throat, but he dodged the attack and pushed Mary aside. A small trickle of blood made its way from Spender's lip. He dropped the gun and raised his fists.

"You have no idea what you're involved in or what's really going on, do you?" he said. "You can't beat the Guangzhou Syndicate. I should know, I tried. It's not too late to join me, you know."

"Yes, it is too late," Mary snapped. "You tried to kill Amy and you tried to kill me. It doesn't get much later than that. Your only smart move now is to give it up, because I won't let you get past me."

"Then you'll wish the bullets were real. It would have been a lot quicker for you."

When *The North Star Express'* bridge exploded, the air became thick with speeding projectiles, mostly broken glass and twisted metallic debris of varying sizes, accompanied by a scorching burst of rapidly moving wind. Ki-Liu had propelled himself behind a bulwark, shielding himself from the blast and debris, but others were not so fortunate. Duyen Trinh was sent flying in the blast, along with Malcolm, Kevin, and Agent Farrell.

The deck of was now a mess of broken glass, debris, fire, and – in places – blood. Ki-Liu stood up and saw Farrell's gun a short distance away. He scrabbled over to it and grabbed it.

"Drop it," Officer Trinh shouted, but Ki-Liu ran along the deck through the black smoke and Trinh no longer had a clear shot at him. Trinh tried to stand but her right leg gave way. She looked down and saw a piece of metal and a shard of glass lodged into her thigh in two places. She had been too adrenaline-fueled and dazed to feel the pain until that moment. She stayed in a crouched position and had her gun in her right hand. She also realized her face was bleeding, as she was able to feel drops of blood running down her face.

Trinh looked to her right and saw Farrell and Kevin lying motionless on the deck. Her vision was a bit blurry but she focused on looking to her left. She saw Malcolm in the process of standing up. He was near the bulwark at the time of the blast and it seemed to allow him to miss the worst of the projectiles. Even so, his clothes were torn and his face was covered with patches of red and black. He was jogging toward her with a pronounced limp.

"Are you going to make it, Officer Trinh?"

"Ki-Liu…" she moaned. "That way," she motioned toward the black smoke with her gun.

"I'll be back for you," Malcolm promised. "Stay awake, no matter what."

He hurried off, staggering into the thick black smoke.

Adam Spender, in a fighting stance, inched toward Mary. Mary stood between him and the rest of the people on board who were at the front of the pontoon. The pontoon had two rows of seats with a narrow aisle between them, so there was no room for Spender to get around or past Mary.

"Hey, tough guy," Mitch yelled out from behind the wheel. "There's four of us and one of you. Give it up, will ya?"

"Mary's the only one I need to worry about, old man," Spender said. "Once she's out of the way the rest of you will be easy pickings."

"Mr. Jorgensen," Mary said, not taking her eyes off Spender. "Your job is to get that engine working properly. Amy, you and Stacy stay behind me no matter what and don't let him get his stinking hands on those files."

Spender inched closer and began to bob and weave as he did so. Mary stood still, completely focused on his movements. Her arms were bent at the elbows, fists raised, and she was in a slight crouch to make herself ready to respond quickly to any attack.

Spender did a rapid one-two punch toward Mary and she deflected both blows and managed to clip his jaw with a return jab.

He immediately followed up with a snap-kick, which connected with the inside of Mary's right forearm. She had no time to shake it off as he went back into throwing rapid punches. She blocked and dodged but was unable to propel him away as his momentum was minimal due to their close proximity to one another. He was careful not to be off-balance and made a point of not over-extended his punches, so as not to give Mary any more openings. The narrow space between the two rows of seats further limited her options. She could only hope he would eventually make a mistake for her to capitalize on.

He advanced on her again, this time with a right-left-right, a snap kick, and then another left. Mary blocked the attacks but the flaring pain she felt in her arms as a result of the blows further challenged her ability to concentrate on the threat before her. Spender launched his next assault. Left-right, then kick. As his snap-kick came in, Mary punched downward on the top of his thigh with as much force as she could muster. She connected and Spender made an 'oomph' sound, but as she punched down, he managed to get in a punch of his own, which connected with the left side of her face.

Mary staggered backward for a moment. Spender tried to launch at her but his leg wasn't responding properly so he ended up staggering a bit himself. As he lurched forward, Mary sent a punch in towards his head but he brushed the blow aside and knocked her off balance. He lunged but she was ready and she shoved him into the side of one of the seats. He grunted in pain.

The two exchanged rapid blows, each deflecting the other's attacks. Mary dodged a lunge by Spender and she kicked into the opening he provided. He was just able to deflect her leg and managed to get his arm underneath it and he lifted with as much force as he could. Mary toppled backwards into the aisle and Spender leapt and landed on top of her, knocking the wind out of her.

Spender sat up and clamped his hands around Mary's throat. She shot her thumbs up into his eyes and he yelled loudly. With his eyes closed, he delivered a hard right punch into the same spot on Mary's face he'd hit before. She screamed in pain and was unable to see anything except exploding stars. Spender rubbed his eyes with his left hand while his right hand secured itself around Mary's throat again. She began making gurgling sounds while she drove her thumbs into the side of his ribs. Spender was wincing from the pain but kept a tight grip while Mary was fighting the creeping darkness. All she needed was one big gasp of air and she could propel him aside, but her airway was being squeezed too hard. She was no longer able to feel her thumbs and her hands were going limp.

"Hey, Whitlock," Metzner shouted. "You want these files so badly?"

He looked up and saw Metzner with her barrette in her hands.

"Don't do anything stupid, Metzner."

"You want this?" she repeated. "Do you?"

"You know I do."

"Then I hope you can swim, you son of a bitch," she said as she threw it into the water.

"No," Spender yelled and his grip relented just enough for Mary to get a partial breath. It wasn't enough to push him aside, but it was enough for her to get her right hand into his face and push hard while her left grabbed his right index finger and bent it back as hard as she could. He grunted as he tried to block out the pain and squeeze the life out of Mary. She pushed his face even further up and he was immediately surprised to see Amy now rushing toward him.

"Let go of my sister, you festering maggot," Amy shouted as she kicked Spender hard in his ribs. "Unhand her now." As Spender doubled over, she raised her foot and stomped the heel of her shoe into the side of his head. He fell over onto the deck, dazed, and he released Mary in the process. Mary gasped and coughed. Spender tried to get up onto his knees but Amy leaped over Mary and charged at him. Like a football player trying for a field goal, Amy delivered her foot solidly between his legs. Spender yelped and fell onto his back, immediately curling himself into a ball. He turned his head, vomited over the side of the pontoon, and was then gasping for air.

Stacy Metzner knelt beside Mary. "Don't talk," she said to Mary. "Your breathing is laboured. Just lie here and let your body recuperate."

"You," Stacy snapped at Mitch. "Do you have any rope? We need to secure that murdering bastard."

"There's no rope, but open the First Aid kit under the seat beside you there," Mitch said. "There's a tensor bandage you can use to tie him up instead."

Metzner nodded and retrieved the kit. There was a long bandage roll there and she brought it to Amy.

"Tie him," Stacy handed the bandage roll to Amy. "And don't be afraid of tying it too tight."

Amy worked quickly, despite her trembling hands, while Stacy held Spender securely. His hands were then tied behind him and he was offering little resistance, engaged as he was with his moaning and gasping.

"Is he secure?" Mitch asked.

"Yes."

"Good," Mitch shouted. "I've got the 'reverse' gear working on the engine, but the 'forward' is still dead."

"Can you drive this thing in reverse?" Metzner asked.

"You bet your ass I can, lady," Mitch said. "Now let's head back to *The North Star Express* and see if there's any survivors we can pick up."

"Amy," Stacy said. "I'll make sure the 'festering maggot', as you called him, doesn't move. Go and see if your sister is okay."

Amy nodded and went to where Mary lay.

"Hey, sis," Amy put her hand on the side of Mary's face. "I'm so sorry about all this. Are you going to be okay?"

"I think so," Mary croaked. "Amy?"

"Yes?"

"You did great," Mary moaned. "Thank you."

Amy smiled.

"Ms. Bristol," Metzner continued to hold tightly onto Spender. "Remember back at the firm when we were evacuating the office? If you recall, I asked you what you would do if we met up with an armed killer. I wish to retract that question because I've seen it for myself and am satisfied with what I saw. As it turns out, you were right: we're in good hands."

Mary sat up, aided by Amy, as the pontoon's engine roared to life and the boat began its journey backwards toward *The North Star Express*.

Mary massaged her throat, which was tender to the touch. She winced and then slowly got to her feet.

"Get back," Mary squeaked to Stacy and Amy. "There's still danger."

Mary knelt behind Adam Spender while Stacy and Amy stood directly behind her.

Malcolm rounded the corner and, through the smoke, saw Ki-Liu looking at something with great interest. Malcolm was not sure what it was, but it was something that made Ki-Liu raise the gun he had taken from Farrell.

Malcolm was able to walk clear of the smoke and he crouched behind the twisted pile of metal that was once the stairwell, which used to lead to the now-non-existent bridge. He was hidden from Ki-Liu's sight, so he took a moment to rub the smoke out of his eyes. He looked to his left to see what Ki-Liu had been watching and was horrified to see the pontoon reversing towards the listing ship he was on.

"No, no, I told you to stay away," he said under his breath. "What the hell are you doing?"

Malcolm cocked his gun but was too late. Ki-Liu had already lined up his shot and fired. Malcolm turned in time to see Adam Spender's bloodied body roll off the pontoon and fall into the water.

"Get down," Malcolm screamed at the pontoon occupants. Mitch had heard the shot and was already steering the boat to starboard in an evasive manoeuvre.

Mary calculated that Ki-Liu was lining up his next shot at Stacy, so she leapt and pushed Stacy aside as he fired. The bullet hit Mary and she spun around and tumbled into the sea. Less than one second later, Amy dove into the water after her.

Malcolm fired at Ki-Liu and his shot hit him in the right shoulder, causing the gun to tumble out of his hand. Ki-Liu fell to his knees, his left arm clutching the fresh and bloody wound.

Malcolm, eyes wide and furious, limped over to Ki-Liu and stood directly in front of him. He raised his gun and aimed for between the eyes.

"You shot Mary, you bastard," Malcolm's voice was breaking and filled with rage. "I'm going to find the slowest and most painful way to kill you and you'll have to forgive me if I enjoy it too much."

"Agent Malcolm," Officer Trinh's voice called out.

Malcolm saw her approaching from his right. Her weapon was aimed at him. She still had the pieces of debris in her thigh and she was leaving a trail of blood behind her. Her clothes were bloodied and torn, but her eyes were focused and filled with determination. "If you shoot him then I will shoot you. Ki-Liu is my mission and not yours. You promised me, yes?"

"The second this bastard took a shot at Mary he became my mission."

Officer Trinh's finger began to tighten on the trigger, but then stopped. She knew Malcolm was not in a rational state of mind. At the same time, she knew she had lost a fair amount of blood and there was no way for her to tell how long it would be before she passed out. A long, tense moment passed.

"Agent Malcolm," Trinh decided to try a different strategy. "Will Mary be okay?"

"I don't know and I can't tell from here. She fell into the water and… if she's dead, I'm going to kill him. I haven't killed anyone in a long time, but I'm pretty sure I still remember how. Once it's done, you can do whatever you want to me."

Ki-Liu knelt silently on the deck, apart from the occasional moan of pain as he continued clutching at his shoulder.

"Agent Malcolm," Trinh called out. "How long have you been with Mary?"

"What?" Malcolm's focus kept shifting from Ki-Liu to Duyen Trinh and then back. "More than twenty years. Why are you asking me this?"

Trinh ignored his question. "Do you have any children?"

Malcolm did not answer, but Trinh could see how the question had changed his stance and posture.

"How many do you have?" she asked, making sure there was ample kindness in her now-soft voice.

"One," Malcolm said.

"I am sure you wish to see him again, yes?"

"Her," Malcolm corrected.

"A girl, how precious," Trinh said. "She is probably beautiful, yes? How old is she?"

"A little over two years."

"Ah, that is such a critical stage of her life," Trinh nodded, still pointing her weapon at Malcolm. "A daughter really needs her father at that age, yes? It is so important that you are able to return to her to guide her through her life's journey and teach her what she needs to know in order to live a good life."

"Yes," Malcolm said eventually.

"Just make certain that someone other than you teaches her English."

"I…," Malcolm began to say, but was unable to form any additional words.

"I am certain it would be most difficult for such a young child to understand why her father was not coming home to be with her. I do not wish to think of how she will feel when she is told her father perished while committing the murder of a captured suspect."

"It's not murder," Malcolm tried to snap in response but it was half-hearted. Her words were like long, icy daggers in his heart. "It's justice."

"No, a trial would be justice," Trinh said. "What you are doing now is murder and your motive is nothing but pure mindless revenge. Revenge for Mary, even though, I must add, you are not certain of her current condition. If you are willing to assist me, then I will take Ki-Liu back to Vietnam with me where he will face trial. He is wanted by my government and he will not be able to avoid receiving a harsh sentence. If China finds out we have him, they will want to punish him even more severely. Either way, you will have your justice and you can also go home and see your daughter again, yes?"

Malcolm nodded after a moment's pause and then lowered his gun.

"You're right," he whispered. He pinched the bridge of his nose and then rubbed his eyes. "What the hell came over me?"

Ki-Liu twisted his left wrist and a stiletto dropped into his hand from his sleeve. He lunged at Malcolm and swung the blade at him. Malcolm propelled himself backwards and he fell to the deck. Officer Trinh fired a shot and hit Ki-Liu in the middle of his forehead. He fell onto his back and lay motionless, as his blood began spreading across the buckling metal of the ship's deck.

"That is very disappointing," Officer Trinh said.

"What is?"

"I managed to persuade you to not kill Ki-Liu and then I ended up killing him myself," Officer Trinh sighed and shook her head. "That was a waste of a good speech."

"It really was a good speech, I agree."

"And all done with proper English words, you will notice," Trinh looked at him. "You could learn to speak properly from me, yes?"

"She's been hit," Amy gasped from the water, pulling Mary towards the boat. "I don't know if she's alive. Help me."

"You," Mitch called out to Stacy. "Grab hold of this wheel, missy, and don't let it move."

Stacy Metzner nodded and stepped over to the boat's steering wheel, holding it firm and pretending she did not notice he had addressed her as 'missy'. The wheel was more difficult to hold firm than she anticipated, so she widened her stance and tightened her grip.

"Here," Mitch called out while tossing a life ring into the water beside Amy. "Grab hold of that and I'll pull you both in."

Mitch Jorgensen pulled on the rope and brought the two women up to the side of the boat.

"Grab my hand," Mitch said, leaning over the side.

"But Mary's hurt."

"I've got her, but I'll need you up here with me first so we can pull her up together. It'll take the both of us."

Amy pulled herself up onto the pontoon deck while Mitch held onto Mary from under her arm.

"I'm so cold," Amy's teeth were chattering and her voice shook.

"Can you grab her other arm?"

"Yes, I've got it."

"Alright then we'll pull her up on three," Mitch said. "One, two, three, pull."

They pulled Mary into the boat and put her gently onto the pontoon's deck.

"Is she alive?" Stacy called from the wheel.

"It seems so," Mitch said, hand on Mary's neck. "There's an arterial pulse but it's not strong. We'll lose her if we don't move quickly. There's blood on her jacket sleeve. Let's get it off her and see how badly she's hit."

Amy and Mitch struggled but managed to remove Mary's soaked jacket. Mitch found the bullet wound immediately. He nodded. "I'll patch her arm up to stop the bleeding. Pass me the medical kit we got the bandages from."

Amy retrieved it and brought it to Mitch.

"Now grab yourself a blanket from the bin over there and bundle up. Then toss me one for her."

Amy wrapped herself in a wool blanket and then gently tossed another towards Mitch.

"This is all my fault," Amy sniffed. "If she dies I'll never forgive myself."

"You can't blame yourself, Amy," Stacy said. "She came here to protect you and that's what she did."

"Looks like the bullet went right through, from what I can see," Mitch said, wrapping a bandage around Mary's upper arm. "It'll need to be disinfected just in case. Between the loss of blood and the shock of hitting the cold water, I'm guessing that's why she's unconscious. We'll somehow have to keep her as warm as we can to prevent hypothermia from setting in. Now we just need the damned Coast Guard to show up."

"Is he dead?" Malcolm asked, looking at Ki-Liu.

"It would appear so," Trinh said, lowering her weapon. "He probably died the moment my shot hit him."

"The last time he *probably died* he came back into play. I'm not giving him the chance to pull another *Lazarus* on me. I'm not leaving here until I'm certain he's dead."

"Then look closely and check him," Trinh pointed.

Malcolm stepped over and knelt beside Ki-Liu's body.

"He's dead, alright," Malcolm said after checking for pulses and a heartbeat but finding neither. "I need to get onto that pontoon boat out there to see if Mary's okay. That last explosion blew a hole in the side of the only lifeboat left on the ship. We have no way to get off this thing before it sinks."

Malcolm noticed Officer Trinh had not been listening. She was swaying and her eyes were closed. "I am not feeling well," she said as she collapsed onto the deck.

As Malcolm made his way toward Trinh, he noticed the entire prow of the ship was now under water, and the sea was inching its way toward his feet.

"Damn it," he muttered and he began to drag Trinh toward the stern of the ship. "I'm on my own again."

Mitch turned and looked to the horizon as he heard a ship's horn cry out. He could not see the ship in the darkness, but there was a search light scanning the waves. Mitch opened the storage bin under the pilot seat and retrieved a flare gun. He prepped it and fired a smoky-red flare into the sky. The distant ship sounded its horn twice and the search light was now partially illuminating the pontoon.

As the boat drew closer, Mitch waved his arms. It was a large fishing trawler, probably about a hundred and twenty feet long. A man waved back to Mitch as it pulled alongside the pontoon.

"We need assistance," Mitch said.

"Yes, I managed to figure that out for myself," the man said. "I'm looking for a Malcolm or a Mary."

"Mary's here and she needs immediate medical attention," Stacy said. "If Malcolm is alive, he's on that flaming wreck over there."

"I'll check it out," the man nodded. "But let's get you all on board first."

"Glad you happened to be out here," Mitch said as he helped the man get onto the pontoon. "I'm Mitch Jorgensen. Who are you?"

"I'm George Simpson from Haida Gwaii," he said as he signaled for a second man to come on board. "I didn't 'happen' to be out here at all. I was hired by a Melanie Waterman to find you all."

"Never heard of her," Mitch said. "How did you know where to find us?"

"Between Ms. Waterman and myself, we were able to triangulate your approximate course and position based on Mary's satellite phone transmissions," George said as he and his shipmate gently lifted Mary together. "Once I plotted a logical course, I asked her if there was a quick way to track you from there. She said if Malcolm and Mary were both on board, chances are all I'd need to do was to look for billowing smoke, flames, or the sound of explosions. I thought she was joking."

It had been mostly quiet on the lifeboats, as people were still coming to terms with everything that had taken place over the past half hour. The life boat was completely enclosed which kept out the elements. Inside, there was a row of seats along the port and starboard sides which faced one another. The seats were all occupied and the mood was sombre by those seated within. Some had been drinking earlier so were still feeling a mix of light-headedness and the stomach-churning nausea that generally occurs after a crisis has passed.

A few people had somehow fallen asleep. Others were in tears. Most were in a state of stunned silence as their brains tried to come to terms with the rapid pace of recent events. Many went from tearing up the dance floor to wearing a life jacket while drifting at sea in under thirty minutes.

Ian Gagnon had been moving from person to person, checking on how they were doing. He was offering comfort and encouragement to as many people as he could, but beneath his reassuring demeanour he was a man feeling lost and confused. He needed to remain busy so as not to break down himself. Ian had noticed the crew member in charge of the lifeboat had received a call, so he'd been keeping his ears open for any hints about what was happening. Once the call was done, Ian saw the crew member put the headset down and then stand up in front of the two rows.

"So, what's the news?" Ian Gagnon asked.

"Ladies and gentlemen, if I may have everyone's attention please," the crewmember said. "I have received word that a fishing trawler has found us and there is a Coast Guard vessel ten minutes behind him which will be picking us up. Please sit tight for now and prepare to be rescued."

There was some enthusiastic chatter along with cheering and applause.

David looked over at Sita. "We're going to make it."

"Yeah," Sita smiled.

"Let's get your stuff together," David said. "I'll get your bag for you, and…"

"You can stop fussing over me, David," Sita laughed. "I think it's over now and I'm fine."

"Sorry," David looked down.

"Don't be," Sita took his hand in hers. "It's cool you're doing all this for me."

"I…"

"We should go out sometime," she smiled as his face turned red. "Like, as a couple. You into it?"

"Um, yes," David said. "I'd like that. I'd like that a lot."

"I figured," Sita patted his hand. "I can't keep waiting for you to ask me out so I thought I might as well do it instead. This day has already been so unreal."

"It really has."

"Any idea where Kevin is?"

"Um, Sita, I need to tell you something," David gulped. "Do you remember all those training projects we did back in college to boost our creativity?"

"You mean all the games and scenarios, right?"

"Yes, those, exactly. As you know, we still do them to generate ideas. And, uh…"

"What?"

"Well, do you remember when the three of us were sitting around last month and we were presenting hypothetical problems to one another? Then we'd all have to creatively find an answer or a comprehensive solution to them?"

"That was so much fun."

"Yes, it was. But do you remember when Kevin asked us how we would commit a murder and get away with it? He gave us a detailed and specific scenario to work with and then we had to figure out how it could be done, remember?"

"Oh yeah, that was a tricky one."

"It really was, but we found a way to do it. As it turns out, what Kevin was describing was Ben Shapner's apartment and Ben was the hypothetical victim."

"What are you…?"

"I'm saying that Kevin wasn't asking us for the sake of a creative exercise. He actually got us to help plot the death of a lawyer and then he and the security guard from our building carried it out."

"Seriously? What makes you think that?"

"Just add it up in your head. Mr. Shapner died, Kevin's been acting all weird and tense since then, and the scenario he gave us matched what happened in exact detail. I wanted Kevin to confess on his own so we could get his accomplice, but he wouldn't. Once I was questioned, I was concerned the security guard would try to blame you and I thought he might try to kill you. I thought if I took the blame, Kevin would snap out of it and help me but he didn't."

"This is a lot to take in. As soon as we dock, you've got to go to the cops and tell them what you just told me."

"I will, I promise. I'm scared, to be honest, but I'll do it."

"Don't worry, I'll go with you. We'll do this together."

"Thank you."

"Uh, David?" Sita said. "This is the part where you act grateful and kiss me."

David's face turned deep red. He nevertheless leaned over and kissed Sita.

Saturday, 10:57pm:

Malcolm looked at his face in the mirror. He had washed the soot off his face and a member of the trawler's crew gave him a soothing gel for the scorch marks on his face, neck, and hands. With the gel applied, his face looked red and shiny.

He looked over at the two cots against the wall. One was occupied by Farrell and the other by Kevin. Neither were conscious and both were in rough shape, each sporting bandages over most of their body. They each bore the full brunt of the spray of glass and debris after the bridge explosion as neither had any protective cover. The medic on board said Farrell would likely survive but only after a painful month or two of surgeries and recovery. Kevin Denbigh, on the other hand, was in critical condition. It was the opinion of the medic that Kevin's best case scenario would be for him to end up alive but with a number of permanent disabilities.

Malcolm exited the room and then walked over to the cabin beside it. He knocked.

"You may enter," Duyen Trinh said.

Malcolm stepped inside and closed the door.

"You are still limping," she said. "How is your leg?"

"The medic said I have some pieces of shrapnel in my thigh, but I feel like an idiot complaining about that when I see what you've got going on."

"And how is Mary?"

"She was punched twice in the face, strangled, shot, and nearly drowned," Malcolm said. "If she'd been poisoned, she'd be one-upping Rasputin."

"I have given up even trying to understand you when you speak," Trinh shook her head. "Just tell me in proper English if she will fully recover."

"I don't know yet," he admitted. "As soon as we dock, I'll need to get her to the hospital to get properly checked out. George told me there'll be an ambulance waiting for us when we get to Queen Charlotte City. The entire left side of her face and her neck looks like one massive and contiguous bruise and it's all swollen. They gave her a shot for the pain and a pill for the swelling, so she's okay until those wear off. What about you? How are you doing, aside from the whole 'I-have-projectiles-sticking-out-of-my-leg' thing?"

"My pain also disappeared after the medical man injected me with a substance. I am currently unable to feel anything in my legs at all."

"I've seen a lot of injuries like yours. You're lucky you didn't sever an artery. Aside from some relatively minor nerve and muscle damage, you'll be fine."

"That is good to hear."

"You look as though you have a lot on your mind."

"So much has happened the past three days," Trinh sighed. "I did not tell you this, but I originally came here to kill Ki-Liu. It was only when I arrived that I realized I could not do it. After some thought, I decided it would be better to capture him alive so he could have a trial. My hope was he would have time to reflect upon his misdeeds and the crimes he committed and hopefully understand his errors."

"That's a nice thought, but people like Ki-Liu don't lose sleep over their own actions. Anything he did, any atrocity he committed, anyone he killed, he viewed as a necessary part of the job. He was beyond redemption."

"Ki-Liu was an assassin but he was still a person. I cannot imagine a person killing someone and not feeling anything."

"I can," Malcolm said. "Some people can kill without feeling anything and Ki-Liu was one of them. He would never have had a change of heart."

"We will never know for certain," Trinh stared at the wall beside her for a moment. "It is strange. When I wanted to kill him, I had no opportunity. When I decided to arrest him instead, I ended up killing him when he tried to kill you. I believe the word in English is 'ironic'. And I mean normal English, not what you speak."

"Thanks for saving my ass, by the way," Malcolm said. "And you're right that a trial would have been better. Death was too easy a way out for a man like Ki-Liu, but if it was a trial, it would have had to have been a secret trial, right? You wouldn't want China to know you had Ki-Liu or they'd want him themselves."

"If I managed to get Ki-Liu back to Vietnam, I would have completed my part of the job," Trinh said. "Once I turned him over, it would then become political and I do not wish to be involved in such things."

"I don't blame you. The problem with politics is that it's the preferred vocation of politicians."

"Very droll, Agent Malcolm, yet also accurate. It would appear we might have some views in common after all. I will make certain your file gets updated."

"Good," Malcolm did a slight nod. "I'd prefer that people know I don't work for the US Government anymore."

"I was thinking more like adding a note suggesting our people plug their ears if approaching you. Between your attempts at humour and your attempts at speaking, the only safe distance is out of earshot."

"Did I just detect a trace of a smile, Officer Trinh?"

"I find that unlikely," she grinned. "However, I wish to extend my compliments to you for helping me with Ki-Liu. You are indeed resourceful."

"Thanks. I'm proud to have worked with you. You're damned good at your job."

"Unfortunately, it would appear I am not good enough," Trinh frowned. "Based on our current situation, I will most likely be arrested by whichever authorities are waiting for us when we dock."

"I don't see why," Malcolm shrugged. "Throw your gun and dagger overboard and then as far as anyone has to know, you're just a bartender from a temp company who escaped the sinking ship."

"You will not report me?"

"No."

"You would do that for me?"

"Yeah, as long as when you get back to Vietnam you update the files you have on me to say I was killed on board during this ordeal. I'd like to have as few people as possible from my past trying to ruin my retirement."

"What about the others?" Trinh said.

"Not too many people saw you as anything except a bartender," Malcolm said. "I'm sure the few who saw otherwise can be persuaded to see what would make the most sense for a solution. I know Mary won't say anything."

"Then perhaps it is an arrangement that would be of benefit to us both," Trinh smiled. "I agree to your proposal."

Saturday, 11:18pm:

Stacy Metzner leaned on the starboard railing and was looking up at the stars, marvelling at the sight of how many there were in the night sky. In the city, you didn't see more than a dozen or two stars on a clear night, but out here… it looked as though she could see the entire galaxy and it was a humbling feeling to realize just how small any given law firm's problems really were in the grand scheme of things.

She heard a sound and looked to her left. Amy was walking toward her.

"What are you still doing up?" Stacy asked.

"I can't sleep yet," Amy stood beside Stacy and leaned on the rail with her. "I'm exhausted but I won't be able to sleep until my mind stops racing."

"I know the feeling."

"Also, I want to apologize," Amy said.

"For what?"

"For breaking down so many times these past forty-eight hours."

Stacy stared at Amy for a few seconds. "I'm not understanding what you're saying. Why on earth would you apologize for that?"

"Because I know how much you look down on weakness."

"No, I look down on *weak people*, not weakness," Metzner said. "There's a distinct difference. You know when I was told of Bill's death, my heart broke. I maintained a brave face until I kicked everyone out of my cabin and then I completely fell apart. I haven't cried like that in a long time. In addition, on that pontoon you weren't weak at all. I'd go so far as to suggest you showed a lot of courage when you attacked Mr. Whitlock who was twice your size."

"Thank you."

"We all have moments when we're not at our strongest, but that doesn't make us weak," Stacy said. "Those moments of vulnerability are how we know we're human."

"You can confide in me when you're feeling down, you know," Amy said. "I'm a good listener and am even better at keeping secrets."

"I appreciate that, I really do," Stacy allowed a small grin to momentarily creep onto her face. "I prefer to keep my emotions to myself, though. I'll take a few days off and grieve at home in private. The problem with being a woman executive is your male colleagues expect you to show no emotion and act like some superficial dumbass."

Amy chuckled. "That's a pretty broad brush you're painting men with."

"Amy, you know I demand a high-level of excellence from everyone I work with. Before you came along, I had a reputation at the firm as someone who couldn't keep an assistant for more than a month. They either weren't tough enough to work with me or their level of work output was inadequate."

"I'm not very tough, but I can work with you even though you can be challenging sometimes."

"You just finished telling me I paint with too broad a brush while you paint with one that's too narrow," Metzner said. "I'm a *difficult person*, Amy, and that's several degrees worse than simply *challenging*. Moreover, I know I'm difficult so don't downplay it or try to dress it up. I hear the whispered comments and the rumours at the firm. I know that when you offered to be the fire warden for our floor the head of the committee said her biggest objection to you joining would be that you'd feel compelled to rescue me if the office was burning."

"You heard about that?"

"Yes, I was serious when I said I've heard all the comments. If I had a dollar for each time someone referred to me as a bitch I'd have been able to retire by now. So it's no secret I'm the most difficult person to work with at the firm. Yet you manage to work with me extraordinarily well. I've worked with you for more than two years now and I've come to rely on you. If you can work with me then I already know you're no weakling. On top of that, you faced a number of life and death situations this weekend and you've come through them. You're an excellent assistant so never make excuses for yourself."

"That means a lot to me," Amy smiled. "You know, I always viewed it as unfair that you were passed over for promotion so many times. You deserved better. Despite all the death and tragedy that occurred this past week, a small silver lining is that most of the people who were holding you back won't be doing that anymore."

"Trust me, that wasn't by design," Stacy shrugged. "It just worked out that way."

"We'll have to see how it all plays out."

"Ah, and it looks like we've got company," Stacy nodded as she looked past her assistant. Amy turned around and saw Malcolm hobbling toward them.

"You're alive," Stacy said. "And those are some serious burns on your face."

"Just first degree, they'll heal," Malcolm said. "Ms. Metzner, can I talk to you in private in Mary's room for a moment?"

"You can call me Stacy," Metzner said. "After everything that's happened, you and Mary have both earned that much. Amy, you and I will chat more tomorrow. Good night."

Stacy and Malcolm walked down the stairs and then along a narrow, dimly lit corridor until they got to where Mary was. Malcolm knocked and then opened the door.

Stacy stepped inside and took a long look at Mary. "She's in pretty rough shape."

"Yeah, she is," Malcolm said. "She and I risked everything to keep you and Amy safe and it could have gone a hell of a lot worse."

"Yes, I'm aware of that," Stacy said. "How are you, Mary?"

Mary simply nodded.

"She looks like she went through hell."

"She did," Malcolm said. "But I know how to make her smile."

Malcolm leaned in close. "Mary? You'll never see that brown leather jacket again because it sank with the ship."

Mary smiled for a moment.

Stacy turned to face Malcolm. "So what did you want to talk to me about?"

"I know why Bill Sutherland came by your house and trusted you with the memory stick," Malcolm said. "You were the one who made him aware of the potential sale."

"Yes, that's true," Stacy said. "I truly didn't know at the time they were looking to sell a client's intellectual property, let alone sell it to some crime syndicate. I pulled out of the deal as soon as I found out and I went directly to Bill and told him."

"Doesn't that break the code of silence your colleagues held sacred?" Malcolm asked.

"By that point, I didn't care," Stacy said. "A code of honour is more important than a code of silence. Besides, I was wanting to leave McKenzie Ferguson to start my own firm anyway."

"You mean start you own firm with Bill Sutherland, don't you?" Malcolm locked eyes with Stacy.

"Yes," Stacy said after a moment's hesitation. "Bill was going to announce his departure from McKenzie Ferguson at the two o'clock meeting. We were going to start our own corporate law firm."

"That night when Bill dropped off the files to you... he stayed the night, didn't he?"

"Not that it's any of your business, but yes, he did," Stacy said. "We were in a relationship. We were keeping it quiet until our departures could be announced."

"So why the sudden interest in leaving the firm?"

"There was nothing sudden about it. I have wanted to have my own firm for years but I've never been able to take that big leap. I'm nearly fifty and have never managed to start my own practice. Do you know what fifty years of disappointment feels like?"

Malcolm shrugged. "I would if I were a Canucks fan."

"So many years trying to prove myself yet I was still the brunt of everyone's jokes," Stacy fumed. "Nobody was willing to take me seriously despite my skills and talents."

"Ah," Malcolm nodded. "Leafs fans understand that one."

"Then Charles Lautzen said there was a big-money, big-profit business deal going down and asked me if I wanted in on it. Thinking only of the money, I foolishly assumed it would be a legal and legitimate proposition, so I agreed to participate before finding out any of the important details. What I was part of, no matter how briefly or unwittingly, was unethical and I'll probably end up disbarred because of it."

"You're the only one from that boardroom meeting still alive," Malcolm leaned against the wall. "I'm not sure anyone is left to lodge a complaint against you. Nobody else knows."

"You and Mary know," Stacy pointed. "Amy knows, too."

"Amy needs a job and likes working for you," Malcolm replied. "I'm sure she won't give your actions a second thought, especially if it involves a pay raise and some extra vacation time. If that happens, then Mary and I can forget any of this happened."

"I'm sure both can be arranged for her at my new firm." The slightest of smiles appeared on Metzner's face. "As soon as we were brought on board this ship I made the decision to finally take that big step and leave McKenzie Ferguson with a handful of lawyers who had previously expressed interest in the idea. I was going to formally ask Amy to come with me tomorrow morning. It would be hard to imagine doing any of this without her."

"Congratulations," Malcolm said.

"The new firm will be a great chance for a fresh start," Mary's voice was rough but audible enough to be understood. "I'm happy for you. As for your own conscience, do your penance at a local charity. There's no shortage of good causes."

"Point taken," Stacy nodded to Mary. "And I will."

"Then we're done here," Malcolm said.

"There's more to you than your appearance would suggest," Stacy nodded at Malcolm. "You show initiative and take risks. I admire those qualities in people. I may have been mistaken to dismiss you out of hand but I have no regrets in calling you reckless."

"That's fair."

"And Ms. Bristol?"

"Yes?"

"Amy's lucky to have you as a sister. I respect loyalty and dedication and you displayed both, especially on the pontoon. You and Amy share those traits and it's why she's invaluable to me as an assistant. I wish you a full and speedy recovery."

Stacy held out her hand. Mary shook it, and then Malcolm shook it as well.

"I appreciate what you both did but I hope to never see you again," Stacy said. "You know how some people can walk into the middle of a chaotic mess and their mere presence calms things down and everything just seems to fall into place?"

"Yeah."

"You two are the exact opposite of that."

Tuesday, 3:56pm: Vancouver, BC

Mary shuffled into the living room and her mother accosted her immediately.

"Maria, you should be resting."

"I'm much better, Mom," Mary said. "Besides, I'm sick of resting."

"Your arms, face, and neck are still very bruised, dear. Does your throat still hurt?"

"Yes, but Malcolm says it's fitting since I'm a pain in the neck."

"He's such a sweet and funny man."

"Not the words I would have chosen, but we'll go with them," Mary sighed. "I'm not complaining, but you built a career putting people who looked like Malcolm into jail yet you seem almost giddy whenever he's around."

"I'm not naïve, Maria, I know he has a past," Irena said. "I may have put people who *looked* like him in prison but not someone who *acted* like him. Some bad people look mean and scary but just as many wear suits and ties and are immaculately groomed. Good people who make mistakes are better suited for community service or restitution no matter what their appearance. Malcolm takes good care of you, he dotes on Alyssa, and he wants us to be a part of your lives. He's good for you."

Mary looked around. "Where is Alyssa, anyway?"

"Your father took her to the park."

"She'll enjoy that. By the way, I weighed Alyssa and she put on a few pounds while we were away."

"She was so skinny, Maria."

"Her weight was above-average for her age and height."

"No, she needed to gain weight," Irena said. "I'm sure of it."

"So instead of trusting the best scientific minds in pediatric development, I'm supposed to rely on the judgement of a woman who lets my daughter snack on cake before dinner."

"I'm not saying I know more than they do, I'm just saying I know what works. You rely too much on those parenting books and not enough on your own intuition."

"I don't read those books to be perfect; I read them so I make fewer mistakes. I want to raise Alyssa right."

"You're a parent, so you'll make mistakes no matter how many of those books you read. God knows, your father and I made our share of mistakes along the way. Develop your instincts and Alyssa will be fine."

"And the cake before dinner thing?"

"It's good for her."

"Your views on cake before dinner have evolved somewhat since I was her age. Anyway, I'd better go upstairs and see if Malcolm needs help packing."

Mary left the living room and headed up the stairs. She walked into her old bedroom and saw Malcolm zipping up his suitcase. "All done?"

"Yeah," he said.

"And did you make your phone calls?"

"Yeah, and I found out quite a bit, including that Spender lied to me about pretty much everything. He wasn't attacked by two members of the Cartel, it was he who attacked them and neither of their deaths were accidental. And he wasn't driving the van to the cops when he was arrested; he was trying to get away."

"But why would he hit members of the Cartel if he was part of it?"

"He wasn't part of it. I really do believe he was working against them at the time. Something happened after the trial, though, and he switched sides. After their deportation, any cartel members of value were taken off the plane in China, given new identities, and then smuggled back into North America along with Ki-Liu to start a new cartel on behalf of the Guangzhou Syndicate."

"So a new cartel is already in place and providing drugs to anyone who wants them," Mary sighed. "Supply and demand in action, I suppose. I'm still upset you figured out Spender was crooked yet you still sent me out on a pontoon boat with him."

"I didn't send him. Like I told you yesterday, he wasn't supposed to be on it at all."

"I guess I shouldn't be surprised he lied to me," Mary said. "I didn't trust him from the start."

"I didn't know he was compromised at first," Malcolm admitted. "I shouldn't have been so eager to trust him. When I first saw him in the stairwell, I should have clued in there was a problem when I mentioned there were blood spatters on the wall by the upstairs landing and he didn't look. How does anyone not look up when you mention that there's fresh blood spattered on a nearby wall? I only finally clued in when he started asking too many questions about the FIRST files and where they were hidden. After that, I handed him a gun with blanks in it and was going to try to entrap him later but never got the chance to fully implement my plan."

"I could have been killed."

"On the pontoon, sure, you could have been killed; but if you'd stayed on the ship, Ki-Liu would have had a clearer shot at you and his gun wouldn't have had blanks in it. Or, you could have possibly been killed in the explosion. Or in the crossfire. I'd have had one more person to protect, one more variable to consider, one more distraction to worry about. At least you had a fighting chance against Spender. Even though I didn't want him on the boat with you, it ended up being the best option out of a bunch of terrible choices."

"No it wasn't," Mary said. "The best choice would have been you coming with me on the pontoon."

"Then what about Ki-Liu?"

"Forget Ki-Liu, *what about me?*"

"I can't forget about Ki-Liu *because he is about you*. If Ki-Liu had escaped, we're loose ends he would have to tie off, like I told you before. Maybe he wouldn't do it today or tomorrow but maybe in a week or a month when we weren't expecting it as much. We'd be living on his terms day-to-day and there's no way in hell I'll accept that. If anybody poses a threat to you or Alyssa, then I'm not taking any chances. They go down now, *on my terms*. I was not leaving that ship until he was dead or in custody."

"Looks like we have this mostly wrapped up."

"Why only mostly?"

"The murder at the lake still doesn't fit," Mary observed. "Grant McKenzie wasn't part of the Tech Law group, he was an Estates lawyer. On top of that, the one thing everyone agreed upon was that McKenzie wasn't involved in any of these schemes whatsoever."

"You're right, he wasn't involved," Malcolm nodded. "Remember when I said I sent Sammy Mendoza to check into it all for us? Once we pulled into Queen Charlotte City, I had access to Wi-Fi again and I noticed Sammy Mendoza had sent me an email about what he found."

"So what did he find?"

"Bottom, line, he was killed and a suspect was taken into custody. Sammy questioned him and found out he was hired by Adam Spender."

"But why kill him?"

"Spender wanted to convince Bill Sutherland to hire him as ship security. He selected a close personal friend of Bill's and had him murdered so it would have enough impact to get Bill to sign off."

"What a piece of work Spender was."

"Remember when I said I wanted a case with no supernatural elements to it? I take it back. If normal means assassins, explosions, enemy agents, murders, betrayals, and seeing you get shot, then forget it. I'll take strange and abnormal any day."

"You didn't get your wish anyway. You did hear a young woman's voice in your head which told you about the bombs and she said she'd be seeing you in two weeks. Maybe it was more than just a dream. It's rather suspicious, isn't it?"

"No, the data behind the anti-vaccine movement is suspicious. A vegan who doesn't tell everyone he's vegan is suspicious. That wouldn't be suspicious, it would be somewhere between highly improbable and impossible."

"Ah, yes," Mary chuckled. "Between highly improbable and the impossible. That's our job description, isn't it?"

"That about sums it up, yeah," Malcolm smiled. "I'm sure we'll encounter something soon which explains the voice I was hearing. Any other loose ends we need to tie up?"

"There…" *are*, Mary was about to say, but instead decided to say "…aren't."

The remaining loose end, Mary thought, was the final villain to be dealt with. This particular loose end, though, was personal and she wanted to deal with it herself and in her own way. Malcolm would over-react, and she would not be able to blame him if he did. Nevertheless, Mary felt a different approach was required, as she did not want to make an already-bad situation so much worse.

"By the way," Mary said. "There was a second message which was from our boss, Melanie Waterman. She simply wrote 'I look forward to reading your report for the mission I didn't send you on'."

"Yeah, we've got some explaining to do. Uh, can I talk to you for a sec?"

"Of course."

"I know we need to discuss the whole Adam Spender thing in more detail, but before we do I want to ask you something."

"This should be good."

"I'm being serious. When I was a kid, I had a few crushes like every other guy in school did but after I ended up on the street, I didn't have much time to think about relationships. During those years, something as basic as dating became a luxury I could no longer even dream of. Every hour of my life, it seemed I was focused only on either looking for my next meal, finding a warm place to sleep, or plotting the next piece of criminal filth I could lash out at."

"Yes, I know what you went through. It was unthinkable and harsh. Where are you going with this?"

"Listen, I know you're upset with me. I usually have exceptional instincts when it comes to people but I'm not perfect. I know I was wrong about Spender at first but I was still right about everyone else and I clued into him eventually as well. I was also right about you from day one. You weren't my first crush but you've been the only woman I've ever loved. I hate it when you're mad because I don't know what to do. Such as right now."

"Relationships aren't easy and neither of us are exactly pros at dealing with people who are close to us. I used to always drive away anyone who tried to get close to me."

"I know you didn't date much but do you remember the first guy you liked?"

"Oh sure, I definitely remember my first real crush," Mary stared ahead. "I was twelve at the time and there was a cute guy in my class who I had a huge crush on. The first time I really noticed him was in gym class one day when we were all outside playing baseball. He looked at me and I batted my eyes. It really hurts when you hit your eyes with the bat like that."

"You see, it's these kinds of anecdotes that remind me of why I am so lucky to be married to you," Malcolm chuckled. "You have a real down-to-earth manner and an innocence I adore."

"What do you mean by innocence?"

"Well, for example, remember this past summer when you jumped up into my arms and wrapped your legs around my waist? Then I said 'I know what you want' to which you replied, 'good, the spider's in the kitchen, go get it'. Do you remember that?"

"Yes, why? Was that wrong?"

"No, but it was very much who you are and I wouldn't change a thing about you. So what do we do now?"

"I'm not sure what it is you're asking me."

"What happens now with us?" Malcolm pointed to her and then himself. "Are you still mad at me?"

"Yes, I'm still a bit angry with you but we'll talk it out and hopefully one of us will learn an important lesson, such as not excluding their partner from important decisions. Once that happens, I'll find the forgiveness needed for us to move on. Without forgiveness, we'd be stuck in never-ending cycle of resentment and it would hold us back in our lives."

"Wow," Amy said, entering the room. "It's almost as if you knew I was eavesdropping."

"I didn't but... I guess it worked out."

"I'll be in the other room so you two can talk," Malcolm said. "I'm going to pretend I have more packing to do so that I can leave you two alone."

"You're a nut," Mary smiled and shook her head.

"Yeah, but you love me anyway."

"God knows why but yes, I do."

Malcolm turned and exited the room. He gently pulled the door closed behind him to give the women some privacy.

"I couldn't help but overhear paert of your discussion," Amy said. "It really impresses me that you two talk things out. That's good. It's healthy to have that kind of open, authentic, exchange. I wasn't expecting that level of frank honesty and vulnerability from either of you."

"We don't have much choice," Mary shrugged. "We either work through things together or we go completely crazy. It took us far too long to figure that out but things got a lot better once we did. If you value the relationship you have with someone, then you need to be prepared to put some hard work into it."

"Another ambiguous bit of wisdom which could be about you and him or about you and me."

"I'd say it was an equal split," Mary winked.

"Listen, I appreciate everything you did on the ship," Amy shifted awkwardly on her feet. "It doesn't even come close to reconciling everything that's happened between us but... when he pointed that gun at you and I heard the shot ring out, all I could think about was how much I wanted you to be okay. I certainly didn't want to end up caring about you; I wanted to go on hating you because everything would have been so much easier that way. Needless to say, it's safe to say I don't hate you anymore."

"That's progress, I guess, but it's not where I ultimately want things to be with us."

"Sorry, Mary, but I can't even think about our pasts right now. I'm still coming to grips with everything that's happened over the past few days, not to mention my violent outburst on the lifeboat."

"That outburst quite possibly saved our lives," Mary put her hand on Amy's shoulder.

"Does it make me a bad person because it felt so good to kick Whitlock? Because I really liked doing it."

"You subdued a threat," Mary said. "And then I understand you dove into the ocean to save me... that was amazing."

"I wasn't even thinking by that point. It was an automatic response."

"Here. Sit down here on the bed. It will be more comfortable."

"Thank you," Amy sat down and Mary sat beside her. "Mary, I've never experienced anything like this past week before. I've booked an appointment with a psychologist because so much has happened and my mind is still reeling. I'm going to burst if I don't get this all out."

"I understand," Mary put her arm around her sister. "It was a lot of stress for you to absorb in such a short period of time. Why don't you see how you feel about everything in a few days when you've had a chance to process what's happened? Maybe then you'll be able to look at our past through a fresh and more objective filter."

"I will," Amy nodded. "I promise you I'll really give it some thought. I don't know if I'll ever be able to let go of everything but maybe we can find a way to have some kind of civil relationship moving forward. In the meantime, though, it wouldn't hurt you to come to my church and check it out."

"Is it one of those churches where they preach about forgiving people, acceptance, and turning the other cheek? If so, then I'm not so sure their sermons are the kind that stick."

"Ouch. I suppose that was a fair shot, but still... ouch."

"Thanks for the offer but for now I'm happy being a lapsed Catholic."

"What about Malcolm?"

"He refers to himself as a non-practicing atheist."

"That doesn't make the slightest bit of sense."

"I know but nothing in our lives do," Mary said. "I wish I could tell you everything but I can't. It would only put you and your whole family in the same danger Malcolm and I face all the time."

"Yes, I saw that on full display."

"No, what you saw was just a tiny appetizer. For a few years, we lived our lives like that every single day and that even on days when we weren't on a job."

"I can't even imagine."

"Just believe me when I tell you we're the good guys."

"It's going to be a while before I can think of Malcolm as a good guy."

"Sometimes, good guys have to get their hands dirty so everyone else can keep theirs clean," Mary shrugged. "It's not ideal but it comes with the territory and Malcolm and I have gotten really good at it. It took me a while to learn that life isn't all black and white."

"Life may not be neatly divided between good and bad but morality is."

"No, morality isn't a real measure of good or bad, it's just a list of the things you say you believe in. The sum of your actual actions rather than your words is a much better measure of character in my opinion."

"You know something, sis? I completely underestimated you. You're smarter than I gave you credit for and you've also become incredibly brave. When I was on that ship, I was in fear for my life almost the whole time while you were so focused and taking action. I don't know how you were able to maintain your wits and do what needed to be done. You've really gotten a lot tougher over the years."

"You got tough yourself on the pontoon when we needed you to. You can let adversity break you or you can learn to rise up and overcome it. We're both walking the paths we've chosen, come what may."

"Well said. I'm glad you can give me some credit."

"I give you a lot. You were a huge influence on me as a kid. I looked up to you my entire childhood."

"Seriously?" Amy wore a sheepish grin. "I always thought you hated me."

"No, I was jealous of you. You always seemed so together."

"Are you kidding? My signature move is walking up ten steps when there are only nine. But you? Look at you now. You're in great shape. You must work out a lot."

"I do, but my main cardio consists of running away from social situations."

"I'm the jealous one now. And you've got a loving husband who looks after you and your daughter is beautiful."

"Yes, she is."

"They grow up fast, so take the time to enjoy it all."

"I will."

"That means staying alive, you know."

"Yes, I get it," Mary laughed. "I don't go looking for trouble, believe me."

"You know, Mary, I'm proud of what you've become, though I'm still appalled at the path you chose to get there."

"Then maybe you need to think about what's more important: the destination or the means by which the person traveled to arrive at it."

"I don't know. Maybe you're right. As I said, I have a lot to think about. I've been doing a lot of praying lately, and it's been helping."

"Glad to hear it."

"Did you really jump into Malcolm's arms because of a spider?"

"Yes."

"That's both hilarious and adorable."

"Thanks, I think," Mary rolled her eyes. "You know, I've heard psychologists are awfully expensive. If you need to talk about what happened and the things you experienced, I'm here right now. Why not try me?"

"I suppose it couldn't hurt to try. Do you still drink tea?"

"I love tea."

"I'll go to the kitchen and put the kettle on. How about you rummage around and see if there's something chocolate we can snack on?"

"I have some treats stashed in my room. Give me a few minutes and I'll be back. There's something I need to do but it won't take long."

Mary walked across to the other side of the house to the small study. The door was ajar, so Mary stood in the doorway and knocked. Christopher was sitting behind a desk and was accompanied by Sarah.

"Oh, hey, Aunt Mary," Sarah smiled and then walked over and hugged her. "It's cool you didn't get my mom killed. Thanks."

"You're welcome," Mary smiled back at Sarah. "Do you mind if I have a moment with your step-dad?"

"Sure, go ahead. I'm heading out anyway. See ya."

Sarah waved and walked out of the room. Mary closed the door and then stood in front of the writing desk Cristopher had his laptop on.

"I need to talk to you about something," Mary said. "Do you have a moment?"

"Certainly," Christopher gestured to a chair. Mary shook her head. "What would you like to talk about?"

"I know you were working for Ki-Liu and if you even try to deny it, I'll be immeasurably insulted."

"Oh dear," Christopher tapped his pen against the desk a few times. "Well, this is rather awkward, isn't it? All right, then. May I ask how you found out?"

"There were a lot of little things that gave it away but the single biggest thing was how Ki-Liu went out of his way not to harm Amy when he was lining up his shot. If he wanted to shoot Stacy, his bullet would have gone through Amy and still hit her," Mary folded her arms. "Stacy was most likely a priority target yet he didn't fire when he had the chance. It's not as if Ki-Liu cares about collateral damage so only one explanation makes any sense. He made a deal with someone who wanted to make sure Amy came to no harm and you were the only likely candidate."

"I swear I didn't know things were going to get so far out of hand," Christopher raised his hands then let them drop again. "Ki-Liu accosted me in the underground parking garage at my workplace. He pointed a gun at me and said either I could help him or he would kill Amy and the kids. He said the only thing I had to do was make sure Ms. Metzner and Amy went on the cruise and I was not to alert the authorities. If I did as he asked, he said he would guarantee the safety of my family."

"You could have told me or Malcolm. We're not the authorities."

"I couldn't take the chance," Christopher sighed. "He was armed and agitated."

"Any idea why he wanted you to do all that?"

"That first day you and Malcolm went to Amy's workplace, Ki-Liu had been watching the building, monitoring the comings and goings of his targets," Christopher met Mary's stare. "He recognized your husband and assumed he was there because of him so he alerted the accomplice he apparently had on the inside. Apparently there is some history between Malcolm and Ki-Liu."

"More than you need to know."

"Right," Christopher cleared his throat. "Ki-Liu was worried your husband would prevent Stacy from going on the cruise. He needed her and the others on board so he made me ensure it happened."

"So you decided to sacrifice Malcolm and me in order to save your own skin and Amy's."

"Like I said when we first met, I'll do anything to protect my family," his tone was matter-of-fact. "It came down to a choice between the lives of Amy and the kids or two alleged criminals whom I didn't know. Amy hated you both so it seemed like a terrible but safe choice to make."

"Ki-Liu wouldn't have let you live," Mary scoffed. "You'd be another loose end he'd have to take care of."

"And you don't think I know that particular detail? Tut-tut, I'm disappointed, Mary. I am all-too aware that the moment I agreed to help Ki-Liu I was living on borrowed time."

"You'd be leaving Amy a widow and the kids without a father figure."

"Yes, but they'd have their lives and that's all that mattered to me," Christopher stood up and leaned on the desk. "If it meant Amy and the kids would be spared, I would gladly give my life. I'm terribly sorry about everything to do with you, though I can appreciate how hollow that apology must sound. It's nowhere near sufficient in this case."

"If I were to tell Amy or Malcolm about any of this, an apology would be nowhere near sufficient for them either," Mary said. "If I wasn't such a believer in non-violence, I'd be so tempted to grab you by that pretentious jacket of yours and throw you into that wall and out through the other side."

"And I would allow you to do so because I deserve it," he replied. "Perhaps you forget, Mary, I'm English. We do self-loathing better than anyone and I already feel miserable about what I've done. I regret putting you in harm's way but I have no regrets about putting my family first. I admit I was wrong about you and Malcolm. No matter what else you may be, you're not criminals. So, with all that said, what happens now?"

"I have to get back to Amy," Mary unfolded her arms and gestured toward the door. "She and I are going to have a long talk over tea and chocolate about everything she went through this past weekend. While we're doing that, I'd like for you to think of something really nice you can do for your family in exchange for my silence. Some day you might earn my trust back but it won't be today."

"Mary, if I may."

"What?"

"I was right about you," Christopher smiled and wagged a finger. "When we first met I told you I saw a kind, well-spoken person who seemed genuinely interested in helping Amy. Like I said: I'm a good judge of character."

"Thank you," Mary's expression relaxed somewhat. "Now think of how grateful you are to be part of Amy's family and then think of a way to show them how much you appreciate them. Believe me, I'll be watching."

"I don't doubt it."

Mary left the room and pulled the door closed behind her. She stood in the hallway for a moment, thinking about Amy and Christopher, and envied the normalcy they both seemed to experience on a daily basis. She then began walking back toward her room.

Mary was often mystified that other couples were able to lead routine lives. They shopped for groceries, focused on their mortgage and car payments, got their kids to soccer practice on time, and made sure the homework was done.

As she climbed the stairs, she couldn't help but wonder: *what must that be like?*

For that matter, Mary was equally baffled about what such people would have to discuss at dinnertime. When she and Malcolm talked about their days, it usually involved homicides, unexplained events, spies, organized crime, or foreign governments. Discussing the cable bill after that would seem downright trite and banal.

She envied people whose biggest problem was how much the cost of gasoline went up that day.

She would sometimes see her neighbours having backyard grill-outs and barbecues and they would invite their friends over to join them. There would be plastic cups, paper plates, and… whatever else was involved in such things.

One of Mary's biggest fears was to be invited to any sort of social event like that. She imagined being there with other families and parents who were able to walk to the corner store without first having to make sure they were not being followed.

What could she possibly talk about with other people? She would not know what to say and she'd spend the entire event being quiet and feeling awkward.

Other people would probably talk openly about their jobs and their trips abroad whereas Mary would not be allowed to share anything of the kind. One parent's big news might be that they had to deal with a flat tire or they had burned the cookies they were preparing for the bake sale. When Mary had big news, it was often something life threatening, like coming to blows with two Russian snipers, or evading that North Korean assassin, or her fairly recent life-or-death fight with a serial killer.

A month ago, another mom had seen Mary at the pharmacy with Alyssa and tried to make small talk. During the conversation, the mom said, 'I took my daughter to see a magician yesterday, what did you get up to?' and the honest answer would have been 'I sent a virus worm into the computer system of a Russian mafia cell and then presented a full list of names, contacts, and addresses to the FBI' but instead all Mary actually said was 'not much, really' and left it at that. The conversation ended awkwardly and abruptly shortly after that.

Being an introvert made it difficult for Mary to relate to others at the best of times, but being an introvert with a lot of secrets to hide only made sharing life experiences with others that much more difficult. The one thing she had heard but never understood was people blessed with calm, peaceful lives who actually craved excitement. If she were more socially inclined she would walk up to such people and tell them how immeasurably overrated excitement really was.

She entered her room, retrieved the chocolate biscuits she had stashed, and then headed down the stairs to the kitchen where Amy was pouring the tea.

"Those look delicious," Amy said at the sight of the biscuits. "I'll be right back. I just got a text message I need to pass along to Christopher.

"No problem," Mary said as she sat down.

Amy left the room and then scurried over to the study. As she entered the room, Christopher looked up.

"Well?" Amy said as she closed the door behind her.

"You were right," Christopher sighed. "She's much more clever than we anticipated."

"What does she know?"

"She knows about our connection to my associates in Guangzhou," Christopher said. "But she thinks it was me who was forced to make the deal with Ki-Liu. She doesn't suspect you at all."

"That's a relief," Amy said. "Does she know she was targeted?"

"No, she thought Ki-Liu was trying to kill Stacy, not her. Maybe with Ki-Liu dead, she'll simply view it as all wrapped up."

"What about Kevin Denbigh?"

"He never regained consciousness and died of his injuries in the hospital this morning," Christopher smiled. "With Whitlock gone, we can't be tied to Ki-Liu or Guangzhou and with Denbigh gone, nobody can prove Ben Shapner didn't jump to his own death. We're completely in the clear."

"Let's hope so. I'm really starting to like Mary now, so I'm glad she lived. We didn't end up with the files, but nobody else did either. Things didn't work out as planned but with Ki-Liu dead and me getting my sister back, they worked out surprisingly well regardless."

"Except, of course, for Bill Sutherland."

"Yes," Amy frowned. "Spender deserved what happened to him for doing that."

"Whitlock, you mean," Christopher winked. "We're not supposed to know who he is, remember?"

"The important thing is to make sure nobody ever finds out about any of this," Amy began to smile but then her brow furrowed. "Darling, is that your thermos on the shelf?"

Christopher turned and looked over at the strangely conspicuous item on the bookshelf.

"Heavens no," he said. "I'm not sure whose that is."

Wednesday, 9:18am: Seattle, WA

Malcolm scanned the cheque with an app on his phone and sent the money directly into his business account.

"Thanks for your prompt deposit, Mrs. Bell-Anger," Malcolm gave a nod to his client sitting opposite him.

"Half up front is highway robbery," she sniffed, "but I have neither the time nor the patience to explain this to anyone else right now. Regrettably, you'll have to do."

"And thank you also for that overwhelming vote of confidence."

"However, for that amount of money, I'm going to insist you resolve the case in a week and no later," she shook her finger at him. "There is no reason it should take any longer than that."

"I agree to your terms."

"If it's not resolved in a week's time then I don't pay you a penny more than I already have."

"Fine, as long as you promise to sign this cheque for the balance in full as soon as we resolve it."

"As long as it's within the week, then of course."

"Good," Malcolm stood up. "Because I've already solved the case."

"Don't be so flippant," she snapped. "You haven't even started yet. I find your mockery outrageous and offensive."

"I'm not mocking you and not just because it would pose no challenge," Malcolm retrieved a file from on top of the filing cabinet beside him. "On our own initiative, we've been working on the case since we last spoke and the case really is solved for you."

"Very well then. Let's hear it."

"Walter did commit suicide and he deliberately arranged things so you wouldn't get the insurance money."

"That's outrageous. I've never heard such nonsensical drivel."

"Here are the facts," Malcolm opened the file and his eyes scanned the summary page he had inserted. "You stated that a mysterious person had visited your husband two days before he passed away. I have records which show Walter requested Howard Blakie, a prominent Wills and Estates lawyer, to attend his bedside at the hospital. According to the billing from Blakie, their discussion centred on how his life insurance policy would work in various scenarios. Documents were signed and witnessed and the attending physician vouched that Walter was of sound mind. Walter was also quite vocal with his closest friends and colleagues about how unhappy he was with your extravagant spending on vanity items for yourself. We have multiple sworn statements by his friends and colleagues to that effect. Your husband knew exactly what he was doing, Mrs. Bell-Anger. He refused a doctor-assisted suicide specifically because his policy would still pay out. Instead, he took a cocktail of pills just before his scheduled morphine shot and he was gone in minutes. He died this way specifically to spite you. You've inherited his estate and assets but he went out of his way to deny you the large insurance pay out."

Malcolm closed the file and put it back on the cabinet.

"That's outrageous."

"Somehow I knew you'd say that," Malcolm said as he sat down. "As I anticipated this outrageous conversation, I have taken the liberty of having an outrageous pen ready for you to endorse the cheque for the outrageous balance owing, as agreed."

"This is completely outr... *unacceptable*. This is not what I hired you for."

"Yes it is," Malcolm placed the pen on top of the cheque and slid it across the desk towards Belanger. "You hired us to find out what happened and that's exactly what we did. It's not our fault if you don't like what we discovered."

"I won't sign."

"The balance owing is cheaper than hiring a lawyer for a long, protracted court case."

"I have a lawyer on retainer. I dare say you do not."

"No, but I happen to be tight with Stacy Metzner, who is the managing partner at Metzner and Company. She owes me a really big favour and I'm sure if I asked her she would be willing to represent me pro-bono in this matter. We'll then counter-sue you for a half-million to make up for the emotional stress I'm experiencing having to engage in this conversation with you."

"Ugh. This is outrageous."

"No, a man wearing his hair in a bun is outrageous," Malcolm said. "This is just business."

"Here. I have signed your accursed cheque. I shall never hire you again."

"I sure as hell hope that's a promise."

Wednesday, 8:11pm: Seattle, WA

"Alyssa's asleep," Malcolm said as he came into the bedroom where Mary was hanging up the last of their clothes.

"That was quick," Mary nodded.

"Get the recipe for your father's lasagne," Malcolm grinned. "If it induces sleep, then next time I'll bring more leftovers home so I can have some myself."

"While you were tucking her in, I got a message from Director Waterman," Mary held up her phone. "She's agreed to pay our expenses for our time on board *The North Star Express,* less the cost of the satellite phone that was ruined when I fell into the ocean."

"Great, but what changed her mind?"

"It turns out after I submitted our report, she got a call from her contact at the ATF who was asking if we knew about a drug enforcer named Ki-Liu."

"Convenient."

"It is convenient," Mary smiled. "They'd heard he'd come to North America but had lost track of him and they wanted to hire ARIES to find out where he was. She was able to solve their case and submit a billing in less than twenty-four hours."

"Great," Malcolm stood in front of the bed. "Is your arm any better today?"

"Yes, but it still stings a lot," she glanced at the bandage on her upper arm. "I know you've been shot a few times over the years, but this was my first time and it was much worse than I imagined."

"You never really get used to it. Good thing it didn't hit an artery or shatter a bone. As bullet-wounds go, it was a good one to start you off with."

"Start me off with? No, thank you, I'd rather not get used to being shot. By the way, let me ask you something. What do you think of the outfit I'm wearing?"

"Oh, this is a trick question, I can tell."

"Yes it is," Mary put her hands on her hips. "However, it still requires a completely honest answer so I don't want to hear any of that 'you have so many other outfits that suit you better' nonsense."

"The outfit you're wearing totally suits you."

"Alright, now explain what your comment means."

"Well, it's not something I would have thought of and yet you've made it look perfect."

"Oh, good answer, you smooth talker."

"You shouldn't care what I think of your outfits," Malcolm said. "Wear what you want to wear and to hell with what anyone else thinks."

"Around you it's not an issue. You let me be real."

"No, you let *yourself* be real around me. You can choose to be real around others as well."

"I'd be too worried about what people thought, to be honest. I know I shouldn't but I can't help it."

"Chances are those same people have their own insecurities and closets full of skeletons so who cares? At some point, somebody needs to break the self-conscious cycle. Life's too short to be anything except who you want to be."

"Sometimes you have really deep moments, you know."

Malcolm grinned but his mind was still largely preoccupied by the conversation he'd overheard the day before. He now regretted placing his thermos in the study, even though his mistrust had compelled him to do it. He wasn't prepared for what he'd overheard nor did he want to be burdened with the knowledge he now possessed. He had no idea what he should do about it.

Well, that wasn't entirely true.

The one thing he knew for certain was he had to tell Mary about this. She deserved to know and she had the right to know, even if the information would cause her pain.

Once he told her, they would determine a course of action together. After all, he thought, that's what you should do when you're in a relationship. After everything that had happened and after all the resulting problems that came out of withholding information, full disclosure was the only sensible option.

Mary suddenly shrieked and then leapt up into Malcolm's arms. His legs buckled and he fell backwards onto the bed.

"Seriously?" Malcolm groaned. "You can subdue an attacker twice your size but you're still afraid of spiders?"

"What spider?" Mary said as she leaned in and kissed him.

Made in the USA
Middletown, DE
27 June 2019